Praise for J. L. Langley's *The Tin Star*

"*The Tin Star* by J.L. Langley is a contempor~~y~~ romance. Ms. Langley has taken a western contemporary problem to enhance th~~e~~ ~~ne~~ interaction between Ethan and James is v~~ery~~ ~~very~~ hot!

"Ms. Langley should be commended for writing not only beautiful story, but one that has huge social ramifications. This book is a Recommended Read!"

—Teresa, *Fallen Angel Reviews*

"*The Tin Star* is a gripping saga of two cowboys, and their deep abiding love for one another. This emotionally charged erotic novel shows the pure depth, richness, sensuality and warmth that can be shared between two men. If you loved the movie *Brokeback Mountain*, this novel will sweep you off your feet. Ethan and Jamie are unforgettable characters that make you remember what true love is all about."

—Qetesh, *TCM Reviews*

"JL Langley's *The Tin Star* is a must read for anyone who loves non-traditional/homo-erotic/gay stories. This fabulous tale will make your eyes tear at its poignancy and laughter will regularly escape from you throughout. The chemistry between the characters is sizzling; the sex is so hot it'll scorch you if given half the chance. Various twists in the plot keep the storyline fresh and unpredictable. I love these characters, and their close friends and family, too. I can't wait for more from JL Langley!"

—Elizabeth, *Euro-Reviews*

LooseId ®

ISBN 10: 1-59632-327-2
ISBN 13: 978-1-59632-327-8
THE TIN STAR
Copyright © 2006 J L Langley
Originally released in e-book format in January 2006

Cover Art by April Martinez

Printed in the U.S.A. by
Lightning Source, Inc.
1246 Heil Quaker Blvd
La Vergne TN 37086
www.lightningsource.com

THE TIN STAR

J. L. Langley

Dedication

To Ann Lory. I knew you could do it! Congrats! You worked hard, and you deserve it!

Chapter One

Ethan had sat in front of the computer too damned long again. That was the one thing he hated about managing the ranch; he'd much rather be outside working with the livestock. He looked up from the monitor as he heard a truck pull up the dirt drive and around the back of the house, then he listened to the autumn leaves rustling as someone stomped through them and onto the back porch.

"Fuck! Fuck! Shit! Damn!" Ethan frowned at the sound of John's voice. The back door slammed, followed by the opening and shutting of cabinet doors.

That wasn't good. Not good at all. The outburst of profanity was not unexpected. After all, John had always had a temper, but he had never sounded on the verge of tears before. In fact, he could only remember John crying once during the past twenty-six years, and that was when his mama had died three years ago.

"Oh, hell."

Ethan saved his last changes to the herd record, then made his way into the kitchen to find out what was eating John, his friend since first grade. He supposed that the occasional emotional upheaval from your best friend was a small price to pay for having someone you could trust and depend on live only a bit down the road from you.

"Ethan! Are you here, man? Where is the fucking whiskey?!"

He walked in just as John's tan Stetson slid across the kitchen table. Ethan caught it before it hit the floor. "Top of the pantry, there's a fifth of Jack." He padded barefoot across the room, got down two glasses and brought them back to the table.

John set the bottle down on the table, spun the ladder-back chair around, and straddled it. He didn't look at Ethan, just crossed his arms over the chair back and laid his head on his forearms.

Ethan poured a couple swallows in each glass, then slid John's to him. He knew John well enough to give his friend time. John would tell him what was up when he was ready; pressuring him would only delay the inevitable.

John glanced up, his blue eyes bloodshot, and tossed the whiskey back in one swallow. He brushed the back of his hand over his mouth, then pushed the glass toward Ethan, motioning for a refill.

Ethan poured some more and watched as John swigged it down, then grabbed the bottle. He sighed and took a sip of his own whiskey. *Man, that burns.* He propped his legs up on the chair next to him and waited for John to finish drinking.

Finally, John lifted his head, running his fingers through his short black hair, making it stand straight up. "Jamie is gay."

Ethan's eyes widened and he gulped down the lump in his throat. His feet slid off the chair and hit the wooden floor with a thump. What the hell was he supposed to say to that? He reached out and grabbed the rest of his own whiskey and drank it down.

James Killian. Jamie. John's younger brother had always followed in their footsteps when he was younger. They hadn't been able to go anywhere without the kid trying to tag along. Hell, Jamie was a good guy…even if he wasn't exactly a child anymore. He'd turned twenty-one the past fall.

"He freakin' walks in the office this morning while Dad and I are going over the books, sits down on the old leather couch, and says he needs to tell us something."

"So…he what? Has a boyfriend he wants to bring home or something?"

John stared at him for a few minutes, then shook his head. "Don't know. I don't have any fucking idea. Hell, for a minute there, I thought he was just yanking our chain."

"Well, what happened?"

"What do you mean what happened? He told us he's gay and Dad kicked his ass out. He kicked Jamie out, Ethan! Out of the house, off the Quad J!"

Ethan blinked. Jamie was not only John's brother, he was also the ranch foreman. Although their sister, Julia, had moved to San Antonio and was working as a nurse, the brothers worked on their family's ranch, the Quadruple J. Jamie had stayed on to help John run the place when their dad, Jacob, had retired. John was ranch manager now, while their dad oversaw both their work. Jacob claimed he wanted to make sure they got it right.

"What? Isn't that a little extreme? He's family!"

John nodded and took another big swig from the bottle. "Yup, he told him to get 'is freak assth out."

"What the hell are you going to do for a foreman? Shit, John! That's just fucked!"

His friend shrugged, listed a little to the side before he jerked himself back up. "Well, whah can I do? I don't know...jus' don' wan' tink 'bout it n-now...anyway."

Ethan could barely understand the slurred words. He stood up and paced. "What the fuck, man? He's your brother! Where the hell is he gonna go?"

John lifted one shoulder and almost fell out of his chair again. "Don' know...jiss hope hiss otay."

Ethan rushed over to prop him up. "Have you had anything to eat today?"

John shook his head. "Jiss dis whiskey."

No wonder he'd gotten so shit-faced so fast. Ethan pulled him up and steered him toward the living room.

John didn't resist, but reached out and grabbed the bottle of Jack on the way past the table. "Where's we go'n'?"

"To the couch before you fall over." Ethan got John settled on the couch, then flopped down on chair next to it. "Damn!"

John's head wobbled in what Ethan supposed was a nod. "Yup...'S fuckin' increb-ib-id-ble. My baby brubber...had no 'dea. Can you 'lieve it? And jis like you, the girls fuckin' lub 'im. In't that funn..."

Ethan shook his head, then looked up as the whiskey bottle slid out of John's hand, catching it before it spilled. He put the liquor down on the coffee table, then sat back down in his chair, running his hands down his face. *What a mess!*

Ethan dropped his head into his hands. Jamie was a good man...*a good-looking man, too.* John was right, his younger brother certainly had his fair share of women trying to catch his eye—and probably men, too, for that matter. Jamie didn't deserve to lose his family over something so...insignificant. Neither did John. His friend might be in shock now, not to mention drunk, but Ethan knew John would try to find Jamie once he had a chance to think straight...however the hell long that would take. *Damn old man Killian! Stubborn, opinionated bastard!*

Ethan knew better than most what it was like to be without family. He and his Aunt Margaret were all that were left of his. His mother had died in a car accident when he was three, he'd lost his older brother to Desert Storm, then his dad had succumbed to a heart attack five years ago.

John snored loudly, interrupting his thoughts.

Ethan glanced down at himself; he had on his gray sweatpants and white Toby Keith tee-shirt. He needed to dress and leave the house, get some air and time to think before he went stir crazy. But first he had to see if he could help John...and Jamie. He didn't know what he could do...but he had to try something. Jacob Killian kickin' his own son to the curb just didn't sit right with Ethan. He had a ranch; the least he could do was offer the kid a job and a place to sleep in the bunkhouse. The Tin Star could always use another good cowboy.

Leaving his friend to sleep it off on the couch, Ethan went into his office and dug through his Rolodex of addresses until he found Jamie's cell phone number.

Damn! He'd always been fond of the kid, but who'd have ever thought...

* * *

Jamie pulled off to the side of the road and cut the engine. Where the hell was he going? He had fifty-two dollars and thirty-seven cents in his wallet. Everything he owned was back at the Quad J, everything except the clothes he had on and his truck. He had no job, no friends who weren't ranch hands, and his sister's place was an hour and a half away. And that was assuming Jules would have anything to do with him. He wondered what she would say. Would she tell him to take a flyin' leap? Or would she risk their daddy's wrath and stand by him?

He pulled his hat off, turned it upside down and set it on the seat beside him, then ran two frustrated hands through his hair.

That had to have been one of the stupidest things he'd ever done. If he could kick his own ass, he would. What the hell had he been thinking? It wasn't like there had been any reason to tell his family. He didn't have anyone special, so it wasn't like he was going to have to worry about bringing a guy home to meet his family.

Except it had been eating at him for years to say something, then last night he'd finally worked up the courage to go ahead with it. He had been going to break the news come hell or high water, because he was tired of keeping secrets, tired of pretending to be something he wasn't. He'd stayed up half the night practicing what he'd say to them. Why couldn't he have just kept his damned fool mouth shut?

He sighed and blinked back tears. He was *not* going to cry over this. *Fuck them!* He'd known they wouldn't be happy; he had even known there'd be a lot of screaming and yelling, but he hadn't expected to be tossed out on his ear. Hell, he knew his dad wasn't the most open-minded man, but he'd always stuck by family…well, he had until now.

There was no help for it; he needed somewhere to stay until he could find a job. He started digging through the console, looking for his phone to call his sister when it started ringing.

Where the hell is it? He found it after about two rings, but when he checked the caller ID, he nearly dropped it.

He hit the steering wheel with his fist. "Fuck!" Of all the people to call him now…What the hell did *he* want? He tapped the on button and put the phone to his ear. "Killian here."

"Jamie?"

"What do you want, Ethan? Did John call you first thing?" He took a quick breath. "Shit, man! If you're planning to tell me that I'm going to hell, or that I'm a freak and my mama is rolling over in her grave, you're going to waste your breath."

He heard a sigh, then that deep, sexy voice came on the line. "Actually he's passed out on my couch drunker 'n' a skunk. Where are you, kid?"

"Why the hell do you want to know?"

"Look, Jamie, quit with the attitude. I'm not your enemy. I just called to see if I can help. You got a place to stay?"

Jamie pulled the phone away and stared at it. *What the hell?* His eyes stung again, and he felt something wet slide down his face. All his life he'd idolized Ethan; was it possible that his brother's best friend didn't hate him? Ethan and John had always agreed on everything—how was it possible that they didn't agree on this? Or maybe John was looking for him. Could it be that John wasn't going to chew him up and spit him out like their daddy had? He realized that he didn't actually have an idea what his brother thought. John had just stood there stunned when he'd made his announcement.

"Jamie?"

He took a deep breath and wiped his face with the back of his hand. Returning the phone to his ear, he opened his mouth to answer, but nothing came out.

"Jamie! You there?"

When he found his voice it was barely above a whisper. "Yeah…yeah, I'm here."

"Listen. Your daddy is going to blow a gasket when he finds out I offered, but hopefully he'll come around in the long run. If you need a job and a place to stay until this shit blows over with your family, I've got an empty room in the bunkhouse. And I can always use another good hand."

Jamie swallowed. "You ain't just trying to get me there so you and John can beat some sense into me, are you?"

That deep voice chuckled in his ear. "Nah." There was silence for a few seconds before Ethan asked, "Would it help?"

"Nope. I am what I am, Ethan. I'm tired of pretending, and I don't really give a shit what anyone thinks about it. So, if you and John have some fucked up plan to—"

"Hey! I don't give a damn what your sexual orientation is, Jamie. We've…hell, kid…we've known each other a long time. I just wanted to make sure you had somewhere to go."

Great! Just what he needed: pity.

"'Sides, you'd be doing me a favor. I've been a hand short since Bobby left."

Jamie widened his eyes and stared up at the ceiling to try and keep more tears at bay. Damned if it wasn't just like Ethan to try and save his pride. He grinned. Ethan always did have the people skills his brother lacked. "'Kay. I can be there in an hour. Is that all right?"

"Yeah, that's fine. Like I said, John's here. I think you need to talk to him, 'cept at the moment he really isn't up to doing much. Just go on to the bunkhouse and get your stuff stored away and take it easy. We'll put you to work tomorrow."

Jamie turned on the engine and looked into his rearview mirror. "Actually Ethan, I don't have any gear. Just my truck. I'll go check in with Bill when I get there and see if he has any work for me." He pulled back onto the highway, hoping that Ethan's foreman wouldn't have a problem about taking on a new hand…especially a gay one. Regardless of what Ethan said, Jamie knew damn well that the Tin Star wasn't short a hand, even with Bobby's absence, since Ethan worked the ranch in addition to handling the managerial side of things.

"What do you mean you ain't got any gear?"

He sighed, not really wanting to admit that he'd been in such a hellfire hurry to leave that he hadn't even thought about getting any of his things. "I was kinda in a hurry to leave. Ya know?"

Ethan sighed back at him. "Yeah, I got ya. I have some clothes that will fit you well enough until we can get your things. John can take care of that later. Just come on back to town. I'll let Bill know you're comin'."

After Ethan hung up, Jamie turned his phone off and tossed it back into the console. On his way to the Tin Star, "Feed Jake" came on the radio. *Shit!* That was all he needed, a song about a dog to make him feel guilty about leaving Fred behind. Hell, he'd forgotten all about his girls. Fred and George were still back at the Quad J. Jamie groaned. Why was it that when you were depressed, every danged song on the radio made you even more depressed?

George would cope; she was out in the east pasture with the other horses so she probably wouldn't miss him for at least a day. But Fred...Fred was his baby. He'd brought that little German Shepherd home when she was only six weeks old, and she'd slept at the foot of his bed every night since. She was probably looking for him already. He'd let her out this morning when he'd gone into the office to talk to Dad and John, then forgotten all about her.

Damn! What a messed up day from Hell! Not only was he a screw-up as a son and brother, but he sucked at being a daddy to his babies, too.

Chapter Two

Ethan grabbed his hat off the hook by the back door and headed out to the barn to find his foreman, Bill. After he'd gotten off the phone with Jamie, he'd changed out of his sweats into some jeans, then decided to go find something to do outside, leaving John on the couch to sleep off the whiskey. The herd records could wait. He doubted he'd get much done in the way of paperwork today anyhow. There were way too many things on his mind.

He stepped out into the sunny fall afternoon and pulled his straw hat down a little lower to block the sun from his eyes. You just had to love Texas weather; you never knew what you were gonna get from one year to the next—or even day to day, for that matter. Last year at this time, he'd already been wearing a light jacket. This year, it was still pretty warm outside. He hadn't even switched to his felt hat yet. In fact, it was warm enough that he was in a tee-shirt instead of a button-down.

He found Bill in the machinery barn, tinkering with the engine on one of the tractors. Bill looked up and pulled his ball cap off as Ethan walked in. He swiped his arm across his forehead and put the cap back on. "Well, looky what the cat done dragged out. You finally decided to haul your ass outta bed, boy?"

Ethan grinned at the older man. Bill had been foreman on the Tin Star since Ethan was four and had taught Ethan at least half of everything Ethan knew about being a cowboy and running a ranch.

"I've been out of bed since seven this morning trying to fix the herd records."

Bill shook his head and spit on the ground. "Seven A.M. You always was a lazy thing." The censure was ruined by the grin on the leathery old face.

Ethan chuckled. "Lazy? I'll have you know I was up till three this morning helping Ed and Hayden pull that calf."

Bill nodded. "Yup, you done good, boy. I got a look this mornin'. Mama and baby both seem just fine. And since you beat those cowboys outta bed, I guess I can cut you some slack."

"That's mighty nice of you, Bill. Listen, we got a new hand coming in. I figure he can bunk up with y'all since we've got that extra room in the bunkhouse."

Bill scratched his head, then turned around and reached down into the cooler that sat by the far wall, pulling out a cola. He held it up. "You want one?"

"Nah. I'm good."

Bill popped the top, took a swallow, then leaned his back against the wall. "Why did you hire another hand? We're gettin' 'long just fine with the four."

Well, hell. He'd known Bill would ask, of course, but he hadn't decided yet what he'd tell him. And he knew, just as sure as sky was blue, that Bill would be even more suspicious once he found out who the new guy was. Ethan sighed and leaned his forearms on the tractor.

"It's Jamie. He had a falling out with his daddy, and Killian threw him out."

Bill's eyes widened. "Now why would the old man do a damned fool thing like that? They just made that boy foreman when old Hank up and finally retired. That boy is one helluva cowboy! Hank trained him himself. Jamie's smart as a whip and good with people and animals, too."

Ethan nodded. "Yeah, I know. His daddy will more than likely come to his senses and take him back, but until then, I've offered him work and a place to stay. And if he stays on, well...I might end up making him foreman when you retire."

Pushing away from the tractor, Ethan went to the cooler and grabbed a cola. Hopefully, Bill would leave it at that. He really didn't want to get into the why's and wherefore's of the whole thing. It was a family matter and didn't need to be made public. *Damn it,* the kid should have kept his mouth shut. There was no reason to go telling people your private business.

"I saw John come drivin' up like a bat outta hell a while ago...it must have been a heck of a fight. Well, it's to our advantage, and I've always liked him. The kid is a hard worker, knows his stuff. If you don't have issue with him, then I don't, either. I'll make a place for him."

"Yeah, it'll work out. John downed two thirds of the Jack Daniels I had in the pantry, so he's sleeping it off." Ethan popped the top off his soda, took a long swig, then tossed the can in the trash on his way out of the barn. "Thanks, Bill."

"You're welcome."

Ethan stepped out into the bright sunlight and saw his Appaloosa trotting up to meet him. No sooner had he reached the corral than his cell phone started to ring. He pulled it off his belt and flipped it open. "This is Ethan."

"Oh, my God, Ethan! Daddy just called me. He kicked Jamie out! You've gotta go find him. I can't get a hold of him or Johnny. Jamie's gay, Ethan, and he told Daddy and Johnny, and Daddy kic—"

"Whoa! Hold on! Jules, calm down! John is here, and Jamie is on his way over."

Julia's voice became slightly less frantic, but it didn't slow down any. If anything she gained speed. "Oh, thank the Lord! Is Johnny okay? I mean is he okay with this? Good God! Jamie! I always wondered but, well, I didn't know. Did you? Did you know that Jamie's gay?"

Ethan grinned as he propped a foot up on the bottom rung of the corral gate. Julia always did talk ninety to nothing around family, and she considered him family. No stranger overhearing her away from her job would ever guess she was nurse, and a damn good one. He supposed it came from the fact that she couldn't get a word in edgewise with her daddy and two rambunctious brothers around.

"Now, Jules, if you will take a deep breath, and let me get a word in edgewise, I'll answer your questions."

"I'm sorry, Ethan. I'm just… I worked a double shift, 7p to 7a last night, then Daddy called and woke me up with this. And you know how I worry about my brothers…all three of you."

Yes, he did. Julia was a mother hen, not just to her brothers but to him, too. Didn't matter in the least that she was two years younger than he and John and nine years older than Jamie.

"No! You, worry? Never!"

"Ethan Whitehall! You quit teasing me and tell me what you know. I'm freaking out over here."

"That's kinda obvious, darlin'." He took a deep breath and reached out to pet Spot as the horse came over looking for a treat and nuzzled him. Damned animal was so spoilt he thought Ethan was supposed to bring him something every time he came out of the house.

"Here's what I know. John came by about an hour and half ago, cussing a blue streak. He drank almost a full bottle of whiskey before he could get out that Jamie had told him and your dad that he's gay, then he passed out on my couch. I checked on Jamie; he didn't seem to think he had a place to go, so I told him to come to the Tin Star." Ethan turned and leaned against the gate, crossing an arm over his chest and waited for Jules's next round of questions.

"Well, what did Johnny think of the whole thing? Was he upset at Daddy for throwing Jamie out?"

"Yeah, I think so. He's kinda shook up I think."

Julie sighed. "My poor babies."

Spot nudged his shoulder twice, then grabbed his hat off his head and took off trotting around the corral.

Ethan spun around glaring. "You little shit! Get back here right now!"

"Huh?"

"Not you, Jules. Spot just stole my hat."

"Oh." She snickered. "You know, Ethan, that surprises me."

"That Spot stole my hat?"

She groaned. "No. That horse is a pest; I'm not a bit surprised by that. I would have thought Johnny'd stand up for Jamie."

Spot whinnied, tossing his head up and down as he pranced, Ethan's hat clenched between his teeth.

Ethan sighed and climbed over the fence. It wasn't an easy thing to do while trying to hold the phone to his ear, but he managed. "You don't honestly think he'd go against your daddy, do you? John runs the Quad J and a lot of people are depending on him. He can't just up and quit 'cause your daddy didn't do what John thought he oughta. Besides, all cowboys are homophobic…well, except the ones that are gay. And most of those guys are smart enough to keep quiet about it and pretend to be homophobic. That's why I can't figure out why Jamie didn't keep it to himself."

"Yeah, but Johnny usually protects Jamie. He *is* his baby brother, after all. Besides, he's always been very supportive of you." Ethan heard her take a deep, gulping breath, then suddenly blurt out, "Did you know Jamie is gay?"

He groaned, not sure if it was directed at Julia or Spot, who was dancing around just out of his reach. "No, I didn't know he's gay. As far as I'm aware, there's no such thing as a gay registry. And it's not like I have some extrasensory gaydar or something."

He finally got within reach of his cowboy hat and snatched it out of Spot's mouth. "Give me that, you pain in the butt!"

"Don't be a smart ass, Ethan! I was just asking. How is Daddy going to feel about you taking Jamie in?"

Ethan put his hat back on and started back over the fence. "I don't know, but I couldn't just let the kid... Oh, hell! You, your family and my Aunt Margaret are all I got, Jules. I couldn't let Jamie suffer on his own—even if it's his own fault for telling his personal business. Your daddy will come around eventually...hopefully."

"Now, Ethan, not everyone sees things like you do. There is no reason he can't let his family know he's gay. Heck, he was probably getting tired of me and John shoving girls in front of him all the time." She sighed again. "You and Johnny have been friends forever, and I don't want this to cause problems between you and Daddy. He could stir up all sorts of trouble for you; he might even use his seat on the town council to rile everyone up. And aren't you guys partners in some new steakhouse thing?"

There was a brief pause, then, "He might blame Johnny, too, 'cause you're Johnny's best friend. I'm telling you, Ethan, he's going to be an ass over this...I just know it. I'll take my baby brother in for however long it takes—you don't have to be in the line of fire. Tell him to call me when he gets there. He can come to San Antonio and stay with me."

Ethan walked up the yard a little way, out of Spot's reach and away from his antics. "And do what, Julia? He's a cowboy. He'll go crazy in town. Darlin', you live in a high-rise apartment; you don't even have a cat. Last time I was at your place, your ivy was dying. Jamie'd go stark raving mad within a week. Besides, I can handle your daddy. Don't worry about me."

"I know you're right, but I hate that you're caught up in the middle of this. At least tell Jamie to call me so I can tell him I love him, and I don't give a damn who he sleeps with."

Ethan nodded, then realized that she couldn't see him. "What are friends for, Jules? I'll tell him to call." Ethan looked up to see Jamie's volcanic-red 2005 Dodge pull onto the dirt drive.

"Thanks, Ethan. I'm going back to sleep. Get him settled, deal with John and tell Jamie to call me...after five."

"Get some rest, Jules." Ethan flipped his phone shut and hooked it back onto his belt. Jamie's truck came to a stop and he walked over to greet him.

What a fucked up day! Aunt Margaret might be the only family he had left, but he was beginning to think that that wasn't necessarily a bad thing, after all.

Jamie pulled the keys out of the ignition and looked up. He dreaded running into his older brother. While his dad had let him have it this morning, John had just sat there with his mouth hanging open. What would he do now?

He groaned. He was being ridiculous. There was no sense lollygagging. Either John would see him and lay into him or he wouldn't. He'd made the choice to accept Ethan's offer and come, knowing that John was here. He'd made his bed and he'd lie in it, just the way his mama had always been fond of saying.

Jamie grabbed his gray felt cowboy hat off the seat and opened the door. Putting his hat on, he shut the door and started around the front of the truck.

Ethan was walking toward him. He had a straw hat on over his short black hair that shaded the upper part of his face and his eyes, but Jamie knew those eyes were a deep, milk-chocolate brown. *Damn, the man is fine.* Where he and the Killian men were lean and sinewy, Ethan was a big man, tall and broad shouldered, heavily muscled, lean-hipped and intimidating as hell. Jamie was five foot eleven; Ethan had at least four inches on him.

Ethan wore a black tee-shirt, faded jeans, and black boots. From under his sleeve, the bottom of his tattoo, which he'd gotten as a teen with John, showed. Ethan and John hadn't even been of age, but somehow they'd managed to get it done. Both had had their ranch brands inked on their left biceps. John's comprised four "J's" held together by a bar at the top, and Ethan's was a star with the number ten in the center. Mama and Daddy had yelled for days when John had come home with his. He was pretty sure Ethan had caught hell over it from his daddy, too.

Jamie once had heard that Ethan's mama was half Mexican. It showed; Ethan had a dark tan year round and very little body hair. There was just a smattering on his chest and he didn't think Ethan could grow a full beard if he tried. Thank goodness—it would be a shame to cover up the sheer perfection of that strong jaw line. The man was a walking ad for sex and he had absolutely no clue. Women had practically thrown themselves at his feet for as long as Jamie could remember, and it always seemed to shock Ethan, like he just couldn't believe that women could act like that because of him. Jamie would love to see the look on Ethan's face if he ever realized that he had the same effect on men, because damned if Jamie didn't want to throw himself at Ethan's feet and beg, too.

Jamie shook his head to clear it as he walked toward Ethan. He'd come here for a job, and even if it was given out of pity, it was a damned fine job and one he intended on doing his best to justify Ethan's trust. Ethan might be his brother's best friend, but he was also owner of a hell of a profitable ranch. The Tin Star had been around for four generations and was well known for their longhorns.

Jamie stepped in front of Ethan and was again reminded of his size. *Damn, he's big and, oh, God...he smells so nice!*

He held out his hand and Ethan took it. Instead of shaking it like Jamie had expected, Ethan pulled him against his chest in a sort of half hug and slapped him on the back.

Jamie's breath caught. Oh, the man felt *good.* Jamie's stomach clenched and his cock stirred. *Shit! Get a hold of yourself, Killian!* He'd always had a huge crush on Ethan, which he thought he'd been pretty good at hiding, but for some reason ever since he'd heard Ethan's voice on the phone today, all his senses were on full alert. He was going to have to get a grip. It would never do for Ethan to see the effect he had on him, especially now that he and John knew that Jamie was gay. Before, Ethan might have dismissed it as nothing, but with his newfound knowledge of Jamie's sexual orientation, it was highly unlikely he'd mistake if for anything other than what it was. And it would really suck to get thrown out twice in one day.

Ethan stepped back but didn't let go of his hand right away. "How are you, kid?"

Jamie blinked, trying to concentrate on the conversation. That was odd; it seemed almost like Ethan was reluctant to let go. But finally—and way too soon, as far as Jamie was concerned—Ethan dropped his hand.

"Uh, okay, I guess. Thanks, Ethan. You won't regret this. I'll pull my weight."

Ethan grinned. "I know you will. You've always been a hard worker." He started walking toward the house, tilting his head for Jamie to follow. "You hungry? Why don't you come in and eat some lunch. I was just about to put something together."

Jamie kept stride next to Ethan. "But isn't John inside?"

Ethan stopped and looked at him. "Yeah. Is that a problem?"

"Nah...I just figure I'm probably the last person John wants to see right now."

"Well, chances are he's still asleep, but you should talk to him, and your sister, too. I think you'll be surprised by what they have to say. Give them a chance, Jamie. Jules has already called in a panic to see if I'd heard anything from you. Your daddy phoned her."

"What? Daddy called Julia?"

Ethan nodded.

"Damn!"

"Yeah, she was upset over you not answering your phone. Come on, Jamie, let's get some lunch. Maybe John will be up by the time we're done eating." Ethan began walking again.

Jamie stood there and stared in shock. Was it possible that Julia *and* John were on his side?

That thought was cut off before it got a chance to really get going—Ethan had just stepped up on the porch, wiping his boots on the doormat. Jamie's eyes zeroed in on his butt. Damn, that tight ass looked good in a pair of Wranglers.

"You comin', kid?"

"What? Oh, yeah!" Jamie peeled his eyes off of Ethan's rear end and jogged up to the house. Man, working with Ethan was going to be hard…literally! Hopefully, Daddy would get over his mad…and soon.

Chapter Three

Ethan woke to the sounds of yelling and a dog barking. He didn't even have a dog. He blinked his eyes open and looked at the clock. 2:13 A.M.

What the hell? Oh, right! After John had woken from his stupor, eaten a meal and sobered up some, he'd gone and gotten Jamie some of his things from the Quad J. He'd brought Fred back with him, too.

"Call your dog off, you cocksucking faggot!"

That had Ethan up and moving. He grabbed the jeans he'd worn earlier off the floor and hopped bare-assed over to the window as he struggled to pull them on. His bedroom overlooked the back of the house and gave him a clear view of the bunkhouse.

Two of the ranch hands, Jeff and Carl, were circling Jamie and Fred. Carl had something, some kind of rod, in his hand and was waving it at Fred. Jamie looked like he'd been dragged out of bed. He was in a pair of dark sweatpants and nothing else, while Jeff and Carl were fully dressed. *Wonderful!* he thought caustically.

"Shit, shit, shit!" Ethan got his pants up around his hips and took off down the stairs. He reached the bottom of the back porch just as all hell broke loose, and Bill stepped out of the bunkhouse with a shotgun in hand. "What the holy hell is going on out here?!"

Carl hit Fred with the stick, making her yelp. Jeff tried to rush Jamie, but Jamie side-stepped him and dove at Carl.

"Don't fucking hit my dog, you piece of shit!" Jamie landed two good punches to Carl's face before Jeff jumped him from behind. Fred growled and leaped to her master's defense, grabbing Carl by the balls. He shrieked.

Carl had lost his weapon, there was blood running from his nose, and he was still screaming, trying to get the dog off him.

Ethan didn't slow his pace. He jumped right into the fray, grabbing Jeff—who was sitting on Jamie's back with a handful of thick black hair, trying to beat the kid's head into the ground—and hauling him off Jamie by the shirt collar.

As soon as Jeff was on his feet, he turned on Ethan and swung. Ethan ducked and punched him in the stomach. Just as Jeff dropped to his knees, Jamie reached for him.

Ethan opened his mouth to tell Jamie to leave Jeff alone when a gunshot rang out. Everyone froze, including Fred. She let go of Carl and ran to Jamie, growling out a warning at Jeff, who was apparently too close to her master for her peace of mind.

The two other ranch hands spilled out of the bunkhouse, hastily tucking their shirts into their unzipped jeans, but they turned around when Bill waved a hand at them.

Jamie reached down and dropped a hand to the dog's head. "Shh, it's all right, girl."

Ethan heaved a sigh of relief and dropped his hands to his knees, trying to get air into his lungs. "Somebody want to explain to me what the fuck is going on?"

Jeff clutched his midsection and scrambled out of Fred's reach. Carl flopped down on the bunkhouse porch, holding his balls with one hand and his bloody nose with the other.

Fred finally stopped growling, and Jamie turned to look at Ethan. He pointed at Jeff and Carl. "I was sleeping when these assholes dragged me from bed and out here. They started yelling all sorts of filth—"

Carl interrupted. "Do you know why Killian kicked him out, boss? Do you? He's a goddamned fag!"

Ethan wasn't surprised they'd learned why Jamie had been kicked off the Quad J. Damned ranch hands were as bad as a group of old women in a quilting circle when it came to gossip.

Ethan couldn't help himself. He knew it wasn't going to cool anyone's temper, but he grinned anyway. "Yeah, well, the 'fag' kicked your ass but good, didn't he?"

Jamie chuckled beside him, and Fred punctuated the taunt with a bark.

Bill sighed and glared at Ethan. "That's not helping, boy!" He looked back at the ranch hand. "Carl, I don't rightly care who the youngster sleeps with as long as he does his job. I wasn't aware you had been made ranch police."

Ethan straightened up and took charge. "Jamie, get your stuff, then you and Fred go on up to the house. You can have one of the guest bedrooms."

As soon as Jamie and Fred went into the bunkhouse, he looked at Bill. "Get these two off my property and make sure we aren't going to have any more trouble from them."

Bill gave a brisk nod. "You heard the man, fellas. Get your shit together."

Ethan turned away and returned to the house. A chorus of protests followed in his wake, but he ignored them. No way was he going to keep those two assholes on. Disagreeing with a man's lifestyle was one thing; dragging him out of bed from a dead sleep just to kick his ass because you didn't like it was another matter entirely. He knew cowboys were a bigoted lot, but damn! He just hadn't expected this, especially on his ranch. Oh, hell, maybe he had. Maybe that's why he'd wished Jamie had kept his mouth shut.

Ethan ran his hands up and down his arms. Now that the excitement was over, he could feel the nip in the air. It was too late, or too early, depending on how you looked at it, to deal with this shit.

He was just putting the water in the coffeemaker when he heard Jamie and Fred come through the door.

"I'm sorry, Ethan."

"It wasn't your fault, Jamie. They had no right." He switched on the machine and put the carafe in place, then turned around. Jamie was standing by the entrance and Fred was sitting next to him, wagging her tail. The kid had his cowboy hat on, a duffle bag slung over his shoulder, a pair of boots in one hand, two stainless steel bowls in the other and a bag of dog food under his arm. He was still in his sweats and barefoot, but he had put on a white tee-shirt that was about three sizes too big for him.

Jamie was nearly his size, albeit a little less filled out, but those baggy red sweatpants and the oversized shirt made him looked so damned sweet and innocent that Ethan could barely hold back a grin. He had the sudden urge to give him a hug. "You okay? Is she?" he asked, nodding toward Fred.

Jamie grimaced. "Yeah, nothing hurt but my pride. I should have expected something like that to happen. Guess I should never have never said anything in the first place, huh?"

"Yeah, you shouldn't have."

Jamie dropped his head and shuffled his feet.

Damn! That air of defeat went right to his gut. He should've kept his own piehole shut instead of making the kid feel worse than he already did.

"Go put your stuff away. I suggest using the room next to mine; it's the next biggest." He grabbed the bowls and the bag of dog food. "Go on. I'll take care of Fred. Come back down when you're done, and we'll have a cup of coffee and talk."

Jamie left the kitchen, and Fred followed her bowls, tail still wagging cheerfully.

Ethan put one bowl in the sink under the faucet and set the dog food and other bowl on the counter. He turned the water on, then petted Fred's head.

"That's a good girl! Going to Daddy's rescue like that. Let's see if we can find the good girl a treat." Fred must have understood, because she gave him a happy bark and sat up really pretty. Ethan chuckled and scratched behind her ears. He'd always loved dogs.

He turned off the water, then went to rummage through the pantry. There was some beef jerky in there somewhere. When he found it, Fred gave him a bark of excitement and nearly knocked herself over with the force of her wagging tail. He laughed and tossed her a piece. "Here you go, pretty girl."

By the time he got Fred's bowls to the laundry room right off the kitchen, the coffee was ready. He poured two cups and sat down at the table to wait. He didn't know what the kid took in his coffee, so he left it black.

Jamie came back and flopped down in the seat across from him. He glanced at the laundry room where Fred was eating and smiled. "She convince you she was starving to death?"

"Nah. Just thought she deserved a little something. She's a good dog."

"Yes, she is. You don't mind having her in the house?"

Ethan took a sip of coffee and shook his head. "No. I miss not having a dog around. It damned near broke my heart when Mutt died, but I've been thinking about getting another. I teeter between missing the companionship and keeping my heart intact. Know what I mean?"

"Yeah. It'd just kill me if something happened to Fred. Fortunately, she's only a year old, so we've still got a lot of years together."

Ethan looked at the large German Shepherd and let out a low whistle. "Damn, she's gonna be big! You know big dogs grow until they're two, right?"

Jamie grabbed his coffee and took a sip. "Yup, I know. She ever grows into her paws, she's gonna be a monster."

"You got that right." Ethan sipped from his mug. "You have a female dog named Fred and a mare named George. I know George is short for Georgia, but you keep it up, you're going to have people thinking you've got some perverse fondness for giving females male names." He winked.

Jamie grinned. "Fred is short for Frederica. I figured she's a German Shepherd, so she should have a German name. I went online and researched German girls' names. I liked Frederica, but it's a mouthful so I call her Fred for short." Suddenly sober, he glanced at Ethan. "Besides, now people will just attribute it to the fact that I like men better than women."

Ethan leaned back in his chair and studied him. Jamie's body was long and lean, muscled without being bulky. At present, Jamie looked several years older than his twenty-one years. The Killian black hair that had a tendency to curl when it got long was hanging in his eyes, which looked tired. There were also bags under those pretty peepers, which were a paler version of his brother's, a crystal-clear blue so light they appeared almost colorless at certain angles. His dark eyebrows and high cheekbones emphasized his good looks, and he had a strong chin, complete with a shallow cleft. A bit of stubble that hadn't been there this afternoon covered his cheeks, and though he was tan from being out in the sun, his complexion was otherwise fair. John's younger brother had grown up into a damned fine-looking man, and the fact that he was exhausted didn't diminish those looks any.

Ethan's gut clenched at his thoughts. Why had he never seen the kid as a man before? Never mind. This wasn't the time.

"Jamie, I won't lie to you. I don't think your being gay should be anybody's business but your own. Still, you know how damned ornery your daddy is. You should have known what he'd do if he found out."

Jamie started to argue, but Ethan held up his hand. "Let me finish. I think you should have stayed in the closet, figuratively speaking, but you damn sure don't deserve how you've been treated. Not just by your daddy, but by Carl and Jeff, too. Hell, it even pisses me off that John didn't stand up for you to your daddy right away." Ethan suddenly grinned and took another sip of his coffee. "But he'd probably be living here and working with us, too, if he did."

Jamie smiled, but it didn't reach those blue eyes. "Yeah. Hell, I was just surprised that John didn't take issue with me. I kind of expected Julia to be supportive, but I really thought John would be as mad as Daddy. I guess he probably feels like you...that I should have kept it to myself."

Ethan nodded. "John's no bigot. Never has been."

Jamie seemed to mull that over a bit. He was quiet for several moments, then he whispered, "I couldn't...I couldn't do it. Couldn't continue to pretend." Those baby blues looked like they were pleading with him to understand.

Ethan sighed. "I get that but, hell, you knew people here would never accept it, right? We live in the freakin' Bible belt, complete with bigots, racists and chauvinists. If you aren't a straight, white, Baptist male, you do your best to pretend you are and blend in."

Jamie stood up abruptly. "Putting your head in the sand don't make it right! How are people's attitudes ever going to change if they aren't forced to deal with it? I just don't get your and John's attitudes!" Fred ran from the laundry room to him, stared at him, then at Ethan, then back at Jamie, clearly trying to decide if there was a threat or not.

"Sit down."

Jamie shook his head, but he sat down anyway. "You just don't get it! It's easy for you to criticize *me*. You won't ever have to worry about hiding who you love. Hell, you can even get married! I can't! At least not legally and not here."

Ethan dropped his head into his hands. *Shit!* He did not want to get into this. Some other time and another place would be more appropriate. He knew where the kid was coming from. He did. He just didn't agree. Didn't make the kid's opinions wrong necessarily, just…not his. He looked up at Jamie.

"I see what you are saying, I do. Believe it or not, I even understand. But you ever heard of the path of least resistance? The question you need to think about is, do you really understand what you've done? We live in a little hick town. You will now be fighting this prejudice until the day you die…or until you move away. Some people will accept you immediately, some will accept you in time, but the majority of people hereabouts never will. The attitudes aren't going to change overnight or even in the next few years. In fact, I doubt we'll live to see the day when gay men can walk hand in hand down Main Street without taking a whole heap of shit for it."

"They have to be made to accept it. You *don't* get it! You and John will never have to hide what you feel for your wives in public."

Had he ever been this young and idealistic? Damned if the kid didn't bring out his protective instincts. He wanted badly to keep him safe and shield him from the hatred he was going to face. And that, almost more than anything else about this whole situation, bothered the hell out of him. He'd never been stirred quite this way before.

Ethan finally held out his hand to Fred, who was still glancing back and forth between them uncertainly. "'S okay, girl. We aren't going to start slapping each other around. Go lie down." She did—after she went back to Jamie—settling down beside her master's chair. That was one smart dog.

He faced Jamie. "Drink your coffee, kid. We'll agree to disagree. I may not see eye to eye with your methods, but I'll stand behind you. You have my word on it. I'll be damned if I let you get your ass kicked or get run out of town. You have a place here and a job as long as you want it."

"Thanks, Ethan...for everything."

"You're welcome."

They sat there drinking their coffee in silence. Ethan wanted to pull Jamie into his lap and comfort him, then felt like kicking himself for the impulse. But the image of Jamie in his lap wouldn't go away. His cock evidently liked the idea, too; he groaned and shifted a little in his seat. That was one of the worst ideas he, *and his cock,* had ever had. Not only was Jamie a good eleven years younger than him, not to mention his best friend's kid brother, but he had also outed himself.

"You okay?"

He looked up into a set of curious blue eyes. "Huh?"

"You groaned. Did you pull something fighting? You probably aren't used to that kind of thing anymore at your age."

Great! He was getting a boner over the kid—who thought he was too old to be fighting. He sighed. "Nah, I'm good. Listen,

I'm going to bed. You and Fred make yourselves at home. *Mi casa es su casa* and all that." He stood up and saw Jamie's gaze slide down his naked chest to his groin and widen. The kid got a dreamy look on his face and his tongue darted out to wet his lips. He blinked up at Ethan, then quickly looked away, blushing, then glanced back.

His interest did nothing to cool Ethan off. His cock jerked and his balls pulled up at the avid attention. He knew he was hard, but was it really that damned noticeable? His jeans weren't all that tight. Ethan looked down and, yes, it *was* that noticeable. He didn't know whether to blush along with Jamie or laugh. Instead, he got a sudden urge to pay the kid back for his comment about his age.

He grinned down at Jamie and said, "Don't start that! My willpower is pretty good, kid, but it ain't that good. That's all I need, for you to out me, too."

Jamie's eyes opened so wide, Ethan was afraid they were going to pop right out of their sockets. Then Jamie dropped his coffee cup on the table. He hastily jumped up to avoid spilling the hot beverage on himself, sending the chair clattering to the floor.

His gaze shot back to Ethan. The blush was gone, now he was pale as a ghost. He stared at Ethan as if he'd sprouted two heads.

Ethan barely held in a satisfied grin. He went and put his cup in the sink. As he walked out the kitchen door, he called over his shoulder, "Night, kid. Clean that up before you go to bed."

Chapter Four

"I can't believe you never told me about Ethan," Jamie whispered into his cell phone, careful not to be overheard by the other two ranch hands.

"It wasn't my secret to tell, Jamie, any more than yours would have been had I known. Frankly, I'm surprised he told you. As far as I'm aware, Jules and I are the only other people who know, and the only reason Jules does is because she saw him out on a date when we were all in college." John sighed. "Look you have more important things to worry about. I heard what happened last night. That was just the beginning, Jamie. Are you sure you want to stay around here?"

"Hell, yes, I'm staying here. This is my home! I have no intention of leaving because of a bunch of asshole bigots. Hold on a sec. I gotta go after this calf."

"What?"

Jamie pulled the phone away and tightened his grip on Spot's reins, ignoring his brother. Spot, in turn, tried his best to ignore Jamie's demand to follow the calf.

"Damn it, Spot! You're not gonna win, so you might as well mind me, you obstinate pain in the ass!" He heeled the horse in the ribs, making him trot along after the stray animal. Once Spot decided to quit fighting him, they herded the calf back into the main group of cattle without much effort. As they fell back behind the herd, Jamie spoke into the phone again. "You still there?"

"Yeah, I'm here. What are you doing?

"I'm helping Hayden and Ed move the cattle to the west pasture. When are you gonna get George over here for me? I'm having to ride Spot."

"What's wrong with Spot?"

"Aside from the fact that he's a thief and he only listens to Ethan?"

John chuckled. "A thief?"

"Yes! He stole my hat and my bottle of water! I went out to call him in, so he waltzed into the corral. Came straight to me and snatched my hat right off my head. He pranced around for ten damn minutes before I finally got it back. Then, damned if he didn't grab the bottle of water I had on the fence post and tease me with it for ten more minutes. It was practically forever before I got him in the barn and saddled up."

John's chuckles turned into full-out laughter, forcing Jamie to pull the phone away.

Ed rode up beside him and grinned. "Just wait till you have to fix a fence with him along. He'll steal your tools, too."

Jamie looked over at the pale, freckle-faced cowboy and groaned. Ed was only a few years older than he was and had bright red hair and a thin, wiry frame. The other man had a reputation as a heck of a good ranch hand and a nice guy. And if this morning was any indication, his good name was well earned. While they had saddled the horses, Ed had made a point of remarking that he "didn't have a problem with gays" and offered him a handshake.

"You're kidding, right?"

"Nope! Last time Ethan and I strung up new barbed wire, Spot took off with the wire cutters. Took Ethan five minutes of cussing and fifteen minutes of chasing to get them back. The rascal loves to play keep-away." Ed grinned, then rode off a little ways to give back Jamie some privacy for his call.

Jamie shook his head and rolled his eyes, then lifted the phone. "When are you bringing George to me?"

John sighed again. "I'll bring her tonight."

"Good. Bring me some more clothes, too, and find Fred's toys."

"Grrr."

"Don't growl at me. It's not like I can come get the stuff myself. Daddy'd likely shoot me on sight."

John snorted. "Yeah, he probably would. Okay, I'll see what I can do. I've gotta look into hiring a new foreman on top of everything else I have to do today."

Jamie started. They were already looking to replace him? That didn't sound good...not at all. "At Daddy's insistence?"

"Hell, yes! You don't think I want to, do you?"

"Nah. I knew better, I was just thinking out loud, I guess."

"I'm sorry, Jamie. I don't want to hire anybody else, but I can't do your job and my own. Daddy has been very vocal about the fact that we need a new foreman."

"Doesn't sound like he's going to accept this, does it?"

John let out a ragged breath. "I don't think so, kid."

Jamie shivered and looked up at the sky. It was nice out today, almost hot, but he still felt the chill from John's words. What if his dad never allowed him to go back home?

He looked around the pasture. It was beautiful, so it would certainly be no hardship staying on here, but…it wasn't home. No, he couldn't think like that. He couldn't think of not going home again.

"I gotta go, John. I'll see you tonight. Thanks."

"Welcome, bro. Later."

Jamie replaced his phone on his belt, then rode on in silence.

Ed drew up even with him again. "We all carry phones. You should get a hands-free thingy like the rest of us." He pointed to the earpiece he had in place. "Does yours do pictures? If not, you need to get one, else Bill will go crazy." He chuckled. "Bill got him one of them and made us go get them, too, so he can send us pictures of things around here. He sends pictures of everything, things he wants fixed, things we fixed already. He and Ethan go nuts at the cattle auctions, sending pictures back and forth of the stock for sale." Ed shook his head, grinned, then trotted back to his side of the herd.

The rest of the ride was pretty uneventful. They got the cattle moved, then rode the fence back, checking for breaks or spots that would need repairs soon. Halfway back, Bill called Hayden's phone to tell them that he had their lunch ready.

When Jamie, Ed, and Hayden rode up to the house, Ethan was standing in the yard with a sandwich in one hand, a yellow tennis ball in the other and Fred watching his every move.

Jamie felt his heart pound in his chest at the sight of Ethan. If the man's obvious enjoyment from playing with Jamie's baby girl didn't do it for him, the man himself sure did. He wore a ball cap, a pair of cutoffs and red tee, and white sneakers. Damn, the man had great legs! Someone should tell him to cut his jeans off higher up than mid-thigh.

Ethan threw the ball and Fred went bounding after it. Ethan laughed at the energetic puppy, and Jamie felt the sound shoot all the way to his soul. He was starting to get hard just from watching Ethan play with his dog.

Jamie blinked and mentally shook himself. He'd had a crush on Ethan for as long as he could remember. Then, when he was older and most of the guys in his class had been drooling over the varsity cheerleaders, he'd been jerking off to fantasies of Ethan. Still, in all that time, he'd never dreamed that Ethan was gay. Now that he knew, it was not helping his infatuation. If anything, it made it much worse.

A chuckle interrupted his thoughts. He glanced over as Hayden moved up beside him. "That dog of yours is something else. You got yourself a good pup there. I heard what she did for you last night. Wish you would've yelled out or something. Any man that would try to hurt a dog for protecting her master ought to get his ass and more kicked. Listen, you have any more trouble like you did last night, you give a shout." He paused, then shrugged. "I don't rightly understand how you don't like women…what's not to like? But I don't think that oughta be reason to hate someone, either. A man shouldn't be dragged outta bed for nonsense like that. Life is too damned short."

Before Jamie could form a thank you, Hayden winked and rode on ahead into the barn. *Well, hell! How do you like that?* The man hadn't said two words to him all morning, so he'd just assumed Hayden had a problem with him, but now it looked he and the remaining men on the Tin Star were gonna get on just fine. Sure was nice to know, and it took a little of the sting out of his and John's conversation earlier. Getting his mind off of Ethan's legs for a few minutes also had helped his boner go away. *What a bonus!*

Jamie took Spot into the barn, unsaddled him, brushed him down, and fed him. Then he went in search of his own nourishment.

Ethan and Fred were still playing ball, while the other men sat at the picnic table where Bill had sandwich fixings laid out.

The foreman looked at him and grinned. "Sorry about the fare, kid. We don't have a housekeeper like y'all do up at your daddy's spread. We pretty much fend for ourselves around here."

"That's all right. Nothing wrong with sandwiches." Jamie grabbed a paper plate and started putting his meal together.

"Good! 'Cause we eat a lot of them. You cook?" Ethan asked hopefully as he sat down at the table.

Jamie looked into deep brown eyes and his belly knotted up. "A little."

88888

8888

8888888

Ethan nodded and took the ball Fred brought to him. "Great. If you're real nice to me, I'll let you cook us supper tonight."

Jamie blinked. Bill and Hayden laughed.

Ed protested, amusement clear in his voice. "No way! If he can cook, you'll have to share him. In fact, we're all coming up to the house to eat! 'S only fair!"

Ethan chuckled. "Oh, no! You guys get your own cook! He's living in my house, so I oughta get something out of it" He grinned at Jamie, whose gut clenched in reaction.

He smiled back at Ethan, then shook his head and went back to preparing his sandwich. He'd give Ethan a whole hell of a lot more than cooking as payment for living in the big house…eagerly, in fact.

"So, do you clean, too?"

"Hell, no! Ethan, I'm gay…not a damn housewife!"

Everybody laughed.

* * *

Ethan was doing the dishes after a wonderful meal of enchiladas, rice, and beans. He'd only been kidding earlier when he'd told Jamie to cook supper, but Jamie had taken him at his word. As soon as they'd all gone in for the evening, Jamie had set to work in the kitchen. Ethan had told the younger man he didn't really have to cook, but Jamie had insisted.

Man, could he cook! When Jamie had pulled out the homemade salsa, Ethan had decided then and there that he'd do just about anything to keep the kid cooking for him. He couldn't remember the last time he'd eaten such a fine meal. Maybe he'd add it to the list of Jamie's duties and pay him a little extra for it. It was a thought and sure beat cold cuts and frozen suppers.

Just as he put the last plate in the dishwasher, Fred came bounding in with the ball he'd found for her earlier. He chuckled and took it from her. "Okay, girl, let's go in the living room where we have space to play without destroying the house." The living room had a huge, open area. Once he and Fred got there, Ethan tossed the ball toward the front door.

Jamie was half sitting, half sprawled on the couch, watching TV. As Fred ran by, nails clicking on the wood floor, he yelled. "Fred! Don't run in the house!"

Ethan chuckled. "It's okay, she's just enjoying herself."

Jamie started, then glanced over his shoulder. Apparently, he hadn't heard Ethan throwing the ball. "Oh. I didn't know you were playing with her. You don't mind her running through the house?"

"Nah. There isn't much she can mess up in here. She wanted to play, so I obliged her."

Jamie grinned. "You know the way to a man's heart is through his dog, right?"

Ethan laughed as he walked to the couch. Before he could sit down, Fred brought the ball back. He tossed it again and made himself comfortable. "Nope, I believe it's through his stomach…and my heart is all yours. Supper was wonderful. Thank you."

Jamie mumbled something that sounded like "I wish," then he flushed and ducked his head a little. "Thanks."

Damn, he was cute when he got all shy like that. Jamie obviously didn't take compliments well, and Ethan vowed to change that. He'd always known that John was the favored son, but damn! Killian's favoritism had always seemed grossly unfair, but it wasn't till recently that it had really started to bother Ethan.

Jamie was a credit to his family and deserved his fair share of praise. It disturbed him to realize that there was just something about the younger man that made him want to coddle him. "You're welcome."

Jamie's hand came up and brushed his dark hair out of his wonderful blue eyes. He cleared his throat nervously, then looked directly at Ethan. "I don't mind doing the cooking, if you'll do the dishes."

Ethan smiled and flung the ball again. "That's a hell of a deal! You're on."

He got a chuckle and an offered hand. Ethan found himself staring at those long fingers and callused palm for a second. Jamie had nice strong hands, a working man's hands. What would they feel like on—?

They shook on the deal, then Jamie watched soberly as Fred scrambled after her toy. "So you really don't mind Fred?"

"No. She's a good dog."

Jamie nodded absently and gestured to Fred, then tossed the ball for her. "Daddy always complained. He doesn't think dogs belong in the house."

Ethan snorted. "No offense, but I'll tell you exactly what I've told John over the years: your daddy can be a real asshole sometimes. Dogs are like family; of course they belong in the house."

Jamie blinked up at him and snickered, blue eyes sparkling and nose crinkled up ever so slightly. It was the sweetest thing Ethan had seen. "Yup. Hell, I'd let George in the house, too, if she'd fit."

Ethan laughed. "Okay, I draw the line at bringing the horses in."

Jamie cracked up. "All right, no horses in the house, I promise. Have you heard from John?"

"No. Why?"

"He was supposed to bring me some more of my things and George, too."

Ethan shook his head. "Last I heard from him was early this morning. Word apparently got back to the Quad J about your fight last night."

Those dark eyebrows arched. "Yeah, I heard. How do you think that happened, anyway? It doesn't seem something Bill, Ed, or Hayden would call people about."

Ethan shrugged and held out his hand as Fred came trotting up. "There's no telling how it got around. I swear ranch hands gossip more than a gaggle of old, blue-haired ladies on bingo night." They shared another laugh. "Carl and Jeff probably whined about being tossed out on their asses. Anyway, one of the ranch hands there told John about it first thing, and he called just around the time you headed out to move the cattle."

Fred came to an abrupt halt, flipped her head up and let go of the ball...which went flying into Jamie's lap.

Jamie sucked in air.

Ethan's eyes zeroed in on Jamie's crotch. *Oh, man!* The green flannel drawstring pajama bottoms Jamie had put on after his shower were tented. *Damn! How long has he been that way?* Jamie shifted. Ethan felt his cock turning rigid at the sight of Jamie's erection.

He realized he was staring and looked up. Jamie cleared his throat, sat up straighter and moved his baggy white tee-shirt over to cover himself. The younger man was biting his full, bottom lip, gaze on Ethan's face. Damn it, he was sexy!

Ethan knew it was a bad idea, but he just had to taste that sensual mouth. He leaned forward, his lips lightly brushing Jamie's. Jamie gasped, and before Ethan knew what hit him, Jamie had taken over, his mouth crushing his, tongue pushing for entrance. He grabbed Ethan's face with both hands and urgently pressed his body against Ethan's, or as near to it as he could get with them both still sitting. He was rough, aggressive, practically swallowing Ethan up as his tongue searched and caressed every bit of Ethan's mouth. Finally, he calmed down a little, gentling the kiss, and Ethan had the chance to kiss him back at last. Jamie's hands slid to his shoulders. Their tongues met and parried. It was like making slow and easy love. Jamie moaned.

It was one of the most erotic things Ethan had ever heard and made him even more painfully erect. His hand slipped down to ease the restriction of his jeans. Jamie dropped his hands from Ethan's face and pulled out of their kiss to look down at him. Ethan looked down, too, as he adjusted himself.

Jamie moaned again, then reached out tentatively to touch Ethan through his jeans. Those clear blue eyes shot up to his, as if he were asking for permission.

"Good God!" Ethan gasped out as Jamie squeezed; then he lost what little control he had. He pushed Jamie backward on

the couch, unfortunately dislodging the grip on his cock in the
process. It didn't matter; nothing mattered except he had to feel
that mouth on his again, taste Jamie again.

He couldn't remember wanting anyone as much as he
wanted Jamie, right here, right now. He knew this wasn't smart.
Jamie was too damned young. He'd also outed himself. And, to
top it all off, he was John's brother. Still, he couldn't help
himself; the kid had had him all twisted up, albeit in a good
way, ever since he'd stepped out of his truck yesterday.

Ethan had always liked Jamie, always found him attractive,
always felt mildly protective of him. But now? Now everything
was so much more intense. He had no idea why things had
changed. Maybe it was knowing that Jamie liked men, too.
Whatever it was, Ethan knew that Jamie was his now.

His lips found Jamie's mouth at the same time his hand
found its way inside those soft pajama bottoms. He wrapped his
hand around that incredibly stiff prick and they both moaned.
God, Jamie was so hard! Ethan could feel the cock pulsing
against his palm.

Jamie's hips bucked.

Ethan had to see him. He broke the kiss and sat back,
pulling Jamie's flannel pants down with his free hand. Jamie
groaned, his pelvis pushing up again, making his dick slide in
Ethan's hand. Ethan released his grip, looking at the prize he'd
claimed. It was hot to the touch and felt like velvet, and was
longer than his own by about an inch or so, but not near as
thick. The deep red color really stood out next to Jamie's much
paler legs, which were a sharp contrast to the dark curls above
his cock. As Ethan watched, fascinated, a drop seeped from the
slit and began to streak down the flared head; another soon

followed. He leaned forward and caught the first drop with his tongue, then the next. Mmm... It was almost sweet, not overly salty.

Jamie's cock jerked in his hand, and he cried out. Ethan opened his mouth to take more of his dick in, to taste him fully.

Fred barked.

They both jumped. Then the back door opened.

He let go of Jamie and sat up. Jamie scrambled to get himself back in his pants and into a sitting position.

"Jamie! Ethan!" John's voice echoed through the house.

Ethan ran his hands down his face and glanced at Jamie, whose face was scarlet. Ethan frowned and whispered, "Stop blushing!" then yelled, "In here!"

"I can't help it!" Jamie hissed back, glaring. That was just too much, Ethan grinned. God, he had it bad!

John stepped into the living room with a pile of stuff in his arms while Fred barked again.

Jamie was digging around the couch cushions.

"What are you doing?" Ethan asked.

Jamie stood up and looked back at the couch. "She wants her ball."

John set down the pile he was carrying onto the coffee table. "I brought Jamie more of his gear."

Jamie finally found the ball and flung it for Fred. Ethan and John both turned their heads to watch the dog scramble on the wood floor, then looked at each other. Ethan took the time to calm his breathing. It wouldn't do for John to notice.

"I bet Fred is loving this," John said, a smile in his voice.

"She is." Jamie started going through the pile of boxes and bags on the table. "What all did you bring?"

"Some clothes, Fred's toys, a few of your books and a box I found in your nightstand." John flopped down on the couch next to Ethan.

Jamie looked up, the flush gone from his face. Ethan thought he looked a little startled, but John didn't seem to notice anything unusual.

Jamie dug through the boxes until he came up with a black lock box. He tried the lid, but when it didn't open, he seemed to relax. *That's weird.* Ethan wondered what Jamie had inside there.

"Did you bring the key?"

"What key?"

"The one hidden under the lamp on the nightstand."

John shook his head. "Nope. Didn't know it was there. I'll bring it tomorrow. What's in the box?"

"Nothing much, just this and that. Did you bring George?"

Ethan blinked. Well that was an evasion if he ever heard one. Now he was even more curious about what was in that box. He glanced at John, who seemed to have missed Jamie's noncommittal reply.

John cleared his throat, and Ethan braced himself. John always cleared his throat when he was nervous, a habit he'd had since they were kids.

Jamie must have realized it, too, because he set the black box down, stood up straight, and put his hands on his hips. Thankfully, his boner was gone. "What?"

"Uh, well, there was a little problem with that."

"You're hedging," Ethan commented.

John's head snapped toward him. "Shut up, Ethan!"

"Well?" Jamie asked.

John sighed and got up, then began pacing. Jamie opened his mouth about to say something, but Ethan shook his head. "He'll get to it."

Jamie groaned and started pacing in the other direction. He stepped over Fred, who'd confiscated a chew toy from one of the boxes.

Ethan grinned. Pacing must be another Killian trait. They all did it the same way, with the same stride, the same carriage. John finally stopped and looked at him. Ethan knew the look; it was John's I-really-don't-want-to-tell-you-the-bad-news look. *Aw, shit!* Ethan raised an eyebrow at him. John sighed and turned to face his brother.

"Dad won't let me take her. He says that if you want the horse, you'll have to buy her."

Jamie's face flushed bright red and his eyebrows lowered. Anger was coming off him in almost visible waves. "That son of a bitch! George is mine! A gift is a gift! He gave her to me for my seventeenth birthday! You can't freakin' charge someone for a fuckin' gift!"

Ethan was speechless. He'd known Jacob Killian could be a mean old bastard, but this was pretty low, holding a man's own horse hostage.

"He can't do that!" Jamie paced rapidly. Fred came up to him, stopping him in mid-stride, and whined, apparently attuned to his mood. He patted her head absently and turned back to John and Ethan. "Can he do that? I mean, can he actually get away with that?"

John shrugged. "Probably. He's the one who actually bought George and you know what they say about possession being nine tenths of the law."

Damn, this sucked! Ethan stood up and walked toward his office, leaving the brothers alone for a minute. Poor baby! All this just because he'd tried to be honest with his family...

Whoa! Ethan stopped. Where the hell had that thought come from? *Poor baby?* Oh, no, no! Jamie wasn't his lover yet and he damned sure wasn't poor or a baby...

Ethan shook his head to clear it and continued to the brandy decanter. He poured a splash into a tumbler, then returned to the living room. The brothers were sitting on opposite ends of the couch. Fred was at Jamie's feet with her chew toy, chomping happily away. Ethan strode over to Jamie and pressed the glass into his hand. "Drink up."

Jamie gulped the contents back, then coughed. He wiped his forehead and handed the glass back. "Thanks."

"Welcome." Ethan set the glass on the coffee table.

"How much does he want for her?" Jamie mumbled.

"Ten thousand."

Jamie shot to his feet. "I don't have that kind of money, damn it!"

John looked up at his brother. "I know. That's not really the issue. I'd already planned on buying her for you, but I had to tell you how Daddy is behaving."

Ethan walked behind the couch, put his hand on Jamie's shoulder and pushed him back down onto the couch. "Don't worry about it, John. I'll write you a check before you go home and you can bring her here tomorrow, or I'll come get her."

Jamie glanced up at him. "Ethan, I can't ask you to do that."

"You didn't ask. I volunteered. You work for me and you need a mount, end of story. Besides, this will keep John and your dad from going at it. I dare say he wouldn't think too kindly of John buying George for you anyway."

Jamie nodded, eyes glistening. "Thanks." He stood up. "Come on, Fred." He walked toward the stairs, shoulders slumped. "I'm going to bed."

Ethan and John watched him leave.

Damn Jacob Killian! Something told Ethan that Jamie would be staying at the Tin Star for good. And strangely enough, all he could feel was a sense of relief.

Chapter Five

Jamie woke up a little disoriented.

Where in the hell am I? Oh, yeah, his daddy had kicked him out. Not only that, now he was refusing to let him have his horse. Why had he ever thought his father would take his announcement without a problem? Sure, Daddy had always favored John, but he'd thought he had loved him, too. How could anybody disown their own flesh and blood? At least his brother and sister were on his side, offering their love and support. When he'd spoken to his sister, Julia had even gone so far as to say that she wasn't speaking to their father until he came to his senses.

Maybe Daddy would get over it…eventually, but Jamie was no longer quite able to believe that. He wasn't stupid—maybe a little naïve at times, but not stupid. The possibility was very real that his dad might never accept him. Surely Julia realized that, too? He knew John did, because he was looking for a new foreman. Even if it was at their father's demand, he'd indicated as much. That had hurt more than Jamie wanted to admit.

Damn. It was times like this that he really missed Mama. She'd always had a way of soothing things over. She'd let Daddy pout and throw a fit for a while, but then she'd rein him in and make him do what was right. Like telling his youngest son that he still loved him, no matter what.

Jamie sighed. This was getting him nowhere. The ball was out of his court and he needed to put it out of his mind. What else could he do?

He looked at the clock: 8 A.M. *Fuck!* How had he slept so late? Fred usually woke him up about 6:30, wanting to go outside. He sat up and looked around. There was no sign of Fred anywhere in the room. Ethan must have let her out.

Jamie rubbed his eyes, then got up and stumbled to the adjoining bathroom. He stood in front of the toilet, waiting for his morning erection to go away so he could take care of business.

Ethan. Jamie had been so upset about his dad that he hadn't even thought about what had happened between the two of them last night.

They'd always gotten along well together and had been friends of a sort. Not close friends, but friends nonetheless. Still, there were so many reasons he should not have kissed Ethan back last night, In fact, getting involved with Ethan was not a good idea any way he looked at it. One, Ethan had his feet firmly planted on the closet floor and had no intention of leaving. Two, Ethan was now his boss. Three, Ethan was his brother's best friend. Four, Ethan was a little over a decade older than him. And, five…well, hell, none of those really mattered at all if Ethan felt the same way he did...because he'd been head over heels in love with Ethan even before he'd realized he was gay.

Shit. Who was he kidding? He'd had a huge crush on Ethan practically since birth. Long before he knew he wasn't "supposed" to feel that way about other guys.

Thoughts of last night with Ethan were not doing anything to make his morning wood go away. So Jamie gave up and turned on the shower. He pulled out a towel and glanced at the door that led to Ethan's room. On a ranch this size, it was a pretty good bet that Ethan had been up for hours and was already working, but Jamie had to check. Who knew? Maybe Ethan would agree to pick up where they'd left off and help him get rid of his little, er, big problem.

He pulled the door open slowly and looked in. Sure enough, it was empty. The room was spotless, the bed made. It was obvious Ethan had been gone for quite some time. He closed the door and climbed into the shower, closing the glass door carefully behind him. He wet his hair, grabbed the shampoo and washed.

What would Ethan say about what they'd done? Would he try to pretend it hadn't happened? Would he tell Jamie that he'd made a mistake and that it wouldn't ever happen again? God, he hoped not.

He wasn't going to give Ethan the chance to stop whatever it was they had started. There was definitely something between them and he was going to talk to him about it before Ethan even had the chance to bring it up. Although he'd been attracted to Ethan for a long time, the previous evening's events were the first inkling he had that Ethan felt something for him, too.

Hopefully, it wasn't just lust. He didn't want this to be only about sex...okay, sex would be a good start, but that wasn't all he wanted. He wanted all of Ethan.

Jamie grabbed the soap—Ethan's soap—and lathered up his hands. He took a deep breath. Mmm. It smelled like the man himself. Shit! If it was possible, he was growing even stiffer. He washed up, then leaned his arm on the shower wall, resting his head on his forearm and letting the water pour over him. With his eyes closed, he grabbed his cock with his other hand and squeezed. Oh, yeah, that felt really great.

It was no surprise that his brain conjured up the image of Ethan's dark head bent over him, licking his cock. God, he had looked so sexy, better than any dream Jamie had ever had, and he had certainly dreamed about this a lot over the years. And it had felt so good. If only Fred hadn't barked and John hadn't come in...

Jamie stroked himself, nice and easy. With the hot water running down over him, his hand slick on his cock, he pictured Ethan taking him all the way in his mouth.

Those full, sensual lips slid all the way down, then sucked lightly on the way back up. One of Ethan's hands played with his balls.

He increased his tempo, pulling faster on his long prick. His testicles drew tighter.

Warm, dark brown eyes peered up at him as Ethan's other hand wandered lower, past Jamie's balls, rubbing up and down his crease. Jamie panted, gripping his prick tighter and pulling faster. *Ethan gathered saliva with his finger as his teeth scraped lightly on Jamie's cock, not enough to hurt, just enough to tease.*

Ethan pressed and pressed against his anus until the finger pushed right into him.

Jamie groaned, his head dropped back against the shower wall, and his hips bucked as his orgasm whipped up his spine and out his cock. "Ethan!" He quickly glanced down and watched as his come washed down the drain.

Both hands braced on the shower wall for support, he breathed in deep gulps and tried to calm his pounding heart. Man! That was just what he had needed. Now if Ethan would only consent, he could have the real thing.

Jamie smiled. Oh, yeah, Ethan was as good as his! He didn't care how long it took; eventually Ethan would belong to him. Not just that luscious body, but his heart, too!

"Jamie."

His head jerked up at the whisper.

* * *

What a sight!

Ethan leaned against the doorframe between Jamie's room and the bathroom. He'd come upstairs to tell Jamie that he'd gone and gotten George and to ask if he wanted to go with him to town and run some errands. Walking in on Jamie jerking off in the shower had been unexpected. The view had been enough to make him hard instantly, but then hearing his name gasped from Jamie's lips as he came... Ethan had almost joined him in blowing his load. He hadn't meant to say anything after he'd seen the other man come, but it had sort of rasped out of his mouth.

Jamie turned off the water, opened the shower door and grabbed the towel off the rack. He gazed right at Ethan as he began drying his shiny black hair, almost as if he were daring Ethan to say something.

Man, he was gorgeous! Jamie's well-defined muscles and lean, athletic build brought to mind a sleek jungle cat. There was just a little hair on his chest, enough to make him appear masculine, a grown man. The hair trailed down and narrowed into a thin line that fanned back out over his groin. And what a groin it was. Jamie's cock was still semi erect; he had to be at least nine inches at full length. Thick, muscled thighs and his long legs were a testimony to hours spent in the saddle.

Despite the resemblance to his brother, Ethan thought the younger man was the better looking of the two. Jamie was easily the most striking man Ethan had seen in quite a while and Jamie staring at him was doing nothing to make Ethan's hard-on go away.

He bit back a groan and glanced at the other man's handsome face. Ethan grinned. Jamie was beet red. *Damn, he's cute when he's embarrassed!*

Jamie finished drying off and wrapped the towel around his hips. He still hadn't said a word and his gaze was still glued to Ethan. He stepped right up to him, bold as you please, and smiled. "Hi, Cowboy."

Ethan smiled back. "Hey, Blue Eyes."

Jamie's eyes shifted down, his gaze roaming over Ethan's body. When his inspection got to the front of Ethan's jeans, he reached out and gripped Ethan's prick, which was more rigid than a steel pipe by now. "You need some help with this?"

"Sssssss…" Ethan groaned and clenched his eyes shut as the pleasure rushed through him. He reveled in the other man's ministrations for a few moments, then opened his eyes. He shifted his weight off the doorframe and stood straight, grabbing Jamie's towel and jerking it loose, tossing it to the floor. Jamie gasped quietly, his eyes going back to meet Ethan's.

Ethan didn't even think about what he was doing or that he shouldn't do it. He reached around and grabbed a handful of that tight little ass and pulled Jamie against him, then bent his head and ground his mouth down over Jamie's, almost dislodging his hat in the process.

Moans filled the quiet bathroom as Jamie kissed him back, hands trailing up Ethan's chest. Ethan could feel Jamie's cock against his thigh, already hardening again. He deepened the kiss for just a minute, their tongues tangling, then he pulled away, letting go of that firm butt.

"We don't have time for this." He dropped a chaste peck on Jamie's lips. "I came to tell you I got George and to ask if you want to come with me into town. I've got some errands to take care of."

"We can run errands after." Jamie wrapped his hands around the back of Ethan's neck and tried to pull him back down.

Ethan chuckled and unwrapped Jamie's hands. "The weather is supposed to get bad and I want to try to get back before it does. So if you want to come with me, get dressed."

Jamie groaned. "Yeah, I wanna come with you. Is that all right with Bill? Doesn't he have work for me to do?"

"Nah. Hayden and Ed can handle it. I told Bill you'd be coming with me."

"Okay." Jamie brushed past him into his bedroom, pressing against him a lot more than necessary to get through the door.

Ethan followed, his eyes focused on that muscled behind. "Damn!"

"What?" Jamie looked over his shoulder with a knowing grin.

The little flirt!

Ethan shook his head and rolled his eyes. "Nothing. Get dressed and meet me downstairs."

As Ethan waited for Jamie, for at least the fiftieth time in the past twenty-four hours, he asked himself what the hell he was doing. He'd tried to convince himself that it was his cock doing the thinking because it had been at least five years since he'd gotten laid, but he really didn't think that was it. He and Jamie clearly had chemistry together.

He'd felt it as soon as Jamie had set foot on the Tin Star two days ago, but the funny thing was that despite having known Jamie for twenty-one years, he had never felt this way about him before. Okay, that wasn't quite true. He *had* noticed Jamie, especially after Jamie had hit puberty and started filling out, but he'd always brushed the feelings aside. He'd filed Jamie away in that part of his brain marked "straight men."

Of course, he'd admired many such men, but he'd known there was no hope for anything else, so he'd never given them too much thought beyond the initial attraction. Yet now that he knew Jamie was gay, too, all those suppressed feelings were emerging. And suddenly the fact that Jamie was John's baby brother didn't seem like that big an obstacle. Hadn't John always said it was too bad he was gay, because if he weren't, Ethan could marry Julia and they'd be brothers? All right, so they'd been kids when he'd said that, but still...

What the hell. He wasn't getting any younger. Over the years, he'd had a few one-night stands during his business trips, but his last serious relationship had been in college with Cliff. And that hadn't stood a chance because John and Cliff had detested each other. Cliff had annoyed the piss out of John, and Ethan's friendship with John had always made Cliff jealous. That wouldn't be an issue with Jamie.

Of course, Jamie did pose another problem, having announced his homosexuality. Ethan really didn't want to deal with the headache of being outed himself. Then there was the issue of a break-up. What if they got together and it didn't last? He wouldn't be able to cut Jamie loose like he had done with Cliff. Ethan still could remember being eleven years old and having to sit down so he could hold Jamie a couple of days after he'd been born. He'd even helped John teach Jamie how to swim. Jamie would always be a part of his life.

"I'm ready. Can I see George before we go?" Jamie walked into the kitchen wearing a dark green, short-sleeved, button-up shirt, a pair of tight Wranglers, and his gray felt hat.

Ethan blinked and felt his cock twitch. Damn, his erection had just gone down and now the sight of Jamie dressed up had it threatening to come back. He groaned silently.

"Yeah. Let's go." He held his hand out toward the door for Jamie to go ahead of him. He told himself he was not going to notice that fine ass encased in those tight jeans, in front of him. Unfortunately, he never had been very good at following his own advice.

* * *

Jamie sat in the passenger seat of Ethan's truck, listening to the radio and watching the land pass by through the windows. After he'd greeted George, he and Ethan had gotten a list of supplies from Bill and taken off in the truck. They hadn't said much yet on the drive. And Jamie was afraid the silence meant Ethan was regretting not just this morning, but last night as well.

Jamie had been embarrassed in the bathroom at first, but he'd taken Ethan's reaction as a good sign. Now he wasn't so sure. At least Ethan hadn't started babbling about how they couldn't do that again. Jamie reached over and turned the volume down on the radio. He had to know where they both stood. "Ethan?"

Ethan glanced over at him, a dark eyebrow arched under the straw hat, before he looked back at the road. "Yeah?"

"I've been thinking. We've definitely got something between us. I think we should pursue it. I can—"

"I agree."

"—be very discreet and…What?"

Ethan chuckled. "I said okay. I agree with you; we should just go with it and see where it leads."

Jamie felt like he'd been hit with a sledgehammer. He'd fully expected to have to argue his case. "You do?"

"Yeah, I do. Am I speaking English?" He smiled.

Jamie chuckled, feeling better than he had in a while. "Smart ass!"

Ethan laughed with him.

"Ethan?"

"Yeah?"

"Thanks…" *Thank you for taking me in, for getting my horse, for giving me a job, and for giving me the chance to be with you.* "…for everything."

Ethan glanced over at him again, then held his hand out. Jamie looked at the big, callused hand for a second, then put his in it. Ethan squeezed. "You're welcome…for everything."

The gesture and words were intimate, held promise. It said everything they didn't…all the questions, the reservations and finally the acceptance. Jamie smiled and finally relaxed. For the first time, he thought that getting kicked out of the only home he'd ever known might not be such a bad thing. Maybe it had happened for a reason. He savored the feel of Ethan's hand holding his for a few more moments, then let go. "So, what all are we doing in town?"

"Other than the long list of supplies Bill gave me, you mean? We are getting you more tack."

"Excuse me? I have a saddle and—"

Ethan shook his head. "Not anymore. Your dad wouldn't so much as give me a rope to load George with this morning. Fortunately, I had some in the back of the truck. And with Fred there, George didn't need much coaxing. Fred herded her right on into the trailer."

"Goddammit!" Jamie took a deep breath. "Will it ever not hurt?"

"I don't know, Jamie… I don't know, but we can hope."

Chapter Six

The saddle was beautifully made, hand-tooled leather and would really put a dent in his savings, but it was well worth the cost. He picked out a new hackamore bit, bridle, halter and saddle blanket, plus all the things he needed for the saddle. Ethan had told him not to bother with anything to do with grooming, had even offered to buy all his tack, but there was no way he was allowing that.

Jamie went ahead and grabbed a currycomb. He had the money now that John had brought him all his belongings and personal effects; he could only take so much charity. Jamie knew he was a hard worker and hiring him wouldn't hurt Ethan's budget in the least, but he also knew darn well that Ethan hadn't been looking for another hand. Charity was still charity. Jamie was going to do his best to make sure Ethan never regretted hiring him on, especially since he'd cost Ethan two experienced workers.

He hauled all his stuff to the front counter.

Ethan was just finishing up his order with Tom Cooke, who had been manager at Hatcher's Feed for years. They were discussing the new gazebo/bandstand that was being built in Town Square.

Tom looked at Jamie. "Why are you still in town?"

Jamie blinked and glanced at Ethan, then back to Tom. "Excuse me?"

"You don't belong here."

Jamie was dumbstruck. He hadn't thought his being gay would matter to the people who knew him. After all, he was still the same person. He gaped at Tom.

Ethan, however, was scowling something fierce. The expression on his face was enough to make Jamie want to step back. No intelligent man would continue talking with a man Ethan's size glaring at him like that. But Tom was clearly not a smart man.

"You should just hightail it on out to California with all the other freaks."

Jamie was so astounded, he couldn't think of a word to say, much less a proper comeback. He'd been coming to Hatcher's Feed since he was a kid. The owner's daughter, Melissa Hatcher, had gone to school with his sister. And he'd known Tom all his life.

"Put the stuff down, Jamie, and let's go." Ethan's eyes met Jamie's and he jerked his head toward the door.

Jamie set the saddle and tack on the floor by the counter and followed Ethan.

From the corner of his eye, he saw the manager's angry face. "Fuckin' faggot," Tom spat out as he walked by.

He was still so amazed at the manager's attitude that he hadn't realized Ethan had stopped short; Jamie's boots slid on the smooth concrete floor as he tried to avoid colliding with him.

Ethan caught his arm, steadying him. Then he let go and looked past Jamie's shoulder with an icy stare. "You go ahead and cancel my order, Mr. Cooke. You can also tell Melissa Hatcher that I'll be taking my business elsewhere here on out."

Once they stepped outside, Ethan turned to him. "You okay?"

Jamie nodded, too flabbergasted to speak.

Ethan tilted his head, looking Jamie up and down as he did so. "Good. Get in the truck. We'll go out to Robert's Feed and Suppl—"

"Ethan! Jamie! Wait!" Melissa Hatcher ran out of the store, her blonde ponytail swinging behind her. "Please don't go. I heard—"

Tom stormed out of the store, grumbling under his breath. He walked right past without acknowledging them. Jamie and Ethan turned their heads in unison to watch him go.

"Sumbitch!" Jamie's eyes widened and his hand flew to his mouth. "Sorry, I didn't mean to say that out loud. Please pardon my language, Melissa."

Melissa giggled. "It's all right, sugar. He *is* a son of a bitch!"

Ethan chuckled. "Did you fire him?"

She shook her head. "Not this time. Just made him take his break. But I sure will if he pulls a stunt like that again." She looked Jamie in the eyes. "I heard the rumors, too, but it don't make no difference to me. You're good people and that's all I care about. I gotta tell you, though, you're gonna catch some flak around here. It ain't right, but it's God's honest truth."

Jamie nodded. "I'm beginning to see that. I'm thinkin' Ethan was right and I should've kept my fool mouth shut."

Melissa glanced at Ethan. "Yeah, well, hindsight and all that, but it still don't give anyone the right to treat you like crap." She huffed and shook her head. "I mean, really, and over something so unimportant. It floors me the things that people take offense at. People's sex lives are private and that's how it should be." She rolled her eyes. "I'm sorry, Jamie. I don't know what got into him. You are always welcome here. Please come back in and let me make it up to you. I'll give you a huge discount, darlin'." She winked and went back inside.

Jamie once again found himself without words as he stared after her. Ethan nudged his arm and stepped into the store. "Well, come on."

All the things Jamie had put the floor were now on the counter. Melissa smiled at them. "So, Jamie, how is Julia? I heard she's working at University Hospital in San Antonio."

"Yes, she is. She seems to like it. I talked to her yesterday and she was tired but doing good, otherwise."

"Good, good. You tell her I said hi and to call me sometime."

"I will."

Melissa grabbed a business card off the counter and started writing, then looked up again. "Now, Ethan, you've been coming here forever. I'd sure hate to lose your business. What if I give you this—" She slid the card across the counter. "— and you call me directly to place your orders. That is my cell phone number and my home number. I'll make sure that I'm here when you come in to get them, too. What do you think?"

Ethan tipped his hat. "That would be perfect, Melissa, thank you. Go ahead and put my order in and give me a call me when it's ready."

"I certainly will. Thanks for the second chance, Ethan." She winked again and started ringing stuff up.

Jamie looked at Ethan, who was grinning. He caught Jamie looking and smiled wider.

Oh, damn! The man was just too sexy for words! Jamie's cock jerked to attention, stiffening. He couldn't wait to get back home. He was pretty sure where he'd be sleeping tonight, given Ethan's easy acceptance in the truck earlier. And that thought was enough to give him butterflies in his stomach. He closed his eyes, willing his prick to behave. He damned sure didn't need to be walking through town with a boner. With the attitudes he'd gotten so far, the townies would probably string him up. Either that or they'd run a mile in the opposite direction to avoid getting near him.

Melissa cleared her throat. "All right, Jamie, I gave you fifty percent off the saddle and twenty-five percent off everything else. How's that sound?"

His eyes shot open and he stared. He was about to tell her that that was too much when Ethan said, "Thank you, Melissa. That is very kind of you."

Jamie looked at him.

Ethan dipped his chin ever so slightly. Those brown eyes peered out from under the straw cowboy hat, one eyebrow arched. Just enough to communicate that Jamie should accept graciously.

"Thank you, Melissa. That's very generous of you. I appreciate it."

"You are very welcome. It's the least I can do."

Jamie grinned and pulled out his bank card and paid while Ethan picked up the saddle and blanket.

Melissa smiled at him, eyes twinkling. "You sure you're gay, honey?"

Jamie blinked. "Uh, yeah."

"Oh, well, a girl can always dream."

She looked over at Ethan. "I do believe he's even prettier than John."

Ethan laughed. "Yes, he is, Melissa! And a whole lot less ornery, too." Ethan winked at him, and Jamie felt his cheeks heat.

Ethan thought he was pretty? *Wait a minute...*"Men aren't pretty!"

"*You* are." Melissa dug around behind her, then put a large box on the counter.

Ethan took the opportunity to give him a good once over from head to toe, practically undressing him with his eyes.

Dang it! There went his cock again. He sighed, loudly. Something told him that getting his libido under control with Ethan around was a lost cause. He wondered how many more errands they had to run and if Bill and the guys would notice if they spent the rest of the day in the house. Hell, he hadn't even gotten to see Ethan naked yet. That just wasn't fair. He was going to have to rectify that as soon as possible.

Melissa put the rest of his tack in the box and said goodbye, apologizing again for Tom's behavior. Jamie thanked her once more for the discounts, then followed Ethan out to the truck.

Ethan put the saddle in the back seat of the quad cab, so Jamie stuck his box there, too. "Damn, Ethan! That was a hell of a deal. It was way too much."

"It's called good business. Besides, haven't you ever heard you aren't supposed to look a gift horse in the mouth?"

Jamie chuckled. "I look George in the mouth all the time."

Ethan groaned, then shut the back door. "Get in, smart ass!"

"Thanks for lunch, Ethan."

Ethan started the truck and put his seatbelt on. "You're welcome. Speaking of food, what are you gonna cook me for supper?"

Jamie grabbed his hat by the crown, pulled it off, raked his hand through those dark curls, then put it back on his head. He caught Ethan's gaze and grinned. "Well, I don't know, Cowboy, what do you want?" He waggled his eyebrows.

Why that little...! Ethan grinned back. Oh, yeah, he was definitely gonna have some of him, but that hadn't been what he was referring to. "I meant food, you tease."

Those blue eyes widened in mock innocence. "What?" Jamie touched his chest. "Me, a tease? I am not. I put out...thank you very much."

Ethan shook his head as a chuckle escaped. He felt comfortable flirting and playing with Jamie, more relaxed in a long time than he had felt with anyone besides John. Of course, he and John didn't flirt, and they'd both been too busy with their work to just go out and have a good time for a while now.

Ethan sobered. His attraction to Jamie made sense. He'd always felt at ease with Jamie, but he hadn't thought further about it, because he'd always regarded him as John's kid brother and off limits. In his mind, John had always been what linked him and Jamie together, but now that he'd had a little time to think about it, he and Jamie did have a lot in common.

Ethan smiled. This was looking more and more promising. He was getting hard just thinking about it. Wouldn't it be great to have not only a lover, but a friend as well? That's what he'd lacked with Cliff. When he wasn't fucking Cliff, he'd always preferred John's company. Cliff had been his lover, but never his friend. Now Jamie…Jamie could be both.

He raised his eyebrows at the younger man. "I'm going to hold you to that, Blue Eyes."

"I like that," Jamie said quietly and looked away. His voice was so soft that Ethan almost didn't hear him.

"Like what?"

Jamie turned his head back and those pretty peepers met his. "You calling me Blue Eyes."

Ethan's stomach tightened and his dick roused fully, throbbing against his suddenly too-tight jeans. He leaned across the space between them.

Jamie leaned in, too, those beautiful eyes staring into his with such longing it made Ethan's breath hitch. Damn, he wanted, just wanted, to push that gray Stetson off Jamie's head, grab those ebony curls, pull that sensual mouth to his and never let go.

He licked his lips and Jamie's eyes zeroed in on them. The younger man was whimpering and wet his lips. The brims of their hats collided. Ethan reached toward that strong, smooth cheek to tilt his head more.

Jamie blinked and jerked back. "We're sitting in the parking lot of Betty's diner," he gasped.

"Shit!" Ethan sat up, put the truck in drive and pulled out of the parking lot. How had he forgotten himself? No other lover had had that effect on him and Jamie wasn't even technically his lover yet. He was going to be the death of Ethan...but what a way to go!

"Sorry 'bout that."

"That was my fault, not yours. I just...damn!"

Jamie laughed. "Yeah. That about sums it up."

Ethan laughed with him, glad to have broken the tension. With any luck, his prick would behave and go back to sleep. "Do you mind if we stop off by my aunt's house?"

"We're going to go see Margie? Heck, no! I love her! Man, I haven't seen her since Mama died. They were friends, you know."

Ethan nodded, smiling at Jamie's enthusiasm. "Yeah, I know. And I call her Aunt Margaret, not Margie. That woman can sure bake, can't she?"

"Oh, heck yeah! I used to beg Mama to let me come to town with her to see Margie, so I could fill up on cookies and brownies and stuff." He chuckled, then got really quiet. "Your Aunt Margaret is a real nice lady. Mama used to argue a lot with Daddy; visiting with Margie always seemed to make her feel better. I guess it's just hard to be in a bad mood around your aunt, you know?"

"Yeah. They broke the mold when they made Aunt Margaret."

It was only a few minutes before they were pulling into her drive. As Ethan put the truck in park, a lady and two cute, redheaded, freckle-faced little girls exited the house with Aunt Margaret right behind them.

Aunt Margaret ran a seamstress shop out of her house so there were always people coming and going during the day. It seemed to make her good money and she was happy doing it. She always made Ethan beautiful shirts for Christmas.

Ethan and Jamie got out of the truck as the two little girls ran toward a waiting minivan. Their mama waved to Aunt Margaret and called something back over her shoulder about taking up a pink petticoat.

Jamie met him at the front of the truck. "Ugh! Pink petticoats." He gave a mock shudder.

Ethan felt the side of his mouth turn up. "I don't know, you'd look kind of cute in a pink petticoat."

"Bite your tongue! The day I wear anything pink will be the day hell freezes over."

"Oh? So it's not the idea of the petticoat so much as the color pink that bothers you?"

Jamie elbowed him in the side. "Ha ha!"

Ethan chuckled.

Aunt Margaret saw them and stepped off the porch with a big grin on her face, arms open wide. "Ethan!"

Ethan saw her about once a week, but she always acted like she hadn't seen him in years. He stepped into her arms and hugged her. Margaret Whitehall was tall and strong for a woman her age. She about crushed the breath out of him. He kissed her wrinkled cheek before he stepped back. "How's my best girl?"

"Why, I'm fine, darl— Jamie? Jamie Killian, is that you? You come give Margie a hug!" She practically pushed Ethan out of the way to get to Jamie. She wrapped him in her arms and kissed him on each cheek and his forehead.

Jamie was grinning from ear to ear. "Hi, Margie."

She pulled back and looked him over. "Oh, honey, you look so handsome and grown up. When I saw you there with Ethan, I thought you were John." She grabbed Jamie's hand and walked toward the house. "Jamie, honey, I haven't seen you since...since..." She stopped inside her doorway and turned.

"Oof." Ethan ran into Jamie, knocking his straw hat off. "Sorry. Didn't know y'all were gonna stop." Of course, if he'd been watching what was going on around him instead of Jamie's tight little ass... Ethan bent down and picked his hat up and put it back on.

Aunt Margaret ignored him and went right on with what she'd been saying. "Since your mama's funeral." She gave Jamie a sad smile, then narrowed her eyes. "You don't need an excuse to drop by every now and again."

Jamie patted her hand. "I know. Do you forgive me for not coming and seeing you sooner?" Jamie dropped to his knees, pulled his hat off and clasped it to his chest dramatically.

She chuckled. "You rascal! Get up from there. You just want cookies!"

Jamie got to his feet and picked Aunt Margaret up, swinging her around. Ethan just barely had time to step aside. "Well, *do* I get cookies, Margie?"

She laughed. "Yes, yes. You can have cookies. Put me down, you scamp!"

Ethan smiled. He'd known, of course, that Jamie knew his aunt; after all, Jamie's mama and his aunt had been friends a long time, but he'd never realized just how well Jamie and she knew each other. It was kind of surprising. John knew his aunt, too, but he didn't seem as easy with her as his brother was. Jamie must have come here quite often as a kid. The affection between the man and woman was quite genuine. Both shared almost the same familiarity that Ethan and his aunt shared.

"What about me, Aunt Margaret? Do I get cookies, too?"

She nodded. "Well, of course, you do, my sweet boy. Y'all come on into the kitchen and tell me what brings you both here. I admit, I'm not used to seeing the two of you together, but I like it."

Ethan frowned at her back. What was that supposed to mean?

Jamie set his hat on the couch as he walked by, reminding Ethan of his own manners. He pulled his off, placing it next to Jamie's.

When he entered the kitchen, Jamie was already sitting at the counter while his aunt poured all three of them a glass of milk and got a plate of cookies out. Jamie looked almost like...well, like a kid in a candy store.

Ethan shook his head. He really had to stop thinking of Jamie as a kid; he was a man now. Good lord, watching him this morning in the shower had proved that beyond a shadow of doubt! Ethan tugged on his collar. He had to get his mind off the younger man. He couldn't get a hard-on in front of his Aunt Margaret. Hell, that would be unbelievably embarrassing.

"Ooh! Oatmeal raisin! My favorite. Margie, you are a goddess!" Jamie's whole face lit up—sparkled, actually. Ethan couldn't help but grin. Jamie was just something else when he was happy.

Aunt Margaret cleared her throat and beamed at Jamie. She went to her seat and Ethan jumped up to pull her bar stool out for her. She patted his cheek. "Thank you, honey."

"You're welcome, Aunt Margaret."

"So tell me what brings my two favorite boys here? And together, no less."

Two favorite boys? Ethan blinked. Wow, she and Jamie really did know each other well. "Well, Jamie is working for me at the Tin Star now. We were just in town running some errands."

Aunt Margaret cocked an eyebrow and looked at Jamie.

Jamie finished chewing his cookie, took a drink and sighed. "Daddy kicked me out and Ethan took me in."

"Uh huh. And just why did that crotchety old bastard kick you out?"

Jamie chuckled. "Well…" He glanced at Ethan.

Ethan shrugged. *You're on your own, Blue Eyes.* It wasn't his place to say anything.

Jamie shifted on the barstool, fidgeting. "Well, Margie. I…uh…um…I told him I'm gay." The word "gay" came out as a squeak. It was all Ethan could do not to laugh.

Aunt Margaret got up and walked around the bar to hug Jamie. "Oh, honey. That man is an ass and you are much better off without him. Besides, if he didn't know already, he's pretty stupid."

Ethan coughed, then continued to eat his cookie, watching the byplay. He was a little surprised that Aunt Margaret knew. Heck, she could have at least shared the info.

Jamie pulled back. "What? You knew? How did you know? I didn't tell anyone until the other day."

"The same way I've always known about Ethan—"

Ethan sucked in a breath, eyes wide, and choked on the cookie in his mouth.

"Ethan, put your hands over your head!" Aunt Margaret rushed to his side and pulled his arms up.

Jamie pounded on his back.

Ethan's eyes filled with tears. He tried to take a deep breath but couldn't between the pounding on his back and his aunt keeping his arms over his head. He tugged his arms down and reached for his milk.

Jamie grabbed his glass and shoved it in his face. "Here, take a drink."

He took a quick sip and some deep breaths. When his coughing stopped, he glared at his aunt. "What do you mean, the same way you always knew about me?"

She blushed. "Sorry, honey, didn't mean to surprise you. It's just that pretty girls come in and out of my house for alterations all the time…and neither of you ever seemed to notice the way John did."

Well, hell, what was there to say? It was true. "Then I guess this means you're okay with us?"

She scoffed. "I can't believe you asked me that. Of course I'm okay with you both. I love you and nothing is ever gonna change that."

* * *

"Ethan, honey? I need to talk to you while Jamie is putting oil and antifreeze in my car."

Ethan looked up at his aunt from under the sink. "Sure. What's up?" He tightened the pipe fitting. "There, that ought to do it. It was just a little loose; this should fix your leak." Ethan slid out, then sat up, pipe wrench still in hand. "Turn the water on."

She reached over and did so. Nothing dripped out as far as he could tell. He smoothed his hands over the pipes, but everything stayed dry.

"Okay, I think you're good to go."

"Thanks, honey. Listen. I need to tell you something. It might come up and since…well, since you're involved with Jamie—"

Ethan grinned and put the wrench back in the toolbox. "Who says I'm involved with Jamie?"

Aunt Margaret smiled back. "You two are perfect for each other, and if you're not together, then you should be."

Ethan chuckled and started replacing the rest of the tools. "Go on. You were saying?"

"Blanche wasn't Jamie's mother."

"What?"

"Jamie is Jacob and his ex-mistress's child."

Ethan sat on the floor, mouth hanging open. He felt like someone had hit him between the eyes with a two-by-four. Holy shit!

"Blanche adopted him at birth. She loved him, but she never did forgive Jacob for his betrayal. I think that's why Jacob has always disliked Jamie so much. He blamed Jamie for Blanche changing toward him. But Blanche, she was such a good woman, she loved that boy despite what her husband had done." She wrung her hands together and glanced out the window at Jamie. "He doesn't know. She forbade Jacob from telling Jamie or her other children. I don't think Blanche told anyone but me. She stayed out at the ranch so much that people didn't see her, and since Jamie's got the Killian looks, no one ever questioned it. But now that Blanche isn't around... For a while, I've been afraid he'd say something, but he hasn't. Now, with Jamie's news, it may be the straw that breaks the camel's back, so to speak."

"You're afraid Jacob will tell him."

It wasn't a question, but she nodded anyway. "Yes, I am. That mean old son of a bitch has never treated that boy right. I suspect he was a little better when Blanche was around, because he did truly love her. I think he figured that if he were ever going to make things right with her, he'd have to accept Jamie. But now that she's gone, he doesn't have any reason to acknowledge Jamie. You would think that Jamie was Blanche's natural child rather than his own."

Ethan stood up, shaking his head. This was really messed up, but it explained so much. Old man Killian had never been outright mean to Jamie, but he'd clearly favored his other two children, and John most of all among them. Jamie had always been left out. Hell, John had always acted more like a father to Jamie than Jacob had…well, John and Hank, the Quad J's ex-foreman.

Aunt Margaret leaned forward and kissed his cheek. "I'm sorry to lay all this on you, honey, but I thought you should know. It's up to you whether you tell Jamie or not."

The screen door slammed.

They both glanced toward the door. Jamie came in smiling, then stopped when he saw them. "What's wrong?"

Ethan cleared his throat, "Noth—"

"Nothing, honey. I was about to get you boys some cookies to take with you. Thank you for getting my car fixed up." She got some tin foil and starting wrapping.

Jamie grinned. "You are very welcome, ma'am! Did Ethan fix your leak?"

"Yup. Was there ever any doubt?" Ethan raised an eyebrow.

"Nope." Jamie's eyes twinkled in what Ethan was coming to realize was a sign of impending mischief. "Ethan's pretty good with his hands." Then the flirt waggled his eyebrows at him. Ethan groaned and shook his head. And he was *not* blushing. He wasn't. Really.

Aunt Margaret laughed and swatted Jamie's behind. "James Wyatt Killian! Shame on you, saying such things in front of an old lady!"

Ethan snorted. "Give me a break! You don't really think we believe you're all delicate and such, do you?" He looked at Jamie, fighting to keep a straight face. "I'll show you good with my hands. I'll wring your scrawny little neck." He stomped in Jamie's direction.

Jamie took off out the door, laughing. "Bye, Margie!"

Ethan smiled after him. Just being around Jamie lightened his mood. He couldn't remember having so much fun in a long time. He really had to hand it to the man. Even with all the crap he'd been through in the last few days, Jamie still knew how to relax and enjoy himself. It said a lot for Jamie's strength of character.

Aunt Margaret handed him the plate of cookies. "What are you grinning about?"

He turned. "Just thinking it's good to see him still so happy despite everything that's happened. Tom snubbed him today at the feed store."

"Well, I always did think Tom is too big for his britches. Jamie's grown into a fine young man. He'll be all right. He's always been a happy child, so nothing will keep him down for long."

Ethan nodded. "Yeah, I admire that about him."

"Me, too, darling, me, too. You best get going or the rascal is liable to take off without you."

"Nah, he isn't going anywhere. I have the keys." He kissed her cheek. "Thanks for the cookies and for letting me know about his mama. I sure don't look forward to telling him, but I reckon it'd be best he hears it from me instead of Jacob."

She kissed him and patted his back as they walked to the front door. "You'll do what's right, baby. You always do."

Yeah, he did, damn it.

* * *

"Oh, hell. I almost forgot. Look in the center console. John left an envelope with his new foreman so I could give it to you this morning when I went to pick up George."

Jamie lifted the lid off the console. "He hired a new foreman already?"

"Yeah, man's name is McCabe. He's from somewhere in West Texas. Seems like a decent guy."

"Hmm. So, where was John? How come he didn't give it to you himself?" He tore open the envelope.

"He had to go into San Antone this morning. What's inside?"

Jamie held up a small key.

Is that a blush? Ethan raised an eyebrow. "What's that for?"

"Oh, nothing, just the key to my box."

Aha! The mysterious black box. "So, what do you keep in the box, anyway?" This time he was sure Jamie blushed. Interesting.

Jamie cleared his throat and pushed his hat down further over his forehead, shielding his eyes. "Toys."

"Toys? What? Like checkers or something?"

"Uh...no. Umm..."

"OH! Those kind of toys!" Ethan threw back his head and laughed. "Well, I'll be damned!"

"Shut up, Ethan!"

Chapter Seven

Jamie two-stepped himself to the pantry to get the potatoes, then back to the sink. This was fun! He'd have to cook with music more often. George Strait was on the radio, Fred was lying on the floor watching him, and Ethan would be back inside in a few minutes after talking to Bill and unloading the supplies they'd bought.

They'd made it back to the Tin Star ahead of the storm, and Jamie had gone straight to cooking. Ethan had gone out to help the hands move supplies into the barn before it rained.

He was singing and peeling potatoes when two strong arms wrapped around his waist and a chin landed on his shoulder. "You have a nice voice."

"Yeah?" Jamie didn't stop peeling.

He felt Ethan grin against his cheek, then kiss it. "Yeah. What do you want me to do?"

Man, he smells great. Jamie took a deep breath, inhaling his scent more deeply. "You can help me peel these if you want. I need to get them on so we can have mashed potatoes. Just have to get these and the rolls, and everything else is done." He pushed his hips back and wiggled his butt a little.

Ethan chuckled and pulled away, swatting his ass. "Cut that out. Supper first." Ethan kissed his cheek again, then moved away to get a knife and help.

Together, they sang along with the radio and finished preparing supper. After Jamie put the potatoes on to boil, they both sat down at the table with cold beers. Fred jumped up and pranced to Ethan as soon as he sat down. The dog was getting spoiled, no two ways about it. She leaned up against him, nudging his hand with her nose until he took the hint and scratched behind her ears. Ethan chuckled and continued to lavish attention on her.

"What is it, girl? Doesn't anybody ever give you any attention? The poor baby is just starving for affection, isn't she?"

Jamie snorted. "Yeah, right!"

Fred hammed it up; she wagged her tail and laid her head on Ethan's thigh, licking his arm. Ethan sipped from his bottle and idly petted Fred's head.

"How did you learn to cook so well?"

"I spent a lot of time with Mama. Daddy was always too busy, and John and Jules were enough older that they didn't want to be bothered with a snot-nosed little brother tagging along all the time. Not that they didn't let me tag along, as you well know, but for the most part I hung out with Mama or Hank. He always seemed to have time for me. I wouldn't know anything about ranching if it weren't for him."

"Yeah, Hank is a good man. Hell of a cowboy. Where is he now?"

Jamie took a sip of his beer, then set the bottle down and leaned back. "Florida. After he retired, he moved out there to be closer to his daughter and her family. He still calls every now and again to see how things are going."

Ethan nodded. "You going to miss not being the Quad J's foreman?"

"Yeah, I guess I will. As long as I can remember, I wanted Hank's job. That's part of the reason I spent so much time with him learning the ropes."

"What else?"

Jamie gave a mirthless laugh. "Unlike Dad, Hank put up with me without telling me I was in the way or to go back inside to Mama."

Jamie stared off into space, not really seeing anything, just thinking back over his childhood. "Dad's never been downright mean except for now, but...well...he's never paid much attention to me one way or the other." He caught Ethan's gaze. "I guess I took that to mean he was tolerant of anything I did. But I'm beginning to think it was just the opposite."

Ethan apparently didn't have a problem following his train of thought, because he nodded. He took a long pull from his bottle and said, "Your daddy isn't the easiest man to get along with. Even for John. And your daddy worships the ground John walks on."

That was true. Daddy had always thought the sun rose and set in John, while he just tolerated him and Julia. "Yeah. I got lucky. John loved...loves me. He always took up for me. I guess in a way, Daddy indulging John is what made me think he cared about me, too. 'Cause John always tried to include me, and Daddy never told him no." Jamie shrugged. There was no use going over the past. It wasn't going to help him now. He was a grown man and he didn't need his father's approval.

They sat in silence for several minutes, Ethan scratching Fred and him drinking his beer. He'd had a great afternoon hanging out with Ethan, then Margie. The only negative of the day had been Tom Cooke's attitude. Well, that and not being able to show affection for Ethan in public. He chuckled. Being out of the closet wasn't as liberating as he'd thought it would be.

"What's so funny?"

"I was just thinking that the whole point of telling my family I'm gay was to not have to hide it and to be accepted. It hasn't really worked out that way."

Ethan grinned. "No, I don't suppose it has. I never thought coming out of the closet would solve anything, actually. It's always seemed to me that it causes more heartache than just keeping it to oneself."

"When did you tell John and Julia?"

Ethan took a swig of beer, then leaned back in his chair with his hands across his stomach. "I never really told them. John just always knew, kind of like I always knew. I mean, we may have discussed it at one time or another. I don't know, it's been so long that I don't remember, but it wasn't like revealing some big secret. When we hit thirteen or thereabouts, he noticed girls, and I noticed boys. That's just how it was between us. We both knew it and that was that."

Jamie felt a sudden stab of jealousy. His brother and Ethan were really close.

"What about Julia?"

The timer dinged and Jamie got up and readied their supper.

Ethan laughed. "Well, when we were in college, I was out on a date and ran into her. Literally. I'd had a little too much to drink and was holding my date's hand, walking back to John and my dorm room. I wasn't watching where I was going and smacked right into her." He shook his head, obviously picturing the scene and smiling widely. He looked at Jamie but didn't seem to see him.

"It was pretty funny actually. I tried to catch her, she grabbed at me to keep from falling, and the next thing I knew, I was rolling down a grass slope on the campus grounds with Julia wrapped around me. Fortunately it wasn't that big a slope. We only got about six feet or so off the sidewalk." He chuckled as Jamie set a plate down in front of him. "Thank you."

"Welcome." Jamie took his seat and grabbed the salt and pepper, dousing his food liberally with both.

"It was hilarious. We landed in a heap, with Julia on top. She looked down at me and smiled really big—I'll never forget it—and, in true Julia fashion, she sat up, straddled my hips and started rattling a mile a minute. She fired so many questions at me I don't even remember them all. 'Who is he, are you gay, how much have you had to drink?' We stared at each other for several seconds, then started cracking up. My date thought I was nuts." He smirked. "I never did see him again. I think Julia scared him off."

Jamie grunted around a mouthful of steak. "That is insane! What are the odds?"

Ethan shook his head and took a bite, then finished chewing. "I don't know, but Julia and I still laugh about it. She and her date were just coming from our dorm."

The thought of Ethan on a date was even worse than thinking about how close he and John were. "Were you ever serious with anyone?" He groaned and stuffed a supper roll in his big mouth. Why had he blurted that out?

Ethan blinked and took another drink.

"I'm sorry, that isn't any of my business."

Ethan quirked an eyebrow, then one side of his mouth turned up. "Yeah, I was, sort of."

"Sort of?"

"Mostly I've just had casual friends who don't mind the occasional roll in the hay. Cliff was a little different. We were together, but not. We never actually agreed to be exclusive, but it just kind of went in that direction my junior and senior year."

"So what happened?"

"John." Ethan got a fork full of potatoes.

"Excuse me?"

He swallowed. "Cliff and John hated each other. To make a long story short, Cliff made the mistake of giving me an ultimatum—him or John. It was no contest. I didn't even have to think about it. John and I have been friends all our lives. And to be perfectly honest, thinking back, I can't imagine what I saw in Cliff anyway. We had nothing in common. Well, nothing but sex."

Okay, now he was jealous of some unknown man *and* his brother. "Wow. Did John know why you dumped the guy?"

"Oh, yeah. I came in that night and I believe his exact words were, "So where's dickhead?" when I told him all about it. Good Lord, your crazy brother actually wrapped his arm around my shoulders and blew kisses at Cliff the next time we saw him. John isn't the most subtle person in the world, in case you hadn't noticed. And like I said, he hated Cliff, so, yeah, he made a big production out of it. Competitive bastard."

Jamie grinned. That sounded just like something John would do. Hell, Ethan should be thankful for the fact that John hadn't stuck his tongue in Ethan's ear, or something equally suggestive, just to get at the other man.

"How about you? You have any serious relationships you've managed to hide from us?"

"Nope. None."

"None, as in no one serious or, none, as in none?"

Oh, boy!

"Spill it, Jamie. You're blushing."

Damn!

"None as in none."

Ethan's eyes widened. "Well, hell, not even girls?"

He frowned. "Now why would there have been girls?"

Ethan rolled his eyes. "Because a lot of men try to tell themselves that they're straight, so they date women."

He snorted. "I've never tried to convince myself I was something I'm not."

Ethan grinned and took another bite of steak.

"What?"

"First sex toys, now this. Anything else you want to throw at me today?"

He groaned and rolled his own eyes at Ethan. "Not that I can think of...no."

"Well, then let's clean up, then go upstairs and start your education. On the other hand, you're the one with toys, so maybe you can teach me a thing or two."

Sometime between putting the last plate in the dishwasher and letting Fred out, they'd started kissing. Jamie was all hands; he brought to mind an octopus, but Ethan decided that he didn't mind being octopus prey. After a few moments of necking in the kitchen, he broke their kiss long enough to get them upstairs. However, as soon as they hit the top landing, Jamie was all over him again. Crushing him into the wall across from his bedroom, devouring his mouth. God, the man was eager. It was pretty heady stuff to be wanted so desperately.

He grabbed two handfuls of that magnificent ass and walked Jamie backward toward his door, never breaking contact. Jamie hit the door and Ethan fumbled for the knob. When he found it and twisted it, they would have toppled to the floor if he hadn't quickly steadied them. Jamie didn't seem to notice. In fact, he doubted Jamie even knew where they were, he was so into their kiss.

Jamie was making sweet little whimpering noises in the back of his throat, and it was all Ethan could do to keep his head about him and get them to the bed. At the edge of the mattress, he pulled away.

Jamie whined and his top teeth nipped that kiss-swollen bottom lip, his hands still clutching at Ethan.

"Gotta get our clothes off, Blue Eyes. And we need stuff."

Jamie blinked those baby blues, hands wandering down the front of Ethan's jeans. "What stuff?"

Damn, his eyes are gorgeous. "What? Oh! Lube, we need lube. Shit! I hope I have some."

"I have some."

"You do?" Ethan caught Jamie's hands, placed them on his shoulders and leaned in to brush a chaste kiss on those puffy lips.

Jamie nodded and kissed him back, wrapping his arms around Ethan's neck. "In my box."

Ethan grinned against his mouth. "Don't suppose you have condoms in there, too?"

Jamie caught Ethan's lower lip between his teeth and shook his head just a little, then let go. "We don't need them, do we?"

Ethan pulled back and looked into those wonderful peepers. "I've never *not* used them." He caressed Jamie's cheek.

"I mean, I've never…I'm clean, Ethan."

"So am I, but you shouldn't take someone's word for it."

The corner of Jamie's lips turned up slowly and those blue eyes twinkled. "But you aren't just anyone. I've known you my entire life. I've never known you to lie or put anyone in any kind of danger."

Damn! Ethan felt like someone had just sucker punched him. That much blind trust was a hell of an aphrodisiac. He pushed Jamie onto the bed and came down on top of him, mashing their mouths together in a hard and bruising kiss.

Jamie was right there with him, his tongue plunging into Ethan's mouth, dueling with his. He pulled at Ethan's shoulders, his hips, anywhere he could grab. Those sexy moans were back and his hips bucked up into Ethan's.

He reciprocated, pushing his pelvis into Jamie's. He could feel Jamie's cock against his hip, right next to his own. He broke their kiss and lifted his upper body off the younger man's, holding himself up on his hands.

Jamie's face was a study in need, cheeks flushed, lips red and shining and his eyes lust-filled and unfocused. His prick was still moving against Ethan's.

Ethan had to slow down. Things were getting out of hand. He was about to go off and they hadn't even managed to get naked. Not that that was a bad thing, but he'd been waiting all day to get Jamie out of his clothes.

"Please, Ethan...please." Jamie writhed and panted beneath him.

"Shh...calm down, baby." He flicked his tongue across Jamie's lips and brushed the black hair off Jamie's forehead, out of his eyes, in a soft caress.

Jamie whimpered.

God, he loved that little sound! Ethan groaned and forced himself to get off Jamie and stand up. He squeezed his eyes closed and took a few deep, even breaths, willing his heart to stop racing and his dick to quit throbbing.

He heard Jamie sit up, then those long, callused fingers were fumbling with his jeans. He felt the air on his belly as Jamie pulled his shirt out of his pants and up. Warm breath brushed across his gut right before Jamie's lips found it. Jamie kissed his abdomen as he unzipped Ethan's jeans and started sliding them down.

Ethan opened his eyes. The dark head against his stomach made his cock jerk. He grabbed Jamie by the chin. Ethan shook his head. "No, baby, go get your box."

Jamie blinked, then nodded, but he didn't move, just stared up at Ethan dazedly.

Ethan grabbed his hands and got him to his feet. He kissed Jamie's forehead, then turned him toward the door that led into the bathroom adjoining their rooms. He nudged Jamie forward. "Go on now. Go get the box."

Jamie snapped to it, hurried out and was back within seconds, the black box in his hands. He gave it and the key to Ethan.

"Get undressed and in bed."

Jamie started stripping immediately, his chest and arm muscles flexing as he whipped the shirt over his head.

Ethan noticed the slight trembling in Jamie's hands when he unfastened his jeans. He couldn't help but stare as Jamie pushed them and his underwear down, freeing his long cock. It bobbed as Jamie kicked the pants aside and climbed onto the bed.

There wasn't an ounce of fat on that sinewy body. His chest and legs were tan, but his groin pale. The black pubic hair stood out in stark contrast against the lighter skin. His cock had a good girth. Not quite as wide as Ethan's, but a real nice size just the same. Jamie had fit in his mouth perfectly. A groan escaped Ethan, and he put the box down on the nightstand. "God, you're beautiful."

Jamie reached for him. "Now, you. Get undressed…please."

He quickly shucked his own clothes, then crawled up over Jamie. He straddled Jamie's thighs and sat back on his legs, Jamie watching his every move. His cock jerked at the feel of Jamie's warm skin against his buttocks and thighs and the sight of the rapt look in Jamie's eyes.

Jamie reached out hesitantly, running a finger down the length of Ethan's cock. "You're so thick."

Ethan sighed and closed his eyes. What was wrong with him that the feel of a fingertip had his balls drawing up tight and ready to explode?

Jamie wrapped his fist around Ethan's cock and tightened his grip. "Oh, Cowboy, you're beautiful, too…" The other hand trailed down across his pecs. "All of you."

His stomach knotted up and his eyes snapped open at the blatant awe in Jamie's voice. Jamie's eyes were wide, his bottom lip caught between his teeth. Ethan leaned down and captured those lips. The younger man's warm body and even warmer cock were delicious against him. Made him shiver in delight. He had to remind himself to slow down, that this was Jamie's first time. He was going to make this a night to remember if it killed him. And it just might. He hadn't been this turned on in…hell, he didn't know how long.

Ethan sat up and reached for the box. He placed it on Jamie's stomach and Jamie hissed out a breath.

"It's cold."

Ethan chuckled. "Good, you need to cool off a bit. You're driving me insane." He reached for the key and unlocked the box. Inside were two dildos, a slender blue one and a flesh-colored realistic one that looked like a nicely sized cock. There was also a small bottle of lube and a red butt plug. Ethan smiled and met Jamie's gaze. "Have you used all these?"

Jamie nodded, a flush creeping up his neck to his face.

Ethan's cock jerked and he groaned thinking about Jamie pleasuring himself with the toys. He took out the lube and the butt plug and set the box back on the nightstand. He laid the objects on the bed and slid down next to Jamie, lying on his side. Jamie started to turn toward him, but he forestalled him, pushing him onto his back again. "Just lie there and relax, baby." He nuzzled Jamie's neck and nibbled his way to Jamie's shoulder.

Jamie was making those noises Ethan loved so much, then he became all arms and hands again. Ethan grinned. Jamie was like a puppy, all enthusiasm without knowing what he was getting into, but having fun anyway.

Ethan grabbed his hands, still kissing Jamie's shoulders and neck. "Put them over your head and be still. You can touch all you want later. Right now, I just want you to feel. Okay?"

Jamie nodded.

"Good." He licked and kissed his way down Jamie's chest to his stomach, trailing his hands over Jamie's sides. He took his time caressing and feeling, learning the lean body beneath him. He used his teeth and tongue, eliciting gasps and moans from Jamie as he went.

God, he has a great stomach. Jamie's abs were even more defined than his own were. Ethan slid his tongue along the ridges and valleys of those chiseled muscles until the wet tip of Jamie's prick nudged his chin. Oh, yeah! Jamie was already leaking precome.

Ethan slid down further and rubbed his face against that hard, hot length, feeling viscous fluid streak his cheek. Jamie gasped, his thigh muscles tensing against Ethan's sides, then he whimpered.

Ethan held Jamie's cock against his face and flicked his tongue over the velvety soft tip. The salty taste of Jamie made his mouth water. He wanted to fully savor Jamie, but he wanted to be deep inside him, too. Ethan released the firm shaft and reached for the lube and plug without looking up.

Jamie shifted his hips in protest.

He grinned and nipped Jamie's hipbone. Jamie squirmed and gasped.

"Ethan, it tickles."

Ethan did it again as he flipped up the lid of the bottle. Jamie yelped and bucked, trying to get away, as Ethan chuckled and pulled Jamie back with one hand. He dabbed some lube on his fingers. Pushing Jamie's legs wider, he dipped his head and ran the tip of his tongue over Jamie's testicles.

"Oh, God! Do that again!" Jamie was panting hard, his head coming off the pillow. He reached for Ethan, but when Ethan met his eyes and shook his head, he dropped back to the bed. *Good boy.*

Ethan pulled one tightly drawn sac into his mouth as he felt beneath Jamie and spread lube on the tight opening he found there. Jamie pulled his knees up, giving him easier access. Ethan breathed deeply, taking in the soft, musky scent of Jamie. The warm skin in his mouth was getting tighter and tighter; it wouldn't be long before Jamie came. And when he did, Ethan wanted it to be in his mouth.

Ethan gripped Jamie's cock and held it up. A drop of semen slid down the base, making Ethan groan and sit up. He lapped at the pearly drop as his finger continued to rub across the slick and puckered skin of Jamie's anus. Ethan took the head of his lover's cock into his mouth as his finger firmly pressed for entry.

Jamie's groan was low and ragged. His thigh muscles jumped and his head rolled back and forth on the pillow.

Ethan's finger slid into Jamie's body and, just like that, Jamie came. He babbled incoherently as Ethan swallowed down the salty mix of his come. Ethan pressed his finger further inside as Jamie ground himself down onto it. Jamie's hips bucked frantically, making Ethan's mouth take more of his cock in. Ethan's finger only seemed to make him wilder, so Ethan took him deeper, to the back of his throat, while he steadily fucked him with his digit.

Ethan had always loved the feel of a hard dick sliding through his lips, caressing his tongue. It was a good thing he didn't gag easily, because otherwise Jamie's frantic movements and the long length of his prick sliding so far back to Ethan's throat would have done so.

Damn, but Jamie was hot! Ethan's own cock jerked in response, throbbing against the bedspread. He was probably seeping come, too. Ethan rode out the pleasure with Jamie, reveling in the fact that he could make his lover lose himself so completely.

Finally, Jamie relaxed a bit. His hand slid into Ethan's hair, stroking languidly. Ethan smiled to himself and continued his idle sucking of Jamie's dick. He worked up and down the hot staff as Jamie's breathing evened back out. Jamie hadn't completely softened, and the more Ethan sucked, the harder he got.

Ethan reached for the lube again and this time coated the plug. He tossed the bottle aside and slid the tip of the plug into Jamie's ass. He gently moved the plug in and out, pressing in a little more each time. The plug wasn't as big around as his cock, but it wasn't that much smaller. If Jamie could take it, then he could take Ethan. All of him.

"Oh, God, that feels incredible. Don't stop, Ethan, please don't stop."

Ethan let go of Jamie's cock with a loud *pop*. "Not gonna, Blue Eyes, so just relax." He watched as the puckered hole took in more and more of the plug. Jamie's prick jerked as the tight little entrance swallowed the plug. Damn, that was a sight to behold! Ethan came up on his knees as he continued to work the plug. Jamie was whimpering and writhing in ecstasy again. He loved every sight, sound, and smell of Jamie's pleasure.

Ethan let go of the plug and slid up Jamie's length. He kissed Jamie's chin, his nose, his eyes. "You okay, baby?" His voice sounded hoarse even to him.

Jamie nodded and opened those beautiful blue eyes. "I'm good, Cowboy. I've never been better, but I'm really needing you to keep going. You've got me all wound up again."

Ethan smiled and rolled onto his back, pulling Jamie with him. He needed to cool off a bit, or he was going to spew before he ever got inside of Jamie.

Jamie gasped and straddled his hips; his hands resting on Ethan's chest. "But I...I..." He frowned and his cheeks turned pink.

Ethan reached up and smoothed the lines from his forehead. "You what?" he whispered.

"I want you inside me."

Ethan groaned. He wasn't going to last long, but, God, he had to have that strong, hot body...now. Ethan snatched the lube and handed it to Jamie. "Me, too. Scoot down and get me ready."

Jamie grinned and backed up so that he could reach Ethan's cock. He took the lube and poured a generous amount into his hands, then closed the bottle and threw it aside, rubbing his hands together.

He held Ethan's cock and it was all Ethan could do not to come. His eyes shut tightly and he silently began to recite the multiplication tables. Jamie stroked his prick in a slow and steady rhythm. God, it was heaven. His balls were so tight, he ached. He needed to come badly. And Jamie wasn't helping his control any. He'd gone way past slicking him up and had moved onto jacking him off. Ethan gritted his teeth and grabbed the other man's hands. "Jamie!" he warned.

Jamie let go. Ethan stared into the handsome face above his as he reached around and tugged on the plug. Jamie groaned, his eyes closing. He leaned forward, putting his sticky hands on Ethan's chest, leaving Ethan no choice but to pull on the plug. As it came out, Jamie's breath hitched. Ethan felt something dripping on his stomach and looked down. Jamie's cock was leaking again.

"Jamie, Jesus, you're gonna be the death of me! I'm trying like hell to go slow and you're doing your damnedest to make me lose my head."

The tease nodded. "Yes! Please! I want you."

Ethan dropped the plug and grabbed his eager prick. With his other hand, he gripped Jamie's hip and guided his butt to his cock. The tip touched Jamie's puckered opening and Ethan had to take a deep breath. He tried to redo the times tables in his head, but Jamie started to push down on him, his body slowly swallowing up Ethan's dick.

Ethan gasped as the tight, hot hole engulfed his cock. Jamie kept pushing steadily down until Ethan thought he'd die of the pleasure. Only when Jamie's ass was nestled against his hips did he let out a breath.

Those pale blue eyes widened. "Oh, God, it feels so good. Better than the toys. 'S so hot. Ooooh..." Then he started to pull up.

Ethan grabbed his arms. "Easy, baby, easy."

Jamie shook his head. "I can't! Gotta move. Gotta...ahh, Ethan..." He plunged himself back down on Ethan's cock. Ethan gasped at the wonderful sensation, his eyes staring endlessly into Jamie's.

Jamie set a hard, even pace, fucking himself on Ethan's dick, riding him furiously. It was too much. Ethan stopped fighting him. He grabbed Jamie's hips, tilting them just so...

Jamie's whole body tensed, squeezing Ethan's prick, hard. "Ethan!"

The hot splash of Jamie's seed hit his stomach an instant before Ethan himself came. He groaned, pulling Jamie down onto his chest, holding him tightly as they both shuddered and gave into their releases. They lay there together, the last tremors of pleasure gradually leaving them.

It seemed like hours later that Jamie stirred. He pushed himself up onto his elbows and Ethan could feel the stare of those baby blues.

Ethan opened his own.

Jamie's pretty peepers were practically dancing. Ethan grinned. "What?"

A smile stretched across Jamie's sensual lips. "Thank you."

"My pleasure." Although he probably should be thanking Jamie instead. That had been the best experience of his life. He pulled Jamie back down, content to keep his Blue Eyes on top of him forever.

Jamie kissed his chin and pushed up again. "If we don't get up, we're gonna get stuck to each other."

"Is that such a bad thing?"

Jamie shook his head. "Nope, but it might be a little awkward once someone realizes we're missing and comes looking for us tomorrow afternoon." Jamie lifted up. Ethan's cock slid from his body.

Ethan groaned. "I'm too relaxed to move."

Jamie chuckled. "Come on, Cowboy." He grabbed Ethan's hands and pulled him up. Ethan tried to get away, but Jamie pulled harder. Before he knew it, he was sitting on the edge of the bed with Jamie yanking him to his feet. Once he was standing, Jamie kissed his jaw and left. He got right inside the bathroom door and looked over his shoulder at Ethan. "Come on."

"If you are always going to be this energetic after sex, I'm making you sleep in your own room."

A laugh echoed from the bathroom.

Chapter Eight

The phone rang.

"Hello?" Ethan said, voice scratchy and sleepy. The phone rang again. He blinked open his eyes, pulling his fist away from his ear. Damn, that had seemed so real. Another shrill tone filled the night. The digital clock read 12:02 A.M.

He reached for the receiver just as an arm flew over him, slapping at the alarm clock, startling him. Realizing it was Jamie, he grinned and grabbed the phone with one hand and Jamie's arm with the other, settling Jamie's arm around his own waist, then placing the phone to his ear.

"Hello?"

"Ethan, what are you doing?"

He glanced at Jamie and felt a sudden stab of guilt. He sure as heck didn't know how to tell John. Eventually, he'd have to, of course, because he had no intention of giving up what was looking more and more like the best thing that would ever happen to him.

Still, first things first. The quality to John's voice had vanquished the last remnants of sleep.

"I was sleeping. What's wrong?"

"Sorry, I didn't think you'd be asleep yet."

"What's going on, you sound pissed."

"I *am* pissed! I had another fight with Daddy."

This was probably going to be a long talk, so he slid up, propped his pillow against the headboard and got comfortable. He absently rubbed Jamie's arm, which had slid to his thighs. "Another?"

"Yeah, we've done nothing but fight since he kicked Jamie out. First, it was over him actually kicking Jamie out. Then somehow my coddling Jamie is what made him gay." He snorted. "Next, it was over you taking Jamie in. That, of course, is *my* fault because I begged you to do it. Oh, and now he wants to meet with you."

"Fine, I'll meet with him, but it isn't going to change anything. Jamie's mine now and I'm keeping him." Ethan winced. Talk about double entendres. "I'll even tell him you had nothing to do with me offering Jamie a job."

"Not that he'll believe you. I think he's going to try and use the steakhouse deal to force you to get rid of Jamie."

Jamie's arm squeezed him tighter, then he nestled even closer and nuzzled his face into Ethan's hip.

Ethan groaned. His cock should have been too tired to take notice, but it wasn't, filling with blood instead. He combed his fingers through the thick black hair, brushing it out of Jamie's face. Damn, he looked so sweet.

"Yeah, tell me about it."

What? Oh, John thought he was groaning over Jacob Killian trying to back out of their business deal. "Why the hell would he trash an agreement that's going to make him a lot of money? To spite me? He'd be doing himself no favors."

Ethan ran his fingertips over Jamie's pale cheek and felt the overnight growth of stubble just beginning to make its appearance. The cheek twitched at the caress, so Ethan went back to combing his fingers through the dark hair.

"He doesn't want him around. Says it would have been best if I'd just let him go, that we don't need 'his kind' 'round here. Can you believe that shit? I can't! And to think I've got that son-of-a-bitch's blood running through my veins."

"The more I hear, the less I like what I'm hearing."

"The more I hear from him, the more I want to kick his ass. I had no idea he could be such a coldhearted bastard. I know he never gave Jules and Jamie the attention he gave me, but still...to disown your own child and over something like this?" John paused to take a deep breath. "That's just fucked! I'm damned close to moving out."

"Why don't you?"

Sky-blue eyes blinked up at him, then a small smile curved Jamie's lips. Ethan smiled back and continued to twine his fingers through his hair. His dick was completely hard now, aching for more of Jamie.

"Hell, Ethan, the Quad J has been in my family for as long as the Tin Star has been in yours. I've been trained practically since birth to run the place. I even got a freakin' degree in agriculture."

"So what? I have a degree in criminal justice. A degree don't mean squat; you can do other things or do the same things elsewhere."

Jamie's hands started to wander, caressing his thighs and hips, then he ducked his head under the covers and lifted himself to settle between Ethan's legs.

John sighed. "Yeah, but that's just it. I don't want to do anything else anywhere else. I'm a rancher, damn it, and this is my home! It's what I was trained to do; it's what I love, and this is where I'm supposed to be. I also have a bunch of people counting on me to keep things together. God knows, left up to Daddy, he'd run off all my best ranch hands. Those men need me to make sure the Quad J doesn't come apart, Ethan."

"Well, if you decide to strike out on your own, you know I'll help you any way I can." He pulled up the covers and looked down at Jamie. The rascal grinned, waggled his eyebrows and tugged at Ethan's cock, squeezing. Ethan barely held in a moan. His eyes rolled back in his head and his stomach clenched in anticipation.

Damn, he couldn't do this now! He was on the phone, with John, for crying out loud. When he mouthed *I'm talking to your brother*, Jamie shrugged. Then, with those big blue eyes staring into his, Jamie's tongue flicked out and swiped across the tip of his engorged prick. Ethan dropped the covers, letting them fall over Jamie's head.

"But that's my point! I *have* a ranch. And, for the most part, I run the place. There is a lot of history here, and I'd hate to leave it. The Quad J is my heritage, my birthright. Hell, I'm the one who has hired most of the staff we have. I can't just up and leave them all. Sure, I could set out on my own, but I wouldn't have enough to pay them all if they came with me."

A breath of warm air trailed down his shaft, followed by a wet tongue. His cock jerked at the sensation. God, that felt good! His balls were nuzzled briefly, then that hot moist mouth closed around them. "Oh, fuck!"

"What?" John asked.

"Nothing I just thought of something I forgot to do." Ethan mentally patted himself. How was that for quick thinking? He lifted the covers again and frowned down at Jamie. Blue eyes twinkled up at him; Jamie's mouth stayed right where it was. Ethan released the sheets.

What had they been talking about? Oh, right. "Well, you could always move into your own place and go back and forth to the Quad J." Shit. That wonderful tongue was back, licking up and down his shaft. It was absolute torture...and absolute pleasure. Ethan lay his head back and closed his eyes.

"I've thought about that, and I gotta tell you it's not a bad idea—assuming the old bastard doesn't disown me, too. Hell, I haven't even told you the *pièce de résistance* yet...he wants me to get married."

"Oh, God!" Ethan wasn't really sure who he said it to, because Jamie's mouth had closed over the head of his cock just as John had dropped that bomb. His eyes popped open and he flipped the covers from his body.

John went on and on about the fight and how his dad kept insisting he get married, but Ethan barely heard him. He was more interested in the mouth working up and down his cock. What a wonderful sight! The hollowed cheeks and the pink mouth leaving a wet trail on every ascent were enough to make his balls pull up tight. What Jamie lacked in technique, he made up in sheer unadulterated enthusiasm. Every time those eager lips moved down on his dick, a soft humming sound of delight escaped them.

Ethan spread his legs a little wider and settled back to watch. Jamie looked up at him, releasing his cock, which flopped out of his mouth and against his stomach. Then those lean fingers brought his shaft back toward that warm mouth. As they stared at each other, Jamie tilted his head and slid his lips up the length of Ethan's cock again.

Ethan shivered. "John. Listen, I'm gonna have to let you go. Try not to fret, and tell your daddy I'll be there around noon."

"You can tell him yourself, I'm not talking to him until I have to." He sighed. "Get some sleep, I'll talk to you tomorrow."

"Later." Ethan put the phone back on the cradle, then glared at his tormentor. "Do you know how hard it is to concentrate with you doing that?"

Jamie pulled his cock out of his mouth and smiled. "I guess that means I'm doing a good job." Abruptly, he swallowed Ethan's cock all the way down, then gagged.

"Yeah, good job. Take a deep breath and try that again."

Jamie inhaled and exhaled, then slid his mouth down until his nose hit the dark curls above Ethan's cock. If the sight of Jamie deep-throating him wasn't enough to make him lose control, the feel of his tongue on his cock was. He grabbed Jamie's head and thrust his hips up.

Jamie choked.

"Use your hand; don't go so far down."

The dark head nodded even as a tight fist squeezed Ethan. Jamie's mouth returned and worked in unison with his hand. It felt amazing and delicious—the firm grip of his lover's hand and the wet heat of his mouth. He watched everything, sweeping his fingers through the dark curls on Jamie's head. Those red, swollen lips worked him fast and hard. He was so close to coming. He could feel it, his balls drawing tighter and tighter, his muscles tensing, his belly tingling.

He tugged at Jamie's head and pulled him off his cock with one hand, then grabbed his prick with the other. "Open your mouth."

Jamie blinked up at him in confusion but did what he was told. Ethan pumped his cock twice, moaned and spurted. A little come landed on Jamie's chin and his cheeks, but the rest went in that wide open mouth. Jamie swallowed it all. He even wiped the semen on his chin with his hand, then licked his fingers clean.

Ethan groaned.

Jamie came to his knees, his own prick rock hard. He reached down and grabbed himself, those pale eyes closing. Ethan swatted him away and fisted that long, hard cock in his hands. He only pulled once before Jamie started thrusting into his hand. He looked absolutely beautiful as he writhed in his pleasure. Within seconds, that lean body tensed and Jamie gasped and came on Ethan's hand, chest and the sheets.

Jamie collapsed face first next to him in a satiated sprawl. "I'm not moving ever again," he mumbled into the mattress. Ethan chuckled and leaned back against the headboard, dropping a hand to Jamie's back. He caressed the smooth skin for several seconds.

God, he felt good. He was so relaxed, he probably could sleep sitting up, but the come on his stomach was sticky and drying on his skin.

He threw his legs over the side of the bed and heaved himself up and into the bathroom. When he came back from washing up, the first thing he saw was Jamie tight, white ass. Jamie was in the same spot he'd left him in, snoring softly. Ethan chuckled and slid into bed. He nudged Jamie over and wiped him off with a warm damp rag, then tossed it toward the bathroom. "Get under the covers."

Jamie snorted and rolled back over onto his stomach. "Huh?"

Ethan pinched him on the butt.

Jamie swatted at him, then turned onto his side with a yawn. He blinked his eyes a few times, then pulled his legs up and lifted himself enough to slide under the sheets. "What was that about? What did John want?"

"Turn over." When Jamie complied, he pulled Jamie against him and wrapped his arm around his waist. Jamie sighed and snuggled into him.

"He had another fight with your father. And now your dad wants to meet with me."

Jamie's head popped up and he turned to look over his shoulder at Ethan. Words poured from him. "What? What about? You don't think he's going to give you any trouble, do you? I won't have it! If I'd known he was going to go after you, I would never have accepted your offer. I'll leave, Ethan. I don't want to cause you problems."

The rapid-fire babble reminded Ethan of Jules. He hid his grin and pushed Jamie back to the mattress. "Like hell you will! I'm not afraid of your daddy, Jamie. He's probably going to threaten to back out of the steakhouse agreement, but so what? There are several others involved in it besides we two. We can find other investors."

"Ethan, I—"

"Stop borrowing trouble, you have enough already. We'll find out what he wants soon enough." He slapped Jamie on the hip. "Go to sleep."

It was quiet for several minutes and Ethan had almost dropped into unconsciousness when Jamie spoke again. "Ethan?"

"Huh?"

"If he backs out, can I be a part of it? Mama left me some money when she died. Technically, I won't get it until I'm twenty-five, but maybe you or John could front me the money and I'll pay it back with interest."

"You want in?"

"Yeah, I do. It sounds like a good investment from what I've heard. I may not have the cattle to contribute to the venture, but I can buy stock in the company, right?"

"Right. Actually, your dad and I weren't putting up the cattle, either. Even combined our cattle operations are too small for that. As far as I'm concerned, if you really want to get involved with this, it doesn't matter whether your dad withdraws or not. A friend of mine from college put it together and I'm the one that brought your dad in. Why don't you sit in on some of the board meetings with me? We'll go over the specifics sometime tomorrow, and if you still think it sounds like a good idea, then we'll contact the others, and I'll front you the money."

"Ethan?"

"Yeah?"

"Thanks."

He grinned and kissed the back of Jamie's neck. "You're welcome, Blue Eyes."

* * *

Ethan stepped up onto the porch of the old Victorian-style house and knocked on the door. It flew open seconds later, and he was nose to nose with Jacob Killian.

It was easy to see where Jamie, John and Julia had gotten their looks. With their black hair and blue eyes, they all bore a strong resemblance to their father. Strangely enough, of the three children, Jamie was the one who looked most like the old man. Looking at Jacob, Ethan could easily imagine what Jamie would look like in forty years. They both had the same lean build and the light blue eyes, and their facial features were almost identical. However, Jacob was a couple of inches taller than his son and, of course, age had added wrinkles at the corners of his eyes and to his face, and his hair was liberally streaked with gray. His eyes also didn't have his youngest child's clarity or openness. Still, he looked relatively young for a man in his sixties. If a person didn't know what an ass he could be, they might consider Jacob very handsome.

Jacob thrust his hand out at him. "Ethan, glad you could meet with me. Come on in."

They shook hands and Ethan removed his hat before he walked inside. Under the circumstances, he hadn't expected the polite greeting, but he wasn't going to be rude. As long as Killian played nice, then so would he. "John didn't know what you wanted to meet about, but he passed the word along."

Killian shook his head and chuckled. "I bet he had an idea or two why I wanted to speak to you, and I'm damned sure he didn't have a problem telling you his thoughts."

So the old man was going to try and pretend everything was as it should be. That they continued to be merely friend and father, respectively, to John, acquaintances, business partners. Ethan grinned. He'd go along with it…for now.

"You're right, he did. But that's neither here nor there. You mind telling why I'm here?"

"Not at all. You know me well enough to know that I don't mince words and never have. I don't have a problem telling people what I think. Let's go on back to the office." Ethan followed Killian and took a seat in the leather chair in front of the desk as Jacob took his seat behind it.

"You and John have been friends a long time, and I appreciate the lengths you'll go to for him, but it isn't necessary."

He quirked an eyebrow. "Meaning?"

"Hiring Jamie. You didn't have to do that. And to be honest, I'd have preferred it if you hadn't. I think it would be better to just let him go his way. That boy never did belong here. He's been a mistake since birth."

His jaw almost hit the floor. "Pardon me?"

"He should never have been born."

Ethan started to twist his hat in his hands before he caught himself and stopped. Really, this shouldn't have surprised him, yet it did. How could anyone look at Jamie and not love him? Jamie was one of the most caring and giving people he knew. "How can you say that? He's your son."

"Yes, he is, unfortunately. With his looks, I can't rightly deny that." The older man looked as if he wished he could have denied it. He got up and paced behind his desk, his gaze on the floor.

"Hell, you'd never know it from the way she doted on him, but James isn't Blanche's son." He sighed and looked up at Ethan. "It's a long story and you don't need to know the particulars, but I had an affair, one I've regretted ever since it happened."

"That's not his fault!"

Jacob blinked. "Excuse me?"

Ethan reined in his anger. Showing one's hand was not a good bet in tight situations. And this certainly qualified as a tense moment. It would not do to let Jacob see how emotionally involved he was with Jamie. "You are blaming him for something that isn't his fault...and not very big of you, quite frankly. He didn't ask to be born."

"You don't know what it's been like to have a constant reminder of a lapse in judgment! You don't even have a wife or kids. And how I treat my children ain't none of your goddamned business."

Ethan stood up and put his hat on. "You're right; I wouldn't know what it's like to have an affair when I already have a wife, much less end up with a son by another woman. And it sure as hell is my business. It became my business when I hired Jamie, and when you got me here and brought up the damned subject. So let me get right to the point and out of your way. I'm not firing him."

"He's a goddamned cock sucker!"

And damned good at it, too! He mentally counted to ten and took a deep breath. Losing his temper wasn't going to help matters. "What he is, is a helluva fine cowboy and a loyal friend. He's welcome on the Tin Star for as long as he wants to stay. This is not open for debate. I needed another hand and I got a damn good one. Your loss is my gain. So if you'll excuse me, I'll show myself out." He turned to leave, but Killian's voice stopped him.

"So that's how it is? You're going to take the little faggot under your wing. Play the hero. Well, don't say I didn't warn you. Folks are gonna take exception to you harboring his kind."

"Then that will be their problem, not mine." He tipped his hat with a rough jerk. "Good day."

Jacob's face turned red. Ethan could swear he was about to start foaming at the mouth.

"It will be your problem, too! You can count me out of the steakhouse! I'll be damned if I do business with some liberal, tree-hugging, gay activist!"

Ethan couldn't help but laugh. He'd known it was coming. Heck, he was actually kind of tickled about it. He'd never been accused of being a liberal before. He nodded. "I figured as much." He turned and walked out the door, closing it firmly behind him. *A liberal? Me?* He was still chuckling when he got in his truck. Being gay was about as liberal as he got.

Chapter Nine

Ethan's humor lasted all of five minutes; he got in his truck and headed home and the anger took over again. How in the hell could a person blame their own child for *their* mistake? Which was essentially what Jacob was doing. *What an ass!* This went way beyond Jamie being gay. Apparently, Jamie coming out was just the icing on the cake.

How did such an unfeeling man end up raising three generous, caring children? Of course, Ethan knew the answer to that…Blanche. Blanche Killian had been a very loving and nurturing individual, and she'd raised three very fine children. How the hell she'd ended up with Jacob as her husband was anyone's guess.

Ethan had always been a little put off by Jacob Killian, but he'd overlooked a lot because Killian had always done right by John. It wasn't until he and John were in their twenties that Ethan realized the fondness he showed John was not offered to his other two children. Looking back, the indifference had always been there in plain sight, but like most young people, if something hadn't affected him directly, Ethan hadn't looked too closely. And, as John's best friend, Ethan always had been afforded a position in Jacob Killian's esteem.

He was actually glad old man Killian was backing out of their business venture. Ethan could barely stand the thought of the man being his neighbor, let alone his business partner. Hell, the only reason he'd invited Killian into the deal was because John had asked him to. John had wanted in on the deal on behalf of the Quad J, so Ethan had included Jacob.

Ethan barely remembered the rest of the quick drive home. He charged inside as soon as he got inside the house. Swiftly making his way to his office, he slammed his fist down on his oak desk as he sat in his chair, then pulled his hat off. He ran a hand through his hair and tossed his hat on to the leather couch that was cattycornered to his desk. How in the hell was he going to tell Jamie the circumstances of his birth? He was pretty certain that Aunt Margaret had hit the nail on the head; with his wife gone, Jacob wasn't going remain silent much longer. It would come out sooner or later, and it was better if Jamie heard it from him first.

"Damn it!" He pounded his desk again, making his keyboard jump. He slumped into his chair, then leaned back and put his hands over his face. How did you tell someone that the parent who'd always been there for him wasn't his natural parent?

Ethan tried to imagine suddenly finding out that his father hadn't really been his father. Rationally he knew that it wouldn't have mattered, that he'd have gotten over it, because his dad had loved him. But it still would have felt like a loss in a way. Like a betrayal by his father.

He dropped his hands and sighed. Propping his booted feet on the desk he closed his eyes. Jamie was a very optimistic person, always had been. Nothing got him down for long, which was probably how he'd survived living with Jacob Killian for twenty-one years. Well, his nature, and John, Jules, and Blanche's love easing his way. Even so, Ethan was willing to bet the news would upset Jamie. He remembered how Jamie had appeared at Blanche's funeral, then again the day Jamie had arrived at the Tin Star. Ethan hated that look and never wanted to see it again on his face.

He was fantasizing about beating the shit out of Jacob Killian when two strong hands settled on his shoulders and began kneading. He opened his eyes and Jamie's pale ones smiled down at him from under a gray cowboy hat. He suddenly felt much better and grinned. "Hey, Blue Eyes."

"Hey. How'd the meeting go? He back out of the deal?"

"Yeah."

"I'm sorry, Ethan."

Ethan shook his head and closed his eyes again. Jamie's hands felt good, and his nearness was lifting more than just Ethan's spirits. "It's fine. I'm actually glad."

The younger man apparently sensed his tension leave, because he asked, "Does that mean you're in a good mood?"

The hesitance in Jamie's voice and the slight pause in the shoulder massage made Ethan open his eyes again. "Why?"

Jamie sighed. "You know that sorrel mare you bought last spring?"

"Yeah?" He asked reluctantly.

"Well, I think she's foundering."

"Damn it! That's all I need, a lame horse!" He took a deep breath and calmed himself. "What makes you think she's got laminitis?"

"Her hooves are warm and I can feel the pulse on the pastern really easily."

Ethan arched a brow. "Okay, I know their hooves are normally cold, but what's with the pulse?"

Jamie arched a brow right back. "You ever try to find a pulse there? Right below the fetlock?"

Ethan's brow wrinkled in contemplation.

"You know the spot below that joint, right before the hoof?"

He rolled his eyes. "I know where the fetlock is. I'm just trying to figure out why anyone would try to find a pulse there."

"I didn't *try* to find it, I felt it when I picked her foot up to check her hoof. I've never felt a pulse there before, so I tried to find it on George, Spot, then Hayden's horse, Gypsy. I couldn't find it in any of them. And I remembered hearing that it can be a sign of foundering. I'm no vet, mind you, and Bill doesn't agree with me, but he called the vet out to take a look at her anyway."

"So when is the vet coming?"

Jamie bent down and kissed him on the lips. "Tomorrow morning. You owe me big time, by the way."

Ethan grinned, dropped his feet off the desk and moved his chair enough to pull Jamie into his lap. His hips bucked up once instinctively as Jamie's hip nudged his growing erection. He took off Jamie's hat and tossed it beside his. "How come?"

Jamie wiggled his hips with a grin, rubbing against his cock. The man was definitely a tease, no two ways about it. Well, okay, as Jamie himself had pointed out, not a tease exactly; he did put out, and deliciously, too.

"Because your ornery horse bit me on the ass when I was trying to find his pulse."

He chuckled, resting his forehead against Jamie's.

Jamie nipped his chin. "That isn't funny. It hurt like hell. Then the beast stole my hat. Again. Why do you keep that brat of a horse around?"

He chuckled again. "The same reason you keep George and Fred around. Besides, you have to admit, pest or not, he has character and good taste…because apparently he must find your ass as delicious as I do."

Jamie snorted. "What he has is an attitude problem."

"Nah, he's trying to play. He just doesn't know when it's appropriate and when he needs to be serious. I think he believes he's a dog or something." Ethan thought for a minute. "Wonder if I could teach him to play fetch? Maybe that would help."

Jamie laughed. "Oh, God, a horse that plays fetch!"

He laughed with Jamie. "You have to admit, it would be kinda cute."

Jamie nodded and wrapped his arms around Ethan's shoulders leaning in for a kiss. "Yeah, it would."

Oh, that mouth felt good! Ethan flicked his tongue across Jamie's lips. He opened for him and flicked back. It wasn't long before Jamie's moans and sighs reached Ethan's ears and his hands began to wander. After a couple of failed attempts to get at Ethan's cock, which he was seated atop of, Jamie settled his hands back around Ethan's neck.

Ethan's hand trailed down to Jamie's lap. He groaned into Jamie's mouth. His Blue Eyes was hard, ready for him. He squeezed, wanting that long prick. Separating their lips so he could see what he was doing, Ethan unzipped Jamie's jeans, then pushed the briefs out of his way, grasping the hot shaft in his fist.

Jamie whimpered and pushed up into his hand. "Oh, please."

"Mmm. I love the way you beg. What do you want?" he whispered against Jamie's lips as he began stroking Jamie's cock.

"Suck me."

Oh, man! That husky plea had Ethan's heart pounding and his dick throbbing. He nudged Jamie out of his lap, then pushed his lover's jeans and briefs past his hips, watching as that long, hard cock bobbed free.

Jamie whimpered and moved forward, nudging Ethan's lips with the moist tip.

He took the head into his mouth and sucked, tasting the salty flavor of Jamie's semen. When Jamie tried to enter further between his lips, he grabbed the slim hips, stilling them. He sucked just the head for several seconds, deliberately tormenting him. Except Jamie wasn't the only one being tormented. Ethan's cock was so hard, it hurt. He reached down and freed himself from his jeans, squeezing his own prick as he took Jamie's all the way into his mouth. Clasping Jamie's dick with his other hand, he worked it up and down in unison with his mouth.

Jamie moaned his pleasure, his cock dripping come onto Ethan's tongue.

He knew Jamie was close to bursting, but Ethan bet he was closer and decided to help Jamie along. He slid his fingers into his mouth beside Jamie's cock, wetting them. He was rewarded with a gasp and shudder when he ran the wet fingers down the crease of Jamie's ass. When his fingers found the tight ring of muscle, he pushed in.

Jamie pushed back. "Oh, God, yes!"

He fucked Jamie with his fingers as Jamie fucked his mouth. The feel of that long, throbbing prick on his tongue sliding past his lips was too much. Ethan's hips thrust into his own hand. He barely managed to cup his hand around the head to keep from making a bigger mess when he came.

Jamie tangled his fingers through Ethan's and rocked himself back and forth between Ethan's mouth and fingers, moaning out his pleasure. "Ethan!" He tensed, his back arched, ass muscles contracting, and spilled his come down the back of Ethan's throat.

Ethan swallowed every last salty drop, reveling in the taste of his Blue Eyes. When Jamie finally relaxed, he slid his mouth and fingers free and watched as Jamie slid to the floor in front of him, resting his head on Ethan's leg.

"Just give me a second, Cowboy, and I'll take care of you." He kissed Ethan's jean-clad knee, then rubbed his face against it like a cat.

Ethan grinned and brushed a hand through Jamie's tousled hair. "No need. I came before you did."

Those blue eyes blinked up at him in surprise, then focused on the hand still cupping the end of his cock. Jamie grinned and came to his knees, kissing Ethan soundly on his lips. "Be right back." He got up, pulled his pants up and went into the bathroom connected to Ethan's office. He came back a few minutes later with his clothing put to rights and a wet rag, then proceeded to clean Ethan up.

Ethan laid his head back, enjoying the feel of Jamie's gentle ministrations. When he felt Jamie putting his sated cock back into his pants, then fastening the jeans, he opened his eyes.

Jamie got back up and took the rag back to the bathroom, then sat down on Ethan's desk facing him when he returned.

"We need to talk."

Jamie nodded. "I kind of figured. You looked like you were trying to figure out a solution to world hunger when I came in. What's on your mind?"

Ethan chuckled and extended his hand to Jamie, wanting him closer. "Nothing quite so far reaching, but probably just as difficult." For him, anyway. Jamie was becoming more and more important to him, and he hated having to give him bad news...well, life-altering news.

Jamie took his hand and allowed himself to be pulled back into Ethan's lap. He sighed and grinned. "I guess if you want me this close, you aren't kicking me out."

"What? Hell, no! You are welcome here. Period. And as to the two of us... I'm not even close to being through with you, Blue Eyes."

Jamie smiled, showing teeth, and visibly relaxed. "Good, because I don't think I'm ever going to be done with you. I'm afraid you may have gotten more than you bargained for. I've wanted you since I was a kid, and now that I have you, I don't plan on letting go. You're stuck with me."

Ethan groaned. Damned if that declaration didn't feel…right. He felt almost giddy. Excited. Hell, he felt both and even more protective than ever. He grabbed Jamie by both sides of his face and kissed him.

Jamie wrapped his arms around Ethan's neck and tilted his head, kissing him back.

"You two are not even going to believe the latest!" John's voice startled them, interrupting their kiss. They looked up.

John came into the study and went straight to the decanter of whiskey on the bookcase, never even looking their direction.

Ethan and Jamie stared at each other. Jamie grinned and kissed his nose. Ethan dropped his hands to Jamie's waist and leaned back in his chair, waiting for John to notice them. Hell, he'd decided he was keeping Jamie, so John was going to have to know. More to the point, John was going to have to stop barging right on into his home whenever he felt like it.

Ethan cringed as he thought about what John would have seen had he walked in unannounced only ten minutes earlier. The sooner John knew about them, the better.

John poured a tumbler of whiskey and turned around as he took a drink. To his credit he didn't choke, his eyes merely widened as he finished swallowing. He set the tumbler on the bookcase and pointed to them. "You two? Since when? I can't believe I'm just finding out about this!"

Ethan nodded. "Since recently…very recently."

"Oh, okay, then I guess you are both relieved of an ass chewing for hiding it from me."

Jamie smiled. "Gee, that's a relief. I think I've fill my quota for having my ass nibbled on today."

John's eyes shot wide and he looked at Ethan.

"Don't look at me. I haven't nibbled on his ass...today. He was talking about the fact that Spot bit him earlier."

John laughed, poured himself another glass and came to sit in one of the two leather chairs in front of Ethan's desk. "Well, hell! So what now? I guess this is where I'm supposed to ask what your intentions are toward my baby brother."

Jamie groaned and rolled his eyes, shifting on Ethan's lap. "Give me a break."

John winked at Ethan, then lifted his chin at Jamie. "You shut up! I'm trying to protect your honor...or is it your virtue?" He shrugged. "Whatever."

"How about protecting my privacy and shutting the hell up?"

"Nah." John shook his head and took a swig.

Jamie groaned and buried his face in Ethan's neck. Ethan couldn't help it; he started laughing. Jamie shook his head and stood up, but he couldn't quite hide his smile.

"Oh, good grief! Now I need a drink." He walked over and poured himself a glass of whiskey, slammed it back, swallowing all of it before he choked. He looked at Ethan and John, his eyes watering. "Good God! How do the two of you drink this shit?"

Ethan laughed harder, and John joined in. Ethan smiled at his friend. "My intentions are quite honorable."

John smiled. "Good. You weren't kidding when you said he was yours and you were keeping him, were you?"

"Nope."

John nodded. "Excellent! Guess we should celebrate. And set to teaching the youngun how to drink."

Ethan groaned. "Oh, no! We are way too old for a drunkfest."

"We're never too old for a drunkfest." John motioned to Jamie. "Bring the decanter and a glass for Ethan. We have some serious drinking to do."

Jamie did as he was told, setting the liquor and tumbler on the desk before he sat in the chair next to his brother. "Don't start that youngun shit! You're not that much older than me." He poured another glass full of whiskey, chugged it down, and winced. "So, what are we never going to believe? What has our illustrious parental unit done now? Beside backing out of the deal with Ethan?"

John shook his head and glanced at Ethan. "I want in on the deal. I was going to use the Quad J's money, but that ain't gonna happen now. He can't tell me what to do with my own money."

Ethan shrugged and poured himself a drink against his better judgment. "Fine. Jamie wants in, too. I doubt Nathan will object. The only reason your father was brought in was because you decided to use the Quad J's money."

John looked at Jamie. "You're in, too?"

Jamie nodded. "Yeah, I heard y'all talking about it. It sounds like a good idea."

Ethan took a swallow and let out a sigh at the burn. "It is. Nathan Canterbury went to college with John and me. He's a whiz in business and investing. He came to me thinking I might be able to put up the cattle, but I told him that though my operation isn't big enough to supply a chain, I'd love to invest. He asked if I knew anyone else who'd want in. So I called John. Of course, there was more to it than that, but that's it in a nutshell. I'll go over the specifics with you later."

"'Kay."

Ethan looked back at John. "So, what is this new development that is going to shock us?"

"Oh, it's a doozie! He wants me to marry Beth Johnson."

Ethan's eyebrows practically disappeared into his hairline.

Jamie slapped a hand over his mouth, but it was pretty obvious he was laughing.

Ethan recovered first. "Ted Johnson's daughter? *That* Beth Johnson? Is she even out of high school yet?"

John shrugged. "I think so. But get this. He and Ted have already discussed wedding plans."

A suspicious sound escaped Jamie. John glared at him. When Ethan looked at Jamie, his face was red, and he was making little muffled, snorting noises.

"What in the hell is so damned funny about this?!" John demanded.

Jamie shook his head and snorted more at intervals.

Ethan bit his bottom lip to keep from smiling at the picture Jamie made. He was sliding out of his chair and had tears in his eyes, he was laughing so hard. Or rather he was trying *not* to laugh so hard. If he didn't stop holding back soon, Ethan was afraid he was going to need CPR.

He turned to John with a grin. "Well, I guess your daddy could have picked a worse bride. Beth is a pretty little thing. Seems feminine and ladylike enough, if you're into that sort of thing."

That was it; the dam broke, metaphorically speaking. Jamie's hand dropped, he hit the floor, then let loose the guffaws he'd been holding in.

John looked down at him, then back to Ethan. "I really don't think dad picking a bride for me is all that funny. How much did he drink?"

Ethan glanced at the empty tumbler on his desk. "Just two glasses."

Jamie flopped backward on the floor and gasped a word at them. It sounded like "thespian."

He and John exchanged puzzled frowns.

"Did he say she's an actor?" John's brow wrinkled.

Jamie laughed even harder. He tried to say something else, but ended up gasping for breath, his face bright red and tear-streaked.

Ethan shrugged. "I don't know, but don't let him have any more to drink. I think he's met his quota for the drunkfest."

Finally, the guffaws slowed to little snickers, and Jamie got back into his chair. His face was still red and his eyes were watery, but he was otherwise composed...until John asked, "What was that about?"

After another protracted bout of laughter, Jamie finally managed to speak. "She's a lesbian! He's trying to get you m-married to prove you aren't gay, but h-he's going to marry you off to a l-lesbian!"

Ethan chuckled. "Are you sure?"

Jamie nodded. "Positive. She's a very good friend of mine. We even joked once about getting married to cover up that w-we're both gay."

John smiled broadly and shook his head. He caught Ethan's gaze. "He's a lightweight, so he isn't going to last the whole night at this rate. Maybe we should all eat something."

Jamie lay on the study floor in front of the fireplace with his socked feet on the couch, his head next to Ethan's and John's. Their boots and belts had long since landed in a pile by the couch, which held all three of their hats. Ethan's feet were in the opposite direction of Jamie's, resting on the hearth. John's feet were perpendicular. All their heads were close, but their legs were spread out, like in a pinwheel. They'd finished off the decanter of whiskey, then started on a bottle of tequila. Well, Ethan and John had, Jamie had had enough sense left to stop with the whiskey.

John was currently singing a Tim McGraw song off-key, and Ethan was...well, giggling was the only way to describe it. Jamie grinned, he'd have never thought that such a sound could come out of Ethan. Then again, he never thought he'd be lying in the middle of Ethan's office watching the walls and ceiling spin...and the couch and the mantel. *Whoa. What's that?*

There was an upside-down picture on the mantel. Well, it wasn't really upside-down, but he was. Still, he'd never seen it before, and he'd been in this office tons of times over the years. He pointed his finger above his head. "Is that a daguerreotype? Where did it come from?"

Ethan lifted his head to peer at the mantel, then dropped his head back down. "Yeah. I found it a couple of weeks ago in one of the family photo albums. It was just too cool to leave there, so I had it framed. That is Theodore Whitehall. My great-granddaddy. He bought the place back in the late 1800's after retiring as a marshal. In the Old West, lawmen often cut their stars out of tin cans, and that's how the ranch got its name."

John broke off from singing and took up the explanation. "Not only was Efan's grape-grandfudder a marshal, but hiss grandfudder was a sher'f and hiss uggle a Tex' Roger. Law 'forcemen' runs in the Whitehall blood. Efan hass a dagger in criminiminal justice, but when Dylan died, he t-took over the Tin Star 'stead."

"Yeah. Sure did. I wanted to be a Texas Ranger, too, but shit happens."

Jamie wasn't sure how long he lay there, but the next thing he knew Fred was licking him in the face. He must have fallen asleep. A quick glance to the left, then the right, assured him that he wasn't the only one who'd nodded off. Ethan and John were both out cold.

Fred whined.

"Hey, pretty girl, what do you want?"

She barked and pranced a bit.

"Outside?"

She barked twice and wagged her tail.

Jamie sat up; his head spun and his stomach rolled. He clutched the bowling ball that was sitting on his neck. "Whoa."

Fred barked.

He winced. "Okay, girl, give me a second." Jamie got to his feet slowly. Once he gained his balance and convinced himself not to heave, he followed Fred through the kitchen to the back door and let her out. Within seconds, she bounded back onto the porch. He let her back in and headed to the office to see what he could do about getting Ethan and John off the floor and into bed. He'd taken three steps out of the kitchen when his leg was jerked backward.

Fred had a hold of his pant leg, tugging.

"What?"

Fred took off into the kitchen, then the laundry room where Ethan had put her food and water dishes.

"Are you hungry?"

She wagged her tail so fast she almost knocked herself over.

He chuckled.

After making sure Fred was fed and had plenty of water, Jamie returned to the office. How was he going to get Ethan and John up to bed? John he might could carry if he had to…but Ethan? No way. He leaned against the doorframe and clapped his hands. "Come on, guys! Up and at 'em! It's bedtime!"

Neither of them stirred.

Jamie sighed. He'd known it wouldn't be that easy, but he had had to at least give it a try. He pushed away from the door. Once he got Ethan in bed, he wasn't coming back downstairs, so John would have to be taken care of first. He toed his brother's arm with his socked foot. "Come on, John. Time for bed."

John snuffled and rolled over, turning his back to Jamie.

Jamie groaned and slowly bent over. He shook John's shoulder. "Rise and shine!"

"Wha? Whaz wrong?" John sat up blinking.

"Nothing, but you can't sleep on the floor. Go up to bed."

John stared blankly at the fireplace.

Jamie waited a few seconds and when it became apparent that his brother wasn't going anywhere, he grabbed him under the arm and started pulling him to his feet. When John finally stood up, he turned his head and looked at Jamie.

"Hey, Jamie."

"Hey, John."

He just stood there shakily. Jamie pushed at his brother's back to get him moving. He managed to nudge John all the way to the guest room before John started to drop.

"Shit!" Jamie slid his shoulder under his brother's arm and grabbed his waist.

John jerked upright and blinked at him. "Hey, Jamie."

"Hey, John."

Jamie maneuvered his brother inside the room and to the bed. "Sit down, John."

His sibling more than complied. He fell flat on his back in the middle of the bed.

Jamie had removed John's boots and his shirt, and was trying to tug his jeans off when his brother opened his eyes again. "Hey, Jamie."

"Didn't we do this already?"

"Huh?"

"Nothing." Jamie finished tugging his brother's jeans off, leaving him in his underwear. He tried to get John off the top of the covers and under them, but finally gave it up as a lost cause and grabbed the opposite corner, pulling the comforter over him.

He went back downstairs for Ethan, who was right where he'd left him—on his back with one arm flung out to the side and the other resting on his abdomen. Jamie leaned down and patted his cheeks. "Come on, Ethan. Time to get up."

Brown eyes blinked open for a moment, then shut. "Jamie, baby, I don't think I can get it up."

Jamie chuckled. "I'm not asking you to, Cowboy. I just want *you* to get upstairs."

Chapter Ten

"Oh, damn." Ethan blinked open his eyes and grabbed his head. What the hell had they been thinkin', to drink that much last night? His eyes finally focused enough to see the ceiling over his bed. Maybe the ceiling would quit spinning any minute now. He turned his head slowly and glanced at the clock on the nightstand. 8:52 A.M.

Ethan realized there was an arm slung over his belly and followed it over to Jamie, who was sound asleep on his stomach. Jamie's black hair was sleep-tousled, he had a morning's growth of stubble on his cheeks and bags under those closed baby blues, but he somehow still managed to look good enough to eat. He hadn't thought Jamie had drunk as much as he and John, but he was still unconscious, so maybe he'd imbibed more than Ethan had thought.

A chuckle came from the doorway. "Oh, hell, that hurts. Gives new meaning to 'only hurts when I laugh,' don't it?"

Ethan slowly rolled onto his side, facing the door and looked at John. "Damn. You look as bad as I feel." And he did, too. His friend's shirt was unbuttoned and untucked, his jeans unsnapped, his hair was all over the place, and he had bags under his eyes as well. But there were two cups of coffee in his hands. "You made coffee?"

John walked in and set a cup on the nightstand. "Nope, Jamie apparently set the timer on the coffeemaker. Here. You got aspirins in the bathroom?"

Ethan moved Jamie's arm off and sat upright. "Yeah, medicine cabinet. Bring me some, too. Hell, bring the whole bottle."

He'd taken his first sip of coffee when John came back out of the bathroom and handed him two aspirins, then set the bottle to the side.

"Thanks. How long you been up?" He tossed the pills in his mouth and washed them down with another sip of coffee.

"About ten minutes. Long enough to go huntin' for coffee and aspirin, and to let Fred out." John sprawled into the chair next to the bed. "Why the hell did we drink that much? Next time I decide to tie one on, would you kindly remind me that I'm not twenty-one anymore?"

Ethan chuckled, then wished he hadn't. "Yeah, well the kid *is* twenty-one and, from the looks of it, he didn't fare any better than we did. And if I remember correctly, I did tell you it was a bad idea." He peered at Jamie, then back at John.

"I didn't think he'd downed as much as we did. Hell, he must have put my ass to bed. Can't imagine I made it there myself."

The man in question reached out toward Ethan. When he found Ethan, he turned onto his side and scooted closer, nuzzling his face into Ethan's hip and wrapping his arm around Ethan's thigh.

Ethan reached down and brushed the hair out of Jamie's face. His brain woke up and shouted, "Hey! John is in the room," before he could caress Jamie's cheek. He pulled his hand back and glanced up at John to see his reaction. His friend had always been supportive of him, but Jamie was his baby brother.

John had been watching Jamie. He looked up and met Ethan's gaze as he took a sip of coffee. "How do you do it?"

"Do what?"

"How do you keep from killing each other?"

Ethan quirked an eyebrow and barely stopped a laugh from escaping. "Well, we try to keep all the guns put up. And Jamie isn't allowed to play with knives."

John smiled. "Oh, ha ha! Very funny! You know what I mean." He took another swallow and shrugged. "I guess it's none of my business. I was just curious, is all." He paused, got a real thoughtful look on his face, then said, "It's just that Jamie isn't always easy to live with, and you sure as hell aren't, and you're both pretty damned hard-headed. The two of you have always gotten along, but I never thought..."

"After living with you for four years, I can handle anything." Ethan shrugged. "I don't know. We just seem to go together." He glanced down at Jamie, who was now smiling in his sleep. Ethan smiled, too, before he could help himself. "To be honest, I think that this is it, the real deal. And it just amazes me that he's been right under my nose all along."

Jamie's hand started drifting, and Ethan had to switch his coffee cup into his other hand before he could stop Jamie's progress. Somehow he didn't think John was ready to see his brother with a handful of cock.

John chuckled.

Ethan was so surprised that he jerked and spilt hot coffee on his bare chest. "Shit! That's hot."

John chuckled louder, but got up and went into the bathroom. He came back with a hand towel and tossed it at Ethan. "Here."

Ethan grabbed the towel and wiped off his chest with one hand, while balancing the cup in his other. He was reaching across to put the towel on the nightstand when Jamie's questing hand wrapped around his prick.

He jumped. "Son of a bitch!" The cup tilted in his hand.

John laughed in earnest now. He got up and rescued Ethan's coffee and set it on the table.

Ethan dropped the towel and removed Jamie's hand, mumbling, "Thanks."

John sat back down, still chuckling. "Damn, Ethan, I haven't seen you blush that red since Brent Fuller pantsed you in P.E class in the fifth grade."

Ethan chuckled. "I'd forgotten all about that. Man, that kid was a jackass. If he wasn't giving people wedgies, he was yanking our pants down! Wonder whatever happened to him."

"Don't know, but he kept his distance from us after you socked him a good one in the nose."

Their laughter disturbed Jamie; he rolled over and faced the other way. Ethan had to catch the covers to keep from being exposed.

When their chuckles died down. Ethan grabbed his coffee from the nightstand and brought it to his lips.

"Does it hurt?" John asked with a straight face.

Ethan's eyes widened and he coughed. It was a damn good thing he hadn't taken a sip yet. He knew John well enough to have followed his train of thought. He should have recognized from the mischievous twinkle in John's eyes that he was fixin' to spring one on him.

"Jesus! What is it with you Killians? First *you* get me drunk. Then I wake up with one hell of a hangover. Then *your brother* tries to molest me in his sleep, making me singe my chest hairs. And now you try to get me to choke to death."

John bit his bottom lip, trying without much success to hide his amusement.

Ethan grinned suddenly. "No. Yes. Sometimes. I don't know. It depends. What do you want me to say, John? Do you really want me to answer that question?"

"Nah, not really, just trying to throw you off balance. We've got a bunch of years together, man, been here for each other through a lot of shit. It's my job to keep you on your toes." John chuckled, then sobered. "Do you remember when we were kids and how I always tried to get you to marry Jules, so you'd be my brother? Well, I guess I got my wish after all, even if it's Jamie and not Julia."

Ethan blinked, caught off-guard by the emotion he felt, and stared up at the ceiling. "Fuck you! You *are* trying to kill me!"

John laughed. "Sorry."

Ethan smiled, looked at John. "Go home! Don't you have a ranch to run?"

John nodded, stood up and slapped Ethan on the shoulder. "Fine, be that way. I can tell when I'm not wanted. Besides, my teeth are fuzzy."

"Gross."

John turned toward the door. "Yeah, it is. My damned breath is about to gag even me." He turned back to Ethan once he was outside the door. His eyes twinkled. "You know, our new foreman isn't bad looking for a guy. Maybe I'll give it a shot. You gonna answer all my questions if I do?"

"Get the hell out of here and stop messing with me! You better behave or I *will* answer all your questions...in graphic detail!" He gave John a great big smile. "Later, that is, when I'm not naked in bed with your brother." Ethan batted his eyelashes innocently.

John groaned and left.

Ethan lay back down and pulled Jamie into his body. His warm breath tickled Jamie's ear. "How long have you been awake?"

Jamie grinned. He hadn't thought Ethan was aware he'd been playing possum. "Long enough to find out my brother might have a crush on the new foreman. That is seriously disturbing, by the way."

Ethan chuckled and nipped his ear, making him jump. "You think it's disturbing; how do you think the new foreman would feel if he knew?"

Jamie snorted and pressed his hips back into the cradle of Ethan's. *Ooh, hard cock!* "True, very true. Please tell me he was joking."

"He was."

"Thank God!"

Ethan kissed his ear with a chuckle. "How very un-open-minded of you, Blue Eyes."

He smiled and proceeded to show Ethan just how open-minded he was by reaching back and squeezing the stiff prick nestled against his backside.

Ethan groaned, reached down, and caught Jamie's cock in his fist.

Jamie couldn't decide whether to buck up into that hand or push back against the cock in his own palm. Ethan made the decision for him by disengaging Jamie's hand from his cock, sliding the rigid organ between Jamie's legs, then pulling on Jamie's penis.

Jamie shuddered and he might have whimpered, but he wouldn't swear to it.

Ethan chuckled in his ear. "What do you want, Jamie?"

"Fuck me."

"Ah, baby, anything you want." Ethan let go of him and leaned over Jamie toward the nightstand, snagging the lube from inside the drawer. He fumbled around behind Jamie for a few seconds; then Jamie felt a cold slickness smear across his anus, a finger stroking against the tight opening.

Jamie shivered in sheer pleasure from the caress. He moaned and pressed back against the teasing digit that was seeking penetration.

A hand clamped down on his hip. "Easy. Slow down, I'm not going anywhere."

He relaxed, sighing in bliss as the finger continued to rub and tease.

"You know, baby, one of these days, you're going to have to fuck *me*." One long finger slid inside him.

Jamie whimpered and pressed back, pushing it deeper. "'Kay. More." A second finger joined the first, plunging in and out slowly. "You like it, Ethan?"

The hot breath against his temple tickled. "Yeah, love the way you feel around my fingers, around my cock."

He shook his head. God, those fingers felt good, filling him, fucking him. "No, not that. Do you like to be fucked? Do you like someone inside you?"

Ethan moaned in his ear. Another finger slipped in, burning for just a second, before giving way to pleasure. "Oh, yeah, babe, I like it. Not as much as you, though. I don't think I've ever met anyone that loves it as much as you do, but yeah, I like it." His fingers stilled. "Are you ready for me?"

Jamie nodded. "Oh, please!"

"Umm, love it when you beg."

The fingers disappeared. He felt the head of Ethan's cock press against him as Ethan used his fingers to spread him open.

"Love it when you fuck me." Jamie bucked backward and felt the tip slide in. "Yes!" He pushed back slowly until he felt Ethan's pubes against his ass.

Ethan hissed out a breath. "I know you do, Blue Eyes. Never had a lover that could get off with penetration alone until you."

"Really?" A shudder wracked Jamie's body, and he squeezed Ethan with his muscles.

"AH!" Ethan started to pull slowly out, his hand clamping around Jamie's hip. "Really. You're so fucking sexy riding my cock." He pushed back in.

Jamie let out a ragged moan. He tried to move, but Ethan held him still, torturing him with long, drawn-out thrusts.

"What's the matter, Blue Eyes?"

Damned ornery cowboy! "Ethan, damn it!"

Ethan chuckled in his ear, then reached down, gripped his cock, and squeezed. *Oh, yeah!* Abruptly the thrusting ceased, and Ethan backed all the way out of him.

He opened his mouth to protest but was pulled over onto his back. Ethan's mouth slanted down over his, and his smooth, hard chest pressed against him. Jamie spread his legs invitingly. He wanted more; he felt very empty, and his cock was stiff with want. Ethan continued to lave his lips, the inside of his mouth, his teeth. "Ethan, please."

Ethan nipped his bottom lip. "Get on your knees, and grab the headboard."

He didn't hesitate.

Just as his hands wrapped around the headboard, something cold slid across his hole again. He jumped and looked back.

Ethan had the lube and was recoating him with it. He looked up into Jamie's eyes as he grabbed his own cock, drizzling lube over it, then tossing the bottle aside. His fist wrapped around his thick penis, smearing the lube across its surface.

A sound gurgled up from the back of Jamie's throat. *Sexy bastard!* He eagerly watched each long, lazy pull. The red prick was already leaking come. Damn, Ethan was scrumptious! He was not going to beg, he wasn't. He whimpered. There, that wasn't begging.

Ethan chuckled and came up on his knees. One hand wrapped around Jamie's hip; the other stayed on that gorgeous cock. He pulled Jamie's hips toward him, nudging him with the wet tip of his cock.

Jamie dropped his head back and closed his eyes. Ethan's dick rubbed up and down his crease teasingly. He thought he might have whimpered again.

The front of Ethan's thighs pressed against the back of his as the slippery, fat crown of his lover's penis slid into him.

He moaned.

So did Ethan.

Inch by torturous inch, Ethan slid forward until Jamie's ass was cradled against his hips. "You ready?"

Jamie nodded.

Ethan pulled out, then thrust back in, picking up a steady rhythm.

Jamie could feel his lover's hard body against his back, muscles rippling with every thrust, the slap of Ethan's balls against his skin. The man was so freakin' amazing. Even more wonderful was the feel of Ethan's cock sliding repeatedly over his prostate. Jamie panted, having a hard time catching his breath. He was close, really, really close to peaking.

Ethan's hand wrapped around Jamie's prick and tugged. Jamie grunted, and his head landed on Ethan's shoulder as Jamie came.

"Fuck, yeah!" Ethan's arm wrapped around Jamie's chest, pressing him close, and he continued to slam into him and pump his cock as Jamie spilled his seed.

Jamie felt the hot breeze of Ethan's breath on his shoulder as he spoke. "Damn, baby, that's it, come all over my hand." Ethan's breath caught. He stiffened against Jamie's back, and Jamie felt the heat of Ethan's release inside him.

Jamie opened his eyes and turned his head toward Ethan, kissing his cheek and chin, willing his own breath to go back to normal.

Ethan slumped back on his heels, taking Jamie with him. Both his arms surrounded Jamie, and his face nuzzled the back of Jamie's neck. "You think Bill would know it if we didn't work today?"

Chapter Eleven

It had been three weeks since the incident with Jacob Killian, and things were perfect...almost a little too perfect. Ethan was waiting for the other shoe to drop.

Jamie was happy, truly happy, and Ethan just couldn't bring himself to ruin the mood around the Tin Star by telling him the facts about his birth. He knew he needed to, but he'd kept putting it off.

It wasn't just Jamie that was happy; so was everyone else. Jamie had that effect on everyone. The ranch hands were happy, Bill was happy, even the animals were happy. Ethan himself was practically freakin' ecstatic. Not that he minded, and apparently neither did anyone else, because he was pretty sure they all knew about him and Jamie.

In the short time he'd been there, Jamie had managed to start giving Bill cooking lessons, which the older man enjoyed and was starting to show in the small spare tire he'd begun to carry around his middle. Ed and Hayden were pretty damned appreciative, too, but they were too young and worked too hard for the excess calories to accumulate.

Jamie had also arranged to get everyone together on Sunday nights for supper, with an open invitation to Aunt Margaret, which she took up. In addition, contrary to his previous protests, Jamie did clean. In fact, the man was a cleaning machine. He'd reorganized the tack room, made a new schedule for feeding the animals, and pretty much taken over the main ranch house and made it his. If something was out of place or lopsided, it got moved, repositioned. Everything was clean and accessible when needed. Jamie ran the place like a well-oiled machine.

The younger man not only pulled his weight around the ranch, he more than made up for the loss of two hands. He did more work in three weeks than Carl and Jeff had done together in three months. The Tin Star hadn't felt the loss of two hands. In fact, with Jamie around it was like gaining new workers. Not only did he shoulder a fair share of the workload, but he seemed to spur Ed and Hayden into working even harder. Ed and Hayden respected Jamie and his work ethic. Because of him they got their work done quicker and more efficiently, and thus had more time off, too.

Ethan didn't have to venture outdoors to take care of work as often as before Jamie had arrived. He still did, of course; there was always something that needed to be taken care of. A man could only take so much sitting in front of a computer, but he knew things were well in hand even without him to oversee everything, which was a first. So much so that Ethan was seriously considering expanding the operation the way he'd always wanted but had been reluctant to do because of the even longer hours and work that would have been needed. He had the land, he had the money, and now he had someone to help him so that he wouldn't have to work himself or his men to death to make it work.

The biggest change was between Ethan and Jamie. They'd settled into a comfortable relationship. There were no doubts that what they had was real. Ethan couldn't remember being so at ease and having so much fun with another person, even John. And the sex? The sex was phenomenal.

Jamie had moved all of his stuff into Ethan's bedroom. At first it had been a little awkward; neither of them was used to sharing such close and intimate space. But they were working it out. In such a brief period, Jamie had not only made a place for himself at the Tin Star, but he'd carved a home in Ethan's heart. Ethan couldn't even imagine going back to his lonely existence. Jamie was much more than his lover; he was his friend, someone he knew he could count on.

There were bound to be a few differences of opinion from time to time, but as a whole they got along great. One of the more notable arguments had been last week when, after a day of work, Jamie had come in and cleaned house. He'd had the main house spotless and supper in the oven. Ethan had followed and taken a shower, then tossed his clothes and his towel on the floor when he was done.

Jamie had gone upstairs to tell him supper was ready, taken one look at the disarray Ethan had left the bathroom in, and snapped. Ethan had thrown a fit of his own, saying he'd worked hard all day. Jamie had put him in his place by merely lifting a brow, as if to say, *And I haven't?*

That had pissed Ethan off even more, because it was true. He'd locked himself in his office without supper, then emerged an hour later to find the house quiet and a note telling him that there was a plate for him in the oven. He'd eaten his supper, gone upstairs, woken Jamie up, and apologized. Jamie had accepted his apology by commenting that since Ethan didn't like cleaning house, he'd best shut up and pick up after himself, or he'd find that he'd have to go back to doing it all himself again. Ethan hated housework, but he damn sure liked a clean house, so he had agreed to do his part to help. Ethan suddenly smiled, remembering the tender lovemaking that had followed his apology.

It really wasn't fair for Jamie to do it all and the cooking, too. Hell, Jamie did too much as it was. Ethan practically had to sit on the man to make him slow down and take a break. Well, in all fairness, blowjobs worked pretty good as an incentive, too, assuming Ethan could get him alone long enough.

Ethan sighed and turned off his computer, stretching his hands over his head. He needed a break. More to the point, Jamie needed a break. He grinned to himself and picked up the phone. He dialed and waited.

Two rings later, a short, clipped, "'Ello?" answered.

"What are you doing?" Ethan stood up and walked to his office window and looked out. Jamie was nowhere in sight. He sighed.

"As little as possible. Why?"

"'Cause Jamie and I need a ride to San Antone."

"What's in San Antone?"

"Will you take us or not?"

"Why aren't you driving? You have a truck and so does Jamie."

Damn! Why did John have to be so nosy? Ethan rolled his eyes. He didn't want Jamie to know why they were going, but he knew John could keep a secret. "I've been looking at the new Ford Mustangs. I think I'm going to get one, but don't tell Jamie. It's a surprise."

"No fuckin' way! You are so NOT buying Jamie a car!"

Ethan pulled the phone away from his ear with a grimace. "Damn! Do you have to be so freakin' loud? I'm not buying it for Jamie. I'm buying it for me."

"Then why are we keeping it a secret from Jamie?"

Ethan sighed.

"Ethan?"

"Oh, hell! Fine, I was going to put his name on the title, too, but I'm buying it for both of us, not just him."

"Shit! That's just not right! I've never had a lover buy me a car. You wanna be my boyfriend?" John was quiet for a second, then added, "You can't fuck me, though."

Ethan pinched the bridge of his nose, trying to decide if John was giving him a headache or not. "Just get your ass over here and pick us up!"

"All right. Be there soon."

Ethan hung up and went in search of Jamie. He started to dial Jamie's cell, but his lover wasn't too far. He decided he needed the exercise.

Jamie was alone in the barn, shoveling out George's stall. He looked up as Ethan came in, leaned on the handle of the shovel, and pushed his gray cowboy hat back a little. Those blue eyes leered at him and his full, kissable lips turned up at the corners. "Hey, Cowboy."

Ethan grinned. "Hey, yourself, Blue Eyes. You think you can leave mucking out the stalls to later and take the rest of the day off?"

One dark eyebrow arched up under the gray felt. "Well, I'm almost done, actually. Can you give me five more minutes?"

"That depends. Can you also shower and redress in less than ten minutes?"

Jamie went back to shoveling, but not before Ethan saw a flash of teeth. "That depends."

Oh, he knew what it depended on, but he wanted to hear the little flirt say it. "On what?"

"On whether you're going to be in the shower with me."

Ethan chuckled and shook his head, turning to leave. "Not this time. I need you ready to leave in fifteen minutes."

"Why so soon?"

"It's a surprise."

"What kind of surprise?"

Ethan shook his head. "Nope. Not gonna tell you."

Jamie sighed. "Okay, I won't pester you about it, if you take a shower with me."

"No time. Hurry up!"

"Okay, fine, be that way! You hog all the hot water anyway!"

Ethan smiled. He could hear the laughter in Jamie's voice as he left the barn.

Twelve minutes later they were in John's truck and pulling out of the driveway. Jamie leaned forward, his elbows on the front seat between Ethan and John's shoulders. "So, where are we going?"

John chuckled and looked at Ethan. "Well, Ethan, where are we going? The youngster wants to know."

Jamie's head snapped around to John. "You're driving. Can't you tell me?"

"Nope. Ethan said I can't."

Jamie's head snapped back around to Ethan.

Ethan rolled his eyes at John and groaned. *Bastard!*

Jamie walked around the dark red GT in awe. He ran his hand down the side of the door. *Nice!* Red was his favorite color. He couldn't believe that Ethan had added his name to the title. He'd been speechless. It hadn't been the car that had made him so breathless and weak-kneed, either. It was the ramifications of Ethan putting something in both their names. It smacked of commitment.

Be still his heart, he wasn't just getting a new car—he was getting Ethan. Technically, he already had Ethan, of course, but this was tantamount to a public declaration for a man who didn't want everyone to know he was gay. At least to Jamie's way of thinking it was.

Damn! His dick was thickening. Maybe later he could talk Ethan into pulling over down the road somewhere and breaking the car in. Shit, thoughts like that were not going to make the ride home a comfortable one. He shifted a little from anyone's view, relieving the press of denim against his crotch. He needed to get his mind off Ethan.

His lover walked out of the dealership, saw him by the car, and smiled. When he got about six feet from Jamie, he tossed him the keys. "Let's go."

Jamie caught the keys with a grin. *Yes!* Ethan was going to let him drive *their* car.

"No fuckin' fair!" John groused behind him. "I drove y'all out here. I should get to drive it home as payment."

Jamie opened the door and slid in. He started up the Mustang and listened to her purr before turning to his brother. "Get your own boyfriend!"

John huffed. "I'm thinking about it! Boyfriends apparently give better gifts than girlfriends."

Jamie grinned at him. "Yeah, and they don't bitch when you watch football, either."

John flipped him off and went back to his truck.

Ethan chuckled. "Oh, Lord!"

"He started it."

Ethan squeezed his shoulder. "Just go to the Riverwalk, so we can all eat something. John's following us. I had actually planned on John just dropping us off, but apparently he's sticking around. I figured the least we can do is feed him."

They made a day of it and hung out with John. They went shopping at the Mercado, visited Julia, ate out. John left soon after. Ethan and Jamie only started home when it began to get dark. On their way back, Ethan's phone rang.

Ethan unhooked it from his belt and looked at the display. "It's Bill." He flipped it open and put it to his ear. "Ethan here." He reached over and rubbed Jamie's thigh.

Jamie grinned, sliding forward in the driver's seat, trying to make Ethan's hand touch his cock.

Ethan's hand stilled, tensed. "WHAT?! How many got out? Did you find all of them?"

Shit! Jamie glanced away from the road for a second. Ethan had a hard set to his jaw and a half frown on his lips. Jamie had a bad feeling about this. What the hell was going on at home?

Ethan sighed. "All right, Bill, we're only about fifteen minutes away. You guys get to work, and we'll be there ASAP." He shut the phone and clipped it back to his belt, then turned toward Jamie. "The fence in the west pasture is down. Bill and the boys are rounding up the cattle that got out. Hayden thinks the wire was cut."

Jamie felt his heart sink. "Damn it!" It was probably his fault. Probably some macho idiot trying to teach the "fag" a lesson.

"Ah, Blue Eyes, don't look like that. We don't know what happened. You know as well as I do that cattle rustling still exists." Ethan reached up and caressed his jaw. "Besides, it isn't just about you anymore. I'm not going to advertise, but I damn sure won't deny us or you."

Jamie gulped and stared at Ethan. Damn, he was not going to get all mushy! He wasn't. His eyes got a little watery, but he wasn't crying. His glance shot back to the road.

"I...I...you're mine, damn it. I'm not giving you up, and I'm certainly not ashamed of you, so I won't hide it and act like I am." Ethan took a deep breath, loud in the taut air inside the car. "I guess what I'm saying is that it's no longer your problem—it's ours. Oh, hell, I guess it always was ours." Ethan's hand slid down his cheek and gripped his arm. "Hurry up and get home; we have cattle to look for."

Jamie gratefully put his foot down on the pedal. He wasn't sure who had the bigger hard-on from driving ninety miles an hour, him or Ethan. Ethan was already giving him shit about "paying an arm and a leg" to insure him to drive the Mustang, so he hadn't gone much over the speed limit. And even then it was only at Ethan's urging. They made it home in record time.

Jamie put the car in park and looked over at Ethan. "Damn, that was fun!"

"Yes, it was. You ready to listen to Bill bitch?"

"Yeah. It's to be expected. I'm none too pleased myself with the prospect of rounding up cattle."

Ethan got out of the car. "Not that. Because we bought a new car. He hates working on anything newer than 1990. Bitches about all the computers in them and such."

Jamie chuckled and fell into step beside him, heading toward the barn. "Well, lucky for us, I am quite mechanically inclined. I don't need Bill to work on it."

"No shit?"

"No shit." He grabbed his saddle, blanket, and bridle and headed out of the barn with Ethan just a few steps behind him, his own gear in hand. Jamie whistled for George, threw his blanket and saddle over the corral fence and climbed over.

Ethan followed. "Is there anything you can't do?

"Nope." Jamie grinned and waggled his eyebrows to remind Ethan what all it was he *could* do.

"Smug bastard." Ethan smiled at him, then looked past him and beyond to where George was running toward them. "Spot! Get over here! I see you, you pain in the ass! Don't you hide behind George!" Spot had pranced over to see where George was going, but as soon as the wily horse had spotted Ethan, he'd ducked back.

Jamie chuckled.

Ethan groaned.

"He has character, remember?"

"Kiss my ass, Jamie!"

* * *

Ethan stepped into the shower and let the water pour down his sore body. He was dead tired.

Thank God Bill and the boys had rounded up all but ten of the missing longhorns. Ed and Hayden had mended the fence, while he and Jamie had looked for the remaining cattle. It had taken the two of them three hours to find the remaining ten. Not too bad, but then again, not great either.

Ethan's ass had fallen asleep an hour ago. The trip to San Antonio was about a four-hour drive there and back. Then he'd sat in the saddle for another three hours, which had managed to turn almost all of him numb.

He ducked his head back under the hot water. Damn! That felt good. He'd desperately wanted a shower for hours now. He'd also wanted Jamie to share it with him, but no such luck.

Jamie was downstairs talking to the sheriff and cussing up a blue streak.

After finally getting all the cattle together again, they'd returned only to find one of the balers vandalized. Bill swore it probably had been like that when they'd left, they just hadn't noticed. Jamie thought otherwise; he was convinced someone had waited for him and Ethan to ride out before they'd painted "faggot" across the machinery.

Bill had taken a real liking to Jamie and would do just about anything to keep him happy. Not that Ethan wouldn't, but he didn't believe in sheltering Jamie the way Bill did, at least aside from the truth of his birth. Bill had tried like hell to steer Jamie away from the baler when he'd noticed the bright red words spray-painted on the side. It hadn't worked. Partly because he'd yelled, "Son of a bitch!" when he'd seen it, and partly from Hayden asking if it was "proof enough that the cattle getting' loose was vandalism." Ed had wisely kept his mouth shut. Bill had glared at them for a full minute before he'd finally gone in to call the sheriff.

Jamie and Hayden had been stalking around on the warpath, looking for more damage, when Ethan had finally gone up to the house. He figured between Jamie and Bill, someone could handle the sheriff.

A click sounded to his right, then Jamie rested his cool cheek on his back between his shoulder blades. Ethan heaved a sigh of relief. He was glad Jamie was here and not still brooding outside. "Hey, Blue Eyes. The sheriff gone?"

"Yeah. He's a nice guy. Said to call if we have any more trouble. I know they all say that, but I think he meant it." Jamie's lips caressed his skin.

"Was it Sheriff Hunter? Or one of his deputies?"

"Hunter."

"Ah. He did mean it, then."

"Why do you say that?"

Ethan shrugged. "He's a great guy. Besides that, I think he's gay, too. I imagine he'll be pretty sympathetic under the circumstances."

Jamie turned him around. Those blue eyes were opened wide. "Really?" Then his dark brows drew together in a scowl. "How the hell do you know that? And why do *you* care?"

Huh. Interesting! Was Jamie jealous? He chuckled and wrapped his arms around Jamie, pulling him tightly against him. He dipped his head and kissed Jamie's nose, then his chin, and finally his lips. "I don't know for sure. It's just a feeling. And I *don't* care. You have nothing to worry about."

Those pale peepers shot him a glare. A frown marred the sensual face. "I'm not jealous!"

Ethan smiled.

Jamie groaned. "Fine, maybe I was…a little, but I've had a really screwed-up evening. I'm entitled to a bit of a mood."

"Are you, now?" Ethan arched a brow.

Jamie shrugged, then began rubbing his rapidly firming cock against Ethan's.

"Oh, yeah! Get under here." He yanked Jamie under the spray. "And let's wash you, then go to bed. I'm betting I know how to get you out of your mood."

"Umm, are we going to play 'ride 'em, cowboy'?"

Ethan chuckled. "Would that do it? Put you in a better mood?"

Jamie leaned up and kissed him. "It might, Cowboy."

Between their kissing and petting, they somehow managed to get Jamie washed, then the two of them dried and into bed. Jamie was sliding down his body, kissing his way below, when a loud pop sounded.

Jamie's head jerked up. "Was that a gunshot?"

Ethan didn't think; he just reacted. He grabbed Jamie and rolled them off the bed and onto the floor. They landed under the bed with Jamie under him.

Three more loud pops sounded.

He looked down at Jamie, reassuring himself that he was fine and in one piece.

"Son of a bitch! That was most definitely gunfire!"

Chapter Twelve

"Jamie, you okay?"

Jamie blinked up at Ethan. Damn, the man had cat-like reflexes. He was still trying to figure out what had happened and why they were under the bed instead of on it, but Ethan had already assessed the situation and was demanding a report. What the fuck was going on? The dog was barking downstairs, but otherwise it was pretty quiet.

"Jamie! Answer me! Are you all right?" Ethan pushed himself up and started running his hands over whatever parts of Jamie he could reach.

Jamie gripped Ethan's hands. "I'm fine. That wasn't really gunfire, was it?" He knew by the look on Ethan's face that he was wrong. Actually, he'd known after hearing the second shot, but he'd wanted Ethan to contradict him. He really, really didn't want it to be gunfire.

"Yeah, baby, it was. Get to the phone and call the bunkhouse. Make sure everyone is okay, then call the sheriff.

Fred, hush!" The barking ceased, and Ethan rolled off of him, then started scooting out from under the bed.

Jamie grabbed his arm. "Where in the hell are you going?"

"To get a rifle and shotgun."

What the hell did he think he was going to do? "You aren't planning on going out there, are you?"

"The thought had occurred to me. But first, I need to make sure no one is just waiting for me to step out the door so they can shoot me."

Oh, okay, yeah. So Ethan had already thought it through. "Get me some clothes and a weapon. I'm going with you."

Ethan nodded and slid out.

Jamie followed. He flipped off the bedside lamp as Ethan turned off the bathroom light. Grabbing the phone, Jamie dialed the bunkhouse.

The phone was answered on the first ring. "Hello?"

"Ed. Everyone okay?"

"Yeah, we're good. Y'all?"

"We're good. Call the sheriff. Ethan and I are going out to go have a look around."

"'Kay. I'll tell Bill not to shoot."

Jamie rolled his eyes and hung up. Great, they were going to have to dodge bullets from Bill as well as the shooter.

"Here." A pile of clothes landed in his lap, and then Ethan left the room.

Jamie mumbled, "Thanks," then dressed in the dark. He got his boots on and went downstairs in search of Ethan. Fred met him at the bottom of the stairs. As he and the dog reached the office, Ethan was coming back out of it. From the dim light of the moon filtering through the curtains he could make out Ethan was dressed in all in black, as was he.

"The guys are all okay. Bill's already out looking around."

Ethan nodded and stopped in front of him and held up what looked like two rifles. "30/30 or twelve gauge?"

"Twelve gauge."

Ethan handed it over, then stuffed something down the front of Jamie's waistband.

Jamie started from the chill, then looked down.

"Here's a .357; there's one in the chamber, and the safety is on." Ethan stuck a handgun in his waistband, as well. "I'm taking the .45. Try not to shoot Bill. I knew that old devil would already be outside checking the place over."

He followed Ethan to the back door, Fred right behind him.

Ethan leaned against the wall, pulled the curtain aside just a bit and peered out. He stayed motionless for several seconds, just watching. "I don't see any movement. Of course, there won't be if it's a sniper, eh?"

"Gee, that's reassuring. You go first."

Ethan chuckled and glanced over at him. "I'd planned on it. Follow me out and get to some cover as soon as possible." He looked down at Fred. "Stay."

Jamie swallowed and nodded. He was not looking forward to this. What if Ethan got shot? What if *he* did?

Ethan opened the door and crept out.

Fred whined, but stayed where she was told.

Shit, here goes nothing. He followed. No shots so far. That was good. He closed the door and quickly went the opposite direction from Ethan. He searched for several minutes without finding anything.

About ten minutes into his hunt, a figure stepped out of the shadows with some sort of rifle. "Y'all can come on out. I've looked; they're long gone."

"Damn it! Bill, you old fool!" Jamie sure hoped to hell that Bill was right, 'cause if he wasn't, they'd shoot the old goat any minute now. What was he thinking to step out in the open like that?

After a few more minutes, no one had shot Bill, and Ethan walked out into the open, too. Jamie wasn't about to leave his cowboy out there by himself. The more targets there were, the less likely Ethan was to get shot. So he stepped away from the barn wall and joined them as well. "Did anyone find anything?"

Bill shuffled his feet and looked everywhere but at him and Ethan.

Ethan cleared his throat.

Bill glanced up. "Ed called the sheriff; he should be here any minute."

Jamie couldn't decide whether to roll his eyes at the evasion or to kick Bill in the shins. "Spill it, Bill! What did you find?"

Bill turned back to Ethan, who nodded.

"They shot your truck, Jamie."

He was stunned. "Beg pardon?"

"Yup. I don't have a good feeling about this. Whoever did it sure don't like our Jamie. Y'all better come take a look." Bill walked off, leaving Ethan and Jamie to follow.

"Son of a bitch!" Ethan abruptly stopped in front of him.

Jamie stepped around Ethan to see how bad it was. He expected a few blown tires or maybe a shot to the engine. What he saw was the windshield spider-webbed right where his head usually was when he drove it. *Damn!*

He chuckled nervously. "Well, I think Bill is right. Whoever did this don't like me much. Any guess as to who that could be?"

Ethan walked around to the driver's side of the truck. He shook his head, then looked up, meeting Jamie's eyes. "I'll kill that son of a bitch if—"

The sheriff pulled into the drive, lights flashing. He stepped out of the car, gun drawn.

Ethan held up his rifle. "It's just us, Gray."

Sheriff Grayson Hunter put away his sidearm, then came toward them. "You find anything?"

Ethan dropped his rifle, pointing it down. "Just this." He indicated Jamie's truck.

The sheriff's brow wrinkled as he walked around and surveyed the damaged windshield. "Looks pretty damned personal, Jamie. You piss off anybody lately besides your daddy?"

Jamie sighed. "Your guess is as good as mine. I imagine there are a lot of people who don't want me here. Cowboys damn near dive off the sidewalk when I go to town nowadays. But no one has been outright hostile…other than my father and Tom Cooke. Well, and Carl and Jeff. Ethan's ex-employees."

Hunter nodded. "We'll look around. I have a couple of my deputies on the way. Anything else I should see?"

Bill shook his head. "Nothing else I came across other than what was done earlier."

"All right. Let me have a look around." Hunter turned to Ethan. "I'm not going to have to arrest you to keep you from going and shooting Jacob Killian, am I?"

Ethan smiled grimly. "I need proof first." He met Jamie's eyes and winked.

Jamie relaxed, feeling a little better.

Bill shook his head. "You might have to arrest me right along with Ethan, if we find out that bastard did this." He patted Jamie's shoulder and gave it a little squeeze. "I'm going to tell Hayden and Ed what's going on." He turned and walked away as the other three watched him.

"Jamie, you have a CHL?" The sheriff brought their attention back to him.

"Yes, sir. I have the license to carry concealed, but I don't have my pistol. It's at the Quad J. I kinda doubt my daddy is going to just give it to me."

Ethan stepped closer to Jamie. "I've got several."

Hunter nodded. "See to it that he doesn't go anywhere unarmed, even out here on the ranch. I don't think there is any question that this and the earlier vandalism were messages to Jamie." He looked Ethan up and down, then grinned. "You might consider carrying, too. It won't take long for people to figure out, if they haven't already, that you two are a couple."

Jamie gasped. How had he known?

Ethan grinned and clapped Hunter on the shoulder. "Damned lawman, can't hide anything from you."

Hunter chuckled. "Yeah, well, you're a lawman yourself, aren't you?"

"Not anymore. I did a year in San Antonio, but came back home to run the Tin Star when my brother was killed in action."

The sheriff gazed at Jamie, then back at Ethan. "If you can talk Jamie into running the ranch for you, I could always use another good deputy."

Ethan's eyes widened, and Jamie could see the excitement there before he quickly masked it again. "Thanks for the offer, but ranching is my job now."

"Well, think about it. From what I've heard, the kid here—" He nodded at Jamie. "—is a helluva rancher." He extended a hand to Ethan.

Ethan shook it. "I'll think about it."

Hunter glanced toward the drive where one of his deputies had just pulled up, then back to them. "I'm going to take a look around. You two let me know if anything else has been disturbed. Dispatch said there were four shots. Any idea where the other three hit?"

Jamie shook his head. "Nope."

"You gentlemen go grab a cup of coffee or something. We'll do the rest, then come and give a full report before we leave." He offered his hand to Jamie. "You remember what I said. Don't go anywhere unarmed or alone. Make sure you have someone with you at all times."

Jamie nodded and shook the man's hand. "Will do. Thanks."

"You're welcome." Hunter turned away and headed up the drive toward the other officer.

Ethan's hand landed on his shoulder. "You all right?"

Jamie tried to give him a reassuring grin even though he was still a little shook up by the night's events. "Yeah, I'm good. Let's go make some coffee."

The phone rang a few hours after they'd finally gone back to bed. Ethan barely managed to get his eyes open by the fourth ring. He jumped groggily when an arm soared over him and smacked the alarm clock. Apparently, Jamie was pretty out of it, too. He usually hit the alarm by the second ring. The funny thing was he never hit the damned thing when it actually was ringing.

Ethan finally managed to grab the phone. "Hello?"

A rapid burst of words followed. "Ethan? Are you okay? How's Jamie? John called me and told me about last night. He said Bill called him to ask if Daddy had anything to do with the cattle getting loose or the word on the baler. Oh, my God, Ethan! I can't believe that! Do you really think Daddy did it? Someone should strangle—"

"Jules! Enough! My brain is too damned tired to keep up. Slow the heck down. Hell, pretend you're at work, and I'm another nurse or a doctor."

"I'm sorry, Ethan. Listen, I'm on my way. It's almost 8:40; I'll be there in about twenty minutes. We'll talk about it then. I'll even make y'all breakfast. Is Jamie awake? Have you seen him this morning? I'll make pancakes and sausage. How's that? If y'all—"

Ethan groaned. *Great! Good fucking morning to me!* Just what he wanted to deal with first thing in the morning after he'd been up most of the night. The only thing worse than Julia's motor mouth was Julia's cooking. The woman was an unmitigated disaster in the kitchen.

"Jules! Not now! My brain is about to explode! I'll see you in a few."

"Oh…okay. Bye, Ethan. See you soon."

Ethan replaced the phone and pulled his pillow over his face. Maybe he could suffocate himself and not have to get up. He had a million things to do today; death would have to wait, he supposed.

He had to call the insurance company and add the new car and Jamie to his policy. He also needed to notify Jamie's insurance about the damage to his truck. The other three shots had been made into the cab, tearing up the seats and dash—also on the driver's side. Hunter was supposed to get back to him this morning. John needed to be informed, even though apparently someone had already let him know all that had happened prior to the shots last night. If anyone knew whether Jacob was involved, it would be John.

Ethan sighed and sat up. He reached over and shook Jamie's shoulder. "Up and at 'em, Blue Eyes!"

Jamie swatted at him and snuggled down further in the covers.

"Come on, Jamie! We have to get up."

"We just went to bed. 'M tired!"

Ethan bent and kissed his cheek, then swatted him on the butt. "Me, too, but your sister is on her way over here."

Jamie rolled over, his blue eyes blinking up at Ethan, then focusing. "Oh, God!"

"Exactly! Come on."

His Blue Eyes groaned, threw the covers off and stomped to the closet, grumbling the whole way.

He grinned and watched. Jamie ended up with his tee-shirt on in reverse, his underwear inside out, and a pair of Ethan's jeans instead of his own. He then grabbed his boots, a pair of socks, and his cowboy hat, thumped the hat on his head—backward—and stormed out of the room.

Ethan chuckled, wondering how long it would take him to fully awaken. He got up and went to the bedroom door, yelling down the stairs. "Unless you want Julia cooking breakfast, you better make something."

A curse came from the kitchen, followed by the clang of pots and pans.

He laughed. Taking his time, he got dressed, then went into the bathroom to take care of business. By the time he was done brushing his teeth, he heard Julia's car pull up. Fred was barking and Jamie was still slamming things around. Ethan shook his head. No time like the present. Either he'd wake up enough to decipher Jules's endless chatter or his head would fall off.

He walked into the kitchen just as Julia stepped in the back door. He waved at her. "Hey, Jules." Fred was trying to lick her to death.

Jamie was at the stove; he never even turned. Maybe he'd fallen back asleep...standing up. Ethan decided he'd better go check. He would hate like hell for Jamie to burn his breakfast, not to mention that that couldn't be too safe.

He checked. Jamie's hat was still on backward, so Ethan turned it around. "You awake?"

All he got was a grunt.

Jules came up behind him and hugged him. "Hi, Ethan." She kissed his cheek, then moved on to Jamie. She wrapped her arms around Jamie's waist. "Oh, honey, you didn't have to cook. I was going to fix y'all breakfast when I got here."

"Why the hell do you think I'm cooking?"

Julia's eyes widened, but she was grinning. She stepped back and pinched Jamie's butt. "James Wyatt Killian, are you saying something about my cooking?"

Jamie's lips turned up at the corners. He flipped an egg over, then reached back and hooked his arm around Julia's neck, bringing her forward to kiss her forehead. "Yeah. You can't cook! In fact, it's a damned good thing you're pretty, because all your domestic skills suck."

She pushed away with a huff and an eye roll. She wrapped her arms around Ethan and kissed his chin. "So I see he's still grumpy in the mornings."

Ethan hugged her back and kissed her cheek. "He doesn't normally give me problems in the morning. Must be you he takes exception to…or maybe it's the thought of your cooking." He gave an exaggerated shudder. "That would do it for me."

Jules chuckled, then stepped out of Ethan's embrace, smacking his arm as she did so. "No respect! I swear! I'm beginning to think that Fred is the only one happy to see me."

Ethan got three cups from the cabinet. Jamie was very predictable about some things, morning coffee being one of them. And damn, it smelled good. "We're happy to see you, Jules. We're just tired. Only had about four—"

"Three," Jamie corrected.

"—three hours of sleep." He glanced at Jules. "You want coffee?"

She nodded. "Damn! I'm sorry. I had no idea. I mean, John told me about the fence getting cut, but I figured it was early enough that y'all got the cattle rounded up and went to bed at a decent hour."

"We did. But then we got woken up by the gunshots." Ethan poured the coffee, then headed for the table.

Julia gasped. "Oh, my God! What gunshots?! John didn't say anything about gunshots!"

Ethan stopped by the stove and handed Jamie his cup. He took a quick thank-you peck on the lips, then went to Jules.

Jules smiled real big and sat down. "OH! You two are perfect for each other! I'm so happy! John told me y'all were together, but—" Her eyebrows pulled together. "What gunshots, Ethan? Why didn't John tell me about them?"

Damn, that woman switched gears fast. Ethan slid her mug to her. "I doubt he knew about them. I imagine Bill called him before it happened. Last night after the cattle were taken care of, we heard some shots. No one was hurt—"

"No one except my truck," Jamie grumbled.

"No one was hurt, thank God. But whoever it was shot up Jamie's truck. The sheriff and his men came back, looked around, took another report. They're investigating."

Julia gasped. "Oh, my God! Who would do such a thing? You don't think... Oh, I'll whip that mean old bastard myself if—"

Ethan held up a hand. "Whoa! We don't know that it was your daddy."

Julia snorted and took a sip. "Who else would it be?"

He sighed and shook his head. "I don't know, Jules. Your dad is my best bet, too, but we can't go around accusing people without evidence. Trust me, after seeing that the bullet went through right where Jamie's head would be if he were driving, I was ready to march over to the Quad J myself. It'd make me feel better to beat the shit outta him, too, but I've had time to think. I know it'd be much more beneficial, if not as satisfying, to press charges and go at him that way. But only after we have proof—"

Jules jumped up and practically ran to Jamie, tucking herself under his arm and into his side. "Oh, baby!" Ethan could hear her sobs from where he sat.

Jamie set down the spatula, pivoted, and wrapped his arms around his sister. He glanced over her head at Ethan with a helpless look on his face.

Ethan grinned. He'd wanted to take Jamie into his arms, too, when he'd first spotted the damaged truck. Wanted to make sure Jamie was safe.

Jamie arched his right brow, silently asking for help.

Ethan took pity on him. He got up and hugged Jules, disengaging her from Jamie. "He's all right, Julia. Let him finish cooking breakfast."

She nodded and returned to her seat, dabbing at her eyes. "I'm okay. I just…it's…that's scary."

Yeah, it was—real scary.

Jamie pulled out plates and filled them. It wasn't long before he joined them at the table. He sat down next to Ethan. "Dig in."

Ethan smiled, watching Jamie do just that. "Thanks." His Blue Eyes was hungry as well as tired, it would seem.

Jules took a bite. She stared at Jamie shoveling food into his mouth for several seconds, then asked, "Jamie, honey, did you know your shirt is on backwards?"

* * *

Ethan kissed the chest under his cheek and laid his head back down. "You talk to Julia when y'all went riding this afternoon?"

Jamie ran his fingers through Ethan's hair. "Yup."

"What did she say?"

"About the shooting?"

Ethan looked up into those pale blue eyes. "Yeah."

Jamie's hand stilled in Ethan's hair, and his head lifted from the pillow. "She thinks Daddy is responsible." Jamie shook his head and lay back on the pillow. "She's even a little pissed at John. She wants John to leave the Quad J. Wants him to leave Daddy."

"To be honest, I'm beginning to think that, too. But I can see why John doesn't want to just up and leave."

The hand in his hair resumed stroking. "He has a lot to lose, Ethan."

"And you didn't?"

"Umm."

"Well?"

"It's not the same."

Ethan raised his head from Jamie's chest, scooted up, and leaned on an elbow. "How so? You lost your home and job. I'd say you lost your father's affection, too, but I'm beginning to think you never had it in the first place."

Jamie turned on his side and leaned on his own elbow. "The Quad J is John's birthright. He was raised—hell, he was *conceived* to take over that ranch. He's been conditioned from birth to run the place. Somewhere along the way, it became what he wanted, too."

Ethan nodded. "I get that, but family is more important than a damned piece of land."

"What about the Tin Star? Would you feel the same if we were talking about the Tin Star?"

"Yeah, I would. I'd trade the ranch in a heartbeat to have Dylan back. Hell, I'd trade it for my daddy, too, but he'd feel like you. He'd kick my ass for even thinking about giving the place away." He sighed "It's just a place, Jamie. It's not who I am."

Jamie leaned over and brushed a kiss across his lips. "But it is to some degree."

Ethan raised a brow.

"It's part of your identity, your history. Your family's history."

"But having it or not having it doesn't change who I am. It and the history surrounding it may have helped make me *me*, but the place isn't my identity. I can go somewhere else, do anything else, and the place and its history is still with me. The memories…all of it is still mine as long as I remember it."

"I hear what you're saying, but would you really want to lose it?"

Ethan shook his head absently. "Not really, no. But I don't value it over the lives of the people I love. It's just a place."

"But, as you pointed out, the memories of the people you love were made here. It was important to your daddy and your family. So shouldn't it be important to you, too?"

"It is important, but it's not everything, Jamie. Think about it, isn't everything you said also true with regard to you and the Quad J? Wasn't it your legacy as well as John's?"

Jamie shrugged nonchalantly, or tried to, but Ethan could see the underlying sadness in his expression. "Not like it is for John or you. I was born last and never meant to have the Quad J."

"That's what bothers you most, isn't it? Losing the ranch. Because it was part of your legacy. You loved it, its history, that you were raised there. It was important, belonging to that history."

Jamie's face went white. "You're right. It's just a place."

Ethan suddenly realized that Jamie hadn't let go. Not really. He still wanted to belong. He was giving all his hard work and his attention to the Tin Star, but his heart still belonged to the Quad J. He didn't want to let go, give up hope. Somewhere in the back of his mind, he probably still thought his daddy would forgive him and ask him to come home.

"Ah, babe! You are important. Not because you're part of some legacy, but because you're you. You can build your own legacy!"

Jamie nodded. "I know. It's just hard. I planned my entire life around working on that ranch."

"How about readjusting those plans and building a legacy here, on this ranch…with me?"

Those pretty blue eyes blinked. "You mean that?"

"Yeah. I do." He kissed Jamie's chin, hoping he was getting through. Jamie had to realize that there was no going back, only forward. "You gotta let it go, baby. It's not going to change. He's not going to forgive you. He's not going to ask you to come back…ever."

Chapter Thirteen

Two days later, Jamie was enjoying his day off. Okay, so cleaning the house wasn't much of a day off. But really, he enjoyed cleaning. There was nothing better than a sparkling house that smelled of fresh pine or lemon. Of course, if Ethan came in and caught him cleaning, he'd probably bitch. Not working today was supposed to be a sort of birthday present. He'd honestly tried to just laze around, but ten minutes of daytime TV was enough to cure him of that. Yikes! The crap they put on TV nowadays.

He'd tried to read a book, too, but that hadn't lasted long. He'd glanced up and seen some dust bunnies under the chair across from the couch. No way could he stay still when the place was dirty. It drove him crazy. And that didn't even include the half-assed cleaning Ethan had done in the kitchen this morning after he'd made and brought Jamie breakfast in bed.

Yeah, the man's heart was in the right place, but he couldn't clean for shit! Actually, he couldn't cook for shit, either. Breakfast had to have been one of the worst French crepes he'd ever eaten. But he'd choked down every bite. Ethan had been so damned excited about making Jamie breakfast in bed that Jamie couldn't stand to disappoint him. He made a mental note to hide the cookbooks to keep the man from attempting more cooking. It was only too obvious that Ethan hadn't had a mama growing up. Luckily for him, Jamie had. God knew one of them had to cook and clean. He was just glad that Ethan was pretty good at doing laundry. Yep, there were definitely worse ways to spend the day than cleaning house and listening to the radio.

Halfway through Clint Black's greatest hits CD and two-thirds through mopping, the phone rang. Jamie grinned. Jules had already called to wish him a happy birthday, so that was probably John. But there was one small problem. He'd mopped his way into a corner and couldn't get to the phone without walking across his freshly cleaned and wet floor. *Damn!* Oh, well, there was nothing to be done; he'd have to re-mop. What were a pair of wet socks and streaked floor in comparison with giving his older brother the satisfaction of wishing him a happy birthday?

Jamie glanced at the caller ID: yup, the Quad J. He picked up the phone with a smile. "Hey, John."

"Well, well, well, if it isn't my bastard son. Just who I wanted to talk to."

Jamie almost dropped the phone. His stomach dropped. He really had not expected this. "Hello, Dad. What can I do for you?"

"Leave."

"Excuse me?"

"You heard me, boy. Leave town. Get out of here and don't come back. In fact, I'll make you a deal."

He swallowed. No way in hell was he going to let his father get the best of him. *Composure, Jamie! Composure!*

"I'm sorry, I'm afraid I can't do that. I like it here, and I'm not interested in any deal you have to offer. So, if that is all you called for, I'm going to have to hang up now. Goodbye."

"You want the money my Blanche left you in her will?"

Jamie blinked. What the hell? Why had he said it like that? His mama had left him, John and Jules fifty thousand dollars apiece when she'd died. The money was already his. Well, technically, it wasn't his until he turned twenty-five, but the money was being held for him, wasn't it? "I beg your pardon?"

"The money, boy! The fifty grand that my wife left in trust for you. You want it?"

Jamie wasn't sure how to answer. What kind of game was the old man playing? "The money is already mine. I can wait three years."

A rusty laugh echoed over the phone. "You think so? You think there will be any of it left by the time you turn twenty-five?"

Okay, now he was getting pissed. His mom had left it for him; who did the old man think he was? And just what the fuck was he trying to threaten? Sure, his dad was in charge of the money until Jamie turned twenty-five, but could he spend it? "Mama left that money to me, not you. It stated in her will that the money was to be—"

"Your *mother* didn't leave you squat! My *wife* left it for you. Your mother was a no-good whore. Hell, the slut is probably still alive."

"What?" Jamie sank to the floor. He hadn't really meant to ask out loud. Jacob was just trying to get to him; he knew that. But, still, why would he say something so terrible?

"You mean your boyfriend and his aunt didn't tell you? My ex-mistress was your mother. The stupid bitch wouldn't agree to an abortion even though she didn't want you, so I had to tell Blanche. Blanche, being the kind woman that she was, agreed to take you in. God rest her soul. My Blanche was a good woman, a little dense at times, but she had a good heart. She never could turn down a stray. Even a bastard one like you."

"That...that's not true. You expect me to believe anything you say?"

"Just ask your lover's dingbat aunt."

Jamie swallowed. How could the man be so nasty as to make up a story like this? "Yeah, I'll ask Margie. I have nothing else to say to you."

Jacob chuckled. "Yeah? Well, I have something to say to you. If you want to see that fifty grand, you better get out of town. Actually, get out of Texas all together. You leave, I'll give you the money now. You stay, and you can kiss every bit of it goodbye. You'll never see one red cent of it, understand? Then and again, you might not make it to twenty-five, either. Think about it." The line went dead.

Jamie wasn't sure how long he sat there with the receiver against his ear, listening to the buzzing sound that signaled the phone was off the hook. Somewhere, Clint Black was still singing in the background, and Fred was barking at the back door, but he barely registered any of it.

What if it were true? All of it. Forget the money; who cared about the money when none of it would bring Mama back, so what was it really worth anyway? And had his father just threatened his life? What about Ethan? Had he truly known Ethan was his lover or was he just mouthing off? Mama. What if...

"Jamie?"

Jamie blinked as the phone was taken out of his hand. He stared at his empty hand. Was it really true? What had he said about Mama? *Ask your lover's dingbat aunt?* Ask Margie? *You mean your boyfriend and his aunt didn't tell you?* Ethan? Ethan knew?

"Jamie? Snap out of it. You're scaring me." Ethan caught his face in his hands, forcing him to look into his eyes. "What's going on? Talk to me."

Damn, his stomach hurt suddenly. Why was it so hard to breathe? "He knows... He wants me to... He said Mama isn't...Blanche isn't... He..." Jamie cleared his throat. God, he couldn't form the horrible words. He looked into Ethan's concerned face. Willing him to understand.

"Ah, babe! Hell." Ethan sat down and pulled him into his lap, pushing his face against the hard wall of his broad chest.

Jamie pulled back. *Why is he coddling me like a damned baby?*

"I think you're a bit in shock. God, I'm so sorry. I should have told you as soon as I found out."

What? Jamie scrambled out of Ethan's lap.

Ethan reached for him. "Jamie?"

"Are you saying it's true? It's not! She's the only one that ever really loved me. It's not true, Ethan!"

"Jamie, you know that isn't true. John and Julia have always loved you. And me, I've always cared about you, too. And Hank and Aunt Margaret." He reached for Jamie again, like he was trying to gentle an animal or something.

Jamie frowned and stood up. How could he not have known that his father hated his guts and wanted him gone, dead even? Then there was what Ethan had said last night. He'd been right; he was never going back to the Quad J, never going home. That part of his life was over, and his life had been a lie. It had never been his home.

He looked down at his recently mopped floor, then at Ethan. It was all too much.

"Get off my fucking wet floor, goddammit!" He turned and stormed off.

"Shit!" Ethan caught up with him at the bottom of the stairs. He didn't say anything, just enfolded Jamie in his arms and kissed the back of his neck.

Jamie stopped mid-stride, gradually relaxing into his embrace. He turned slowly in Ethan's arms, leaned forward and hugged Ethan, too, dropping his head to Ethan's shoulder "I'm sorry. I guess I'm a little...overwhelmed."

"I'm the one that needs to say sorry. I wanted to tell you but I didn't know how, so I just kept putting it off. I could never seem to find the right time...or the right words." He kissed Jamie gently. "I'm really sorry, Blue Eyes, but ignoring it isn't going to make it go away. Talk to me. Tell me what happened."

"Don't suppose you'll leave me alone if I don't."

"Don't suppose I will. So spill it."

Jamie took a deep breath and let it out against Ethan's collarbone. "How much do you know? Or maybe I'll just say what happened, and you can tell me what you know and if it's true or not."

Ethan nodded. "Sounds like a good idea."

Jamie kept his head on Ethan's shoulder. It was somehow soothing. With Ethan so close, it didn't hurt as much to relive the phone call. He went over the entire conversation. "It's true, isn't it? At first, I thought that it was just him trying to get to me, but..."

"Yeah, it's true. Aunt Margaret told me that day we went over to see her. You were putting antifreeze in her car and I was fixing her leak. Your mama never wanted you to know, but Aunt Margaret was afraid that with all the other stuff going on that your dad would probably tell you. Blanche loved you very much, Jamie. Aunt Margaret knew that without a doubt, said that she loved you every bit as much as she did John and Julia. As far as your mama was concerned, you *were* hers. And, really, isn't that all that matters?"

It was, and he knew that Blanche had loved him. No one could have done the things she had done for him if she hadn't loved him. Hell, he'd been accused of being her favorite often enough. He hadn't believed that; Mama wasn't the kind to play favorites, but he had been closer to her than either John or Julia. If only she were here now. Man, he missed her. He missed her a lot. He squeezed Ethan a little tighter.

"Don't worry about the money, babe. We'll have my lawyer look into it. And we've got to call the sheriff about this. Jacob's words sounded too much like a threat to me." Ethan was quiet for several seconds, thoughtful. "Can you forgive me for not telling you? I was going to, I swear. I just...I couldn't stand to see that look you get on your face."

Jamie leaned back. "What look?"

Ethan kissed his nose. "That look, baby." He ran his finger down Jamie's cheek. "This look right here. This defeated look. It never lasts long but, God, I hate it. It breaks my heart."

He grinned and nuzzled into Ethan's caress, feeling a little calmer. Yeah, his life was shit right now, but he still had Ethan. And Ethan clearly cared enough to be upset that he'd heard the bad news from his dad instead of him. Maybe he really did have a future here, a future with Ethan.

"I forgive you if you promise me you'll never keep anything from me again. I know why you did it, and I can even understand it, but promise me, Ethan."

Ethan looked him right in the eye. "I promise."

"I promise, too, 'kay?"

Ethan smiled and kissed him. Maybe life wasn't so shitty after all.

* * *

Jamie sat in the bar with Ed and Hayden, a grin on his face, waiting for Ethan and John, who were at a last-minute meeting about the steakhouse deal. The earlier fiasco was not forgotten, but he wouldn't think about it. At least for now.

After he'd gotten over his shock, Ethan had given him his birthday present: a three-hundred-dollar gift certificate to Sheplers and, of course, half ownership of the Mustang. Then he'd invited everyone out for drinks. Ed and Hayden had readily accepted. Bill had declined. He'd claimed he was going to watch some TV, but Jamie wasn't buying it for a minute. From his recent behavior, Jamie had a sneaking suspicion that Bill and Margie had something going on. Ethan didn't think so, but he didn't seem averse to the idea, either.

After Ethan and John got here, he was going to have Ethan drive by Margie's house. He'd be willing to bet that the old dog's truck was parked out front. Ever since Jamie had started "family supper night" on Sundays, Bill had changed. He'd been eager to learn how to cook, and he took more time on his appearance nowadays. Heck, Jamie had even caught the old codger cleaning the bunkhouse, which had definitely needed it!

"What are you smiling at?" Hayden asked as he slid into the seat across from him, passing him and Ed each another longneck of Shiner.

Jamie grabbed his and tipped his head. "Thanks. I was just thinking about Bill. I think he's taken a shine to Margie."

"Yeah, I think so, too. He sure seems sweet on her, anyhow. You think he went to Margie's tonight?"

"I'm almost sure. Wonder if I can talk Ethan in to letting us all go for a visit when he gets here."

Hayden laughed. "That's pure evil! Now, how would you feel if every time you and Ethan disappeared into the house on the occasional afternoon, we all came knocking? Eh?"

Jamie almost choked on his beer.

Ed chuckled from the other side of him. "He didn't think we knew."

He shook his head. "No, I didn't."

Hayden grinned. "'S okay. I think it's a good thing…"

Jamie raised an eyebrow.

Ed leaned forward. "Yes?"

Hayden flushed and drank his beer. "I mean, I'm cool with it. I like Ethan and I like you, and if y'all are happy, well, then, that's cool. That's all I meant."

Jamie and Ed chuckled. Then Ed added, "Yeah, it's cool. Can't remember seeing the boss man this happy. And speaking of happy…" He held up his beer bottle. "Happy birthday, man."

Hayden did the same with his bottle. "Yeah, happy birthday, Jamie."

Jamie grinned and tapped their bottles with his own. "Thanks!"

They all took a long pull. Then, over the loud music came the opening notes of Shania Twain's "Man, I Feel Like a Woman."

Ed set his beer down and grabbed his phone from his belt. "Hello?"

That was all Jamie heard. He and Hayden looked at each other. They smiled.

Hayden raised his eyebrows. "I'm beginning to feel a little outnumbered…apparently I'm the only straight guy at this table."

Jamie snorted, then grinned and played along, pumping his fist in the air. "Yes! It's working! Come to the dark side! You and Bill are the only ones left now…join us."

Hayden cackled, his face turning red with laughter. "Fuck you!"

"Yeah? Does that mean my Jedi mind powers are working on you, too?"

As Ed talked on his phone, nodding and answering with short yeses and noes, Jamie and Hayden laughed their asses off.

Finally, Ed hung up. "Ethan says turn your phone on, Jamie. What's so funny?"

Jamie kept laughing, tears streaming down his face. He reached down and checked his phone. Yup, it was off.

Ed shrugged. "He said that he and John got tied up in their meeting a little longer than they expected, but they are heading this way. So, what are y'all laughing at?"

Hayden shook his head and doubled over, his shoulders shaking with hilarity.

"Dude! You *cannot* use that song as your ringtone!" Jamie got out between guffaws, barely managing not to fall off his seat.

"What? Why not? I like Shania Twain."

Jamie shook his head. Ed obviously didn't see anything wrong with the picture. "It's just wrong! Pick a different Shania song."

"But I like that one. That one is my fav—"

Hayden held up a hand. "Hey, man, are you trying to tell us something? 'Cause I'm giving it to you straight. If you start prancing around the bunkhouse wearing pink lacy panties, we are going to have issues."

The image of Ed in pink panties had Jamie almost on the floor. "Oh, shit!" He gripped his belly, looked at Ed, then back to Hayden. "You can ask Ethan, but I don't think our health insurance covers sex change operations."

Hayden choked.

Ed sighed, but he was grinning broadly. "Fine! I'll change it! Bill took "Thank God I'm a Country Boy," or I'd've used it!"

They laughed some more and had a good time until two cowgirls came over and asked Hayden and Jamie to dance. Jamie took one look at Hayden and knew the other man was planning to refuse—whether because Hayden was shy or because he thought that Jamie wouldn't want to dance, he didn't know, but Jamie had seen Hayden checking out the two women only seconds before.

Hell, he liked to dance, and it wasn't like they had anything else to do. He quickly stood up and accepted the offer for both of them. "We'd love to."

Ed took one look at the little blonde who had latched onto Jamie's arm and smiled, his eyes twinkling with suppressed mirth.

Jamie rolled his eyes at him and grinned back. "Shut up, and go get us all another beer. Get me a Coors this time."

Hayden smiled at them both, gave Jamie a nod of thanks and eagerly led his partner out to the dance floor.

Jamie nodded back and followed with his partner. The band was playing a Toby Keith song. He introduced himself and learned the blonde was Shelly. She seemed to take it fine when Jamie declined her offer of a little something more than dancing, so he enjoyed a few more songs with her. He was having a good time and had gone back to the table a couple of times to get some beer. Ed was nowhere in sight, but he'd left their beers on the table.

Ed found him two songs later and came right onto the dance floor. "Jamie, we might have a problem."

"Huh? 'Scuse me, Shelly." He looked at Ed. Whoa! Ed was slowly listing back and forth. He blinked, and Ed got fuzzy, too.

"Jamie, I just saw Jeff. He and Carl are at the bar. I think they saw me, but we didn't say anything. I just wanted to let you know. You watch yourself. I already told Hayden."

Why did Ed seem like he was far away?

"Jamie? Jamie, are you okay? What's wrong with you?"

Me? What's wrong with you? You're the one looking all weird and shit.

"Oh, wow! I think the bar might have been picked up in a twister or something." He glanced back at Shelly. "Whoa, now you're all fuzzy, too! How are y'all doing that?"

Ed grabbed his arm. "Excuse us, ma'am, I'm gonna make him sit down for a bit. I think he might have had too much to drink."

"Okay. I didn't think he had that much. Not sure how much he drank before we danced, but he's only had a few quick sips since then. Bye, Jamie."

Jamie smiled and waved over his shoulder as Ed pulled him off the dance floor. "Bye, Shelly!" He giggled. Why was he giggling? Damn, something wasn't right. But he couldn't focus long enough to figure it out. He heard Ed talking, but couldn't make out what he was saying, either.

Hayden came out of nowhere and grabbed his other arm.

Jamie smiled at him. "Hi, Hayden. Did you get her number? Hey, you're all fuzzy, too. Come to think of it, everything is a little on the fuzzy side."

"What the hell is wrong with him?" Hayden stared into his eyes.

Jamie widened them and stared back at Hayden.

"Don't know. He hasn't had that much to drink." Ed pushed him into his chair.

Hayden waved his hand in front of Jamie's face. "His pupils are huge! Call Ethan and find out where the hell they are."

Jamie waved his hand back in front of Hayden. Why was Hayden doing that?

Ethan stepped into the bar and looked around. What the hell was going on? What did Ed mean, "There's something wrong with Jamie"?

He saw someone jump up from the side of the room and wave at him.

He nudged John and pointed. "Over there." As they drew closer, he could see Jamie sitting and staring off into space with a blank look. The knots in his stomach eased a little, until Jamie looked right at him, or rather tried to. He seemed to be having a hard time focusing.

Jamie blinked several times. "Ethan?"

"Yeah, it's me. What's going on, Jamie?"

"Don't know. Feel weird." Jamie shrugged and almost slid to the floor. Ethan grabbed his shoulder to steady him and bent to peer deeper into Jamie's eyes. "Shit, his pupils are too freaking dilated. Someone tell me what the hell happened." Ed and Hayden hadn't noticed anything unusual other than Jamie's current state. According to Ed, Jamie hadn't had much to drink before he'd started dancing and his partner had claimed that he'd only had a few sips between dances.

"Did y'all leave your drinks unattended at any time?"

"Well, yeah. They went and danced and I went to the bathroom." Ed blanched. "Shit, Ethan, that's just for women. People don't drug men's drinks!"

"The hell they don't!" He looked back at Jamie, who was now propped against his hip and yawning.

"I really don't feel so good. Is it gettin' hard to breathe in here?"

Was it his imagination or was Jamie wheezing?

"Jeff and Carl are here."

"What?!"

Ed and Hayden both flinched.

"I just saw them. I went right away to tell Jamie to be careful. That's when I realized he was acting weird. I called as soo—"

Jamie passed out.

"Fuck!" Ethan grabbed him and hauled him up into his arms. He didn't bother to explain himself as he took off for the door, ignoring the odd looks and questions other patrons tossed at him as he passed by. He had to get Jamie to a hospital, immediately.

Damn, he was heavy! Ethan looked down at his lover's pale face as he stepped out of the bar. His breathing was irregular, slow. "Fuck, fuck, fuck!"

John ran in front of him, unlocking the truck and opening the door. John helped him climb in the back seat with Jamie.

"Get us to a goddamned hospital!" Thank God they'd gone into San Antonio instead of staying closer to home.

"Already ahead of you! Hold on, I'm calling Jules." John burned rubber getting out of the parking lot.

Ethan pulled Jamie closer to him, stroking his face. "Come on, Blue Eyes, wake up for me. Baby, hang on."

"Ethan!"

Ethan looked up at the rearview mirror and into John's worried eyes.

"I've got Jules on the phone. She's meeting us at the hospital."

"Tell her he's not breathing right. He's wheezing and having a hard time, and he's sweating like crazy." *Come on, baby. Please. Don't you die on me.*

"Jules, did you hear that? Yeah, I think so. Ethan, are his pupils still dilated?"

"Yeah. At least they were. He's still unconscious." *God, please, don't let him die. I just found him; I can't lose him.*

The drive seemed to take forever, but Ethan knew it was only a matter of minutes before John pulled up to the emergency room entrance.

"We're here!" As soon as the truck jerked to a stop, John jumped out and opened the door. He pulled Jamie out and dashed toward the entrance. "Ethan, go park the truck!"

Ethan ran in behind him. Fuck the truck! Someone could steal it if they wanted to. He'd buy a new one.

A nurse met them just inside the door and directed John into a room to lay Jamie down on a stretcher. Other hospital staff were already there. Ethan and John told them what they suspected. Someone snapped out an order to intubate Jamie and get blood gases, stat. Ethan suddenly felt very ill. Fuck! Jamie was going to need help to breathe.

"Oh, God!" He watched in a daze as the doctors and nurses raced to pull out tubes and machines, and got to work on Jamie. The nurse that had led them into the room ushered them out.

John turned to him, his face white. "I'm going to park the truck."

"Yeah, okay. I'll go wait for Julia."

John nodded and walked off. Ethan stood there for several seconds, then forced himself to move. He went into the waiting area and sat down among the rest of the patients and their families waiting to be treated.

A few minutes later, John sat down beside him. "Anything?"

Ethan shook his head. "Fuck! Did you pick up his hat when it fell off in the parking lot?"

"Yeah, I got it. It's in the truck."

"Good. He'd be pissed if we lost his hat."

"Yeah." John turned to him. "You think Jeff and Carl drugged him?"

"I think it's damned suspicious. Of all the bars, what are the odds that they'd turn up at the one we're at? Especially on a work day. I bet they followed Jamie, Ed, and Hayden when they left the ranch."

"Think they cut the fence and shot Jamie's truck, too?"

Ethan looked at John. "Don't know. Up till now, I thought it was your daddy. He called Jamie today—"

"What? You didn't tell me that!"

"Just did."

"Why the hell didn't you say something earlier?"

He'd thought about it. He'd considered discussing it on the way to their meeting, but had decided against it. He'd promised not to keep things from Jamie, not to try and protect him in other ways. He also didn't want to get into Jamie's parentage. It was Jamie's place to tell his siblings, not his. He shrugged.

"John! Ethan!" Jules came rushing toward them. She was in a pair of jeans and tee-shirt, but her badge was pinned to her shirt. "What's going on?"

John stood up, holding his arms out to her. She hugged him, then Ethan.

"Don't know, Jules. We think he was drugged, but we don't know for sure and we don't have any idea what with."

She nodded. In her work environment, it was clear that Jules was very good at her job. She'd always been that way, calm, cool, and collected, in a real emergency. She thought for a few minutes. "Okay, I'm going back to see what I can find out. I'll come back and get the two of you soon." She walked off through the double doors leading into the ER, waving at one of the other nurses as she went.

Thirty long minutes later, she was back.

Ethan jumped up. "Well?"

She stopped in front of them. "They have him intubated and hooked up to a ventilator, and his blood pressure is up. He's still unconscious, but otherwise stable. Based on his symptoms and what you guys said, we think it was GHB. It gets used as a date-rape drug sometimes."

"Why would someone give him that?" John asked.

Ethan shook his head angrily. "Who the hell knows? Whoever did this—they're sick fucks!" He looked at Julia. "What does GHB do? How's that going to affect him? Is he going to be okay? Why is he hooked up to a ventilator? I know he was having a hard time breathing, but...SHIT! This is serious, isn't it?"

Julia nodded. "It can be. GHB depresses the respiratory system, which is pretty standard in a high dose or when someone has a bad reaction to it. Most people get kind of high on it. But Jamie either got quite a large dose, or his body isn't tolerating it well. Mixing it with alcohol intensifies the effects."

Ethan watched her closely. She wouldn't make eye contact. "What aren't you saying, Jules?"

"You can die from it, but typically someone just suddenly snaps out of it. One minute they're lying there; the next, they're freaking out trying to get the tubes out."

Ethan could swear his heart stopped.

Julia touched his arm. "Ethan, I've seen this before. Jamie's gonna be okay. He's stable. He'll wake up in a bit. Come on, let's go see him." Julia hooked her arms through his and her brother's and led them down the hall and past a nurses' station.

Please let Julia know what she is talking about.

"Hey, Julia! Is this your other brother?"

Jules looked over her shoulder but didn't slow down. "Yeah, Kev, this is John and this is Ethan. Ethan is like a brother, too. I'll be back in a sec. I'm taking them to see Jamie."

"Okay, when you're done, the cops want to talk to them."

She nodded. "Got it!"

If he ever saw Jamie in the hospital again, helpless and hooked up to any number of machines, it'd be too soon. After seeing Jamie, which just about killed him, Ethan and John had told the cops what little they knew, then called Ed and Hayden to get more details. Julia checked on Jamie periodically and reported back that he was still unconscious but having no other problems, which was a good sign.

She'd taken Ethan and John back to the break room after their meeting with the cops. They were drinking coffee, waiting for a change in Jamie's condition.

Ethan was on his fifth cup of coffee when Kevin, the male nurse Jules had talked to earlier, came in. "Hey, guys! Jamie's awake. He's asking for Ethan."

Ethan jumped up.

Kevin laughed. "Slow down, big guy. He isn't going anywhere. The police are with him right now. Come on and I'll take you to him." He winked at Julia. "Y'all coming?" Then he led Ethan out. Ethan followed Kevin down the hall wondering if the man could possibly walk any slower. Jules and John were right behind him. Kevin finally stopped and knocked on the wall beside the door to Jamie's room.

"Knock, knock!"

Jamie looked up. He was sitting on the edge of a hospital bed, and he still looked a bit pale, but he was buttoning his cuff back up. He saw Ethan and grinned, "Where's my hat?"

Oh, thank God! Ethan chuckled, giving a sigh of relief. The claws and cold lump of fear finally left his stomach. Everything was going to be okay.

Chapter Fourteen

Jamie knocked on the office doorframe the morning after they'd returned home and leaned against it just as Ethan hung up the phone.

Ethan smiled. "Hey, Blue Eyes! How you feeling?"

"Much better. That little catnap helped. Throat's still sore, though, and I don't remember much beyond the trip to San Antone." He nodded toward the phone. "Who were you talking to?"

"Sheriff Hunter." Ethan scooted back from his desk and met Jamie at the door. "Thought he should know about the drugging and that Jeff and Carl were at the bar. He's going to question them about the fence-cutting and the shooting. Provided I don't get a hold of them first." He grabbed the open lapels of Jamie's shirt and pulled him forward for a kiss.

Jamie sighed into his mouth. He needed Ethan's touch. He'd had the crappiest birthday on record, but this would go a long way toward making up for it. As Ethan's tongue touched his, he undid the buttons on Ethan's shirt.

Ethan released his lips and cupped his cheek, tilting his face up. "You sure you're okay? You scared the hell outta me."

He nodded. "I'm fine. Honest. Didn't mean to scare you."

"Not your fault." Ethan shook his head and brushed his lips across his again, then pulled him back into his arms. "Jesus, Jamie, when I saw them hooking you up to a respirator and you were so unresponsive... I don't ever wanna feel like that again."

Jamie was torn at how he felt. Part of him hated that Ethan had been so worried, hated to make Ethan feel bad, ever. But the other part was elated that Ethan cared so much. He ran a fingertip down Ethan's cheek then kissed him lightly. "I don't want you to ever feel like that again, either. Wanna come upstairs with me? I'll make it up to ya."

Ethan groaned and dropped his forehead against Jamie's. "You sure you're all right?"

"Yup."

"Let's go!"

He chuckled, grabbed Ethan's hand and headed upstairs.

"Jamie?"

He stopped on the stairs and looked back. "Yeah?"

"Promise me you'll be careful. That you'll stay close to the house until we get this figured out. If something were to happen to you..." Ethan looked away, a muscle jerking in his jaw.

Jamie tugged him the rest of the way up the stairs, then backed him against the hall wall next to their bedroom, kissing him, slow and easy. Taking his time. Caressing and loving and just showing Ethan how much he cared. How much Ethan's concern meant to him.

"I'll stay close to the house until Sheriff Hunter finds out who was responsible. And I'll stay as far away from Jeff and Carl as I can."

Ethan nodded. "Good. I'm going to hold you to that." He snatched Jamie's hand and hauled him into their room and led him to the bed. "I want you to do me, Blue Eyes."

Jamie bit his bottom lip and sat down on the edge of the bed. This was new territory. And he knew it had been a long time for Ethan, too.

"What? You look nervous."

Jamie nodded. "A little, yeah. Don't wanna hurt you."

Ethan grinned and dropped to his knees, kneeling between Jamie's legs. "Does it hurt you?"

"Oh, hell, no!" Okay, put that way, he felt a little silly. But, still, Ethan had said it'd been five years. Jamie might not have had sex before Ethan, but he'd had his toys and used them.

Ethan chuckled and pushed Jamie's shirt off his shoulders. He ran his hand down Jamie's chest, then leaned forward to kiss his belly. "Love your abs."

Jamie's cock hardened more, and his stomach muscles jumped, responding to those lips. "Yeah?" He reached down for Ethan's shirt and pulled it over his head, then dropped a hand to Ethan's belly, stroking. "Kinda fond of yours, too." Really fond. But then, there wasn't a spot on Ethan that wasn't drool worthy. The man was built like a freaking Greek god.

Ethan closed his eyes, burying his face in Jamie's belly for a few seconds and taking a deep breath. "Love the way you smell, too." Then he pulled back and stood up, pulling Jamie up with him. He unbuttoned Jamie's jeans, then pushed them and his briefs down.

Jamie stepped out of his clothes, his cock straining toward his cowboy.

Ethan dropped a kiss on the head of his prick, then got back up, shucking his own jeans. "Relax."

"I'm fine."

"You're nervous, though." Ethan pushed him back until the backs of his legs hit the edge of the bed. That thick, hard-as-nails cock pressed against his as Ethan's mouth came over his.

Before he knew it they were on the bed, and his hands were full of cowboy. Damn, he loved this, couldn't get enough of it. Couldn't stop touching...feeling.

Ethan chuckled. "That's better."

Jamie thought he murmured something about octopuses, too, but he wasn't sure. Ethan had his hands on Jamie's cock, and that's all he could concentrate on. So if the man wanted to discuss marine life, then he was on his own.

Ethan squeezed and fondled for a few moments, then clasped both their pricks in one big hand and started stroking them off. It was absolute heaven, the feel of that hot flesh pressed against his. Jamie was whimpering and moaning and making all sorts of noises, but he didn't care. He couldn't stop; it felt too good. And his cowboy was loving it, too. Those big brown eyes were closed, a look of absolute bliss on that gorgeous, tanned face.

He bit down on Ethan's shoulder and wrapped his own hand around their cocks, helping. His other hand clung to the back of Ethan's neck, holding him close. He was thrusting into their hands when Ethan gasped and let go.

"Slow down, Jamie. Don't want to come yet."

Jamie rolled himself on top of Ethan and straddled Ethan's thighs, reaching for that thick cock.

Ethan shook his head. "No, get the lube. Get me ready."

Jamie nodded and grabbed the bottle off the nightstand, then slid down that long, fine body. He didn't waste any time. His cock was so hard it was about to explode. He was still nervous, but he trusted Ethan to tell him to stop if it didn't feel good.

Ethan slid his knees up, opening for him.

Jamie moaned. Damn, his cowboy was hot. He fumbled with the lid, getting his fingers nice and slick before he gave in to temptation and licked those tightly drawn balls.

"Oh, shit!"

"Mmm." Jamie licked and nuzzled, finally sucking the warm sac into his mouth.

Ethan's head was thrashing back and forth on the bed. He was mumbling incoherently.

Fuck! The man was too damn sexy. Jamie slid his slicked up finger along Ethan's crease, just rubbing. His lover's cock jerked in response and dripped on his own belly.

Jamie groaned. He found the puckered hole with his finger and pushed in slowly as he scooted up Ethan's body. He licked the drops of come off that taut belly and took the head of Ethan's cock in his mouth. *Oh! So fucking good!* He loved the taste of his cowboy.

Ethan was writhing on his finger, head still thrashing. "More."

He knew that feeling, and Ethan usually had him begging for it. He grinned around the prick in his mouth and gave in to the temptation to tease a bit. A little payback was warranted, after all the times he'd been forced to suffer delicious torment. He began moving that lone finger, fucking the tight little hole with it in gradual thrusts.

Ethan groaned again.

He added another finger, hitting a spot that had Ethan's head jerking up and his cock standing at attention.

"Fuck!"

Oh, yeah! Jamie rubbed over the prostate again, watching his cowboy's face. Sheer bliss. He knew damn well how freaking incredible it felt, so he did it again, simultaneously taking Ethan's cock all the way down his throat.

Ethan practically arched off the bed. "Oh, fucking shit, Jamie! Stop! Can't come yet."

Jamie ground his own prick into the mattress, humping just a little bit. He could get off just by watching Ethan, but he didn't want to come that way. Not today, anyway. He wanted to feel that tight little hole stretched around him, needed to know what it was like from the giving end. Wasn't there a saying, something about it being better to give than receive? He wondered if it applied here as well.

He stroked that spot once more, then pulled his fingers out a bit, scissoring his fingers, stretching, just like Ethan always did. "Okay?"

Ethan gave a jerky nod.

"Doesn't hurt?"

"Burns a little. Don't stop. If you stop, I will fucking strangle you."

He chuckled and nipped Ethan's thigh. He set up a nice, even tempo, fucking his cowboy lovingly with just those two fingers until Ethan begged for more, then he added a third finger.

Ethan gasped, his eyes going wide.

Jamie opened his mouth to ask if he was all right, but Ethan cut him off.

"'M fine. Just been a while, is all. Just give me a minute, 'kay?"

Jamie nodded. God give him patience. He was so close to coming already that he wasn't sure he'd make it long enough to get inside Ethan. But he kept giving his man time to adjust. The sight of that tight little opening stretched around his fingers was one of the most erotic things he'd ever seen. He dipped and flicked his tongue around his fingers, over Ethan's skin right above them.

Ethan grunted.

Jamie did it again. He kept licking until Ethan pushed toward him, then he moved his fingers in and out, slowly, testing. His cowboy took it all, his head thrashing again.

Ethan was panting, hard. "Now, Blue Eyes, need..."

He pulled his fingers out and sat up on his knees. Grabbing the lube, he coated his prick liberally, then spread more over Ethan's hole. God! His fingers felt good slicking over his cock; he was too damned close. There was no way he was going to last long.

"Jamie, please…"

He moved forward, aligning the blunt tip of his penis to his cowboy's ass, and gently entered the puckered hole and made his way inside, inch by delicious inch. At first, he tried to watch Ethan's face, but the look of pure pleasure there was too much to withstand on top of the tight heat closing around his cock, so he squeezed his eyes shut. By the time he was all the way in, he was shaking with need, concentrating hard to not spill himself. He took a few deep breaths, got himself under control, and opened his eyes.

Ethan's gaze met his. He reached up and cupped Jamie's cheek. "Come here." He pulled Jamie forward until their lips met. That hot tongue flicked across Jamie's lips, then pushed in.

Jamie whimpered, opening his mouth.

Ethan's tongue caressed his over and over, then explored the rest of his mouth, in a slow sensual glide. It was wonderful, made him feel deeply loved and cherished, forced him to relax a bit. It also took the edge off his hunger and gave him back some of his control. He didn't feel like he was going to come if Ethan so much as took one more breath.

Ethan released him with a sigh, bucking his hips a little. "Move, Blue Eyes."

He did. Flexed his hips, then slowly thrust back in. His balls pulled tighter, making him groan. "Damn, that feels good."

"You like it, huh?"

He nodded, languidly moving his hips. "Yeah." Holding his weight off of Ethan, he set up a steady pace, staring into Ethan's eyes. When Ethan began to meet his thrusts, he lost it. "Oh,

God, Ethan…gotta…oh…" He pumped faster, fucking his cowboy hard.

"Oh, yeah, baby…" Ethan grabbed his own cock, pulling in time with Jamie's thrusts.

Jamie could feel the orgasm start in the base of his spine. His balls pulled tighter and he came, jerking and shooting into the tight, hot body beneath him. Ethan came seconds later, spraying his hand and belly with come. His ass clamped around Jamie, wringing aftershocks from the both of them.

Jamie collapsed on Ethan, knowing his cowboy could take his weight, spreading Ethan's come between them.

Ethan's breath tickled his ear, and he kissed Jamie's cheek, making him smile. "Gonna keep you, Blue Eyes. Ought to brand your ass, like the cattle, so you always get brought back to me."

Jamie chuckled. "Not going anywhere, cowboy. You're stuck with me." He got another kiss to the cheek, then Ethan's tongue flicked inside his ear. He shivered and nipped Ethan's chest.

"Gonna hold you to that. That means no fucking getting poisoned and dying on me, either."

He lifted up, looking down at Ethan. Their eyes met and held for a minute. It was an intense moment; they didn't say a word, didn't have to. Jamie knew both of them were well aware how the other felt.

Ethan finally broke the silence. "I hate to ruin the moment, but I have come dripping down my sides."

Jamie laughed and slid off of his cowboy. "Hold still, I'll bring you a towel." He got off the bed and headed to the bathroom. He heard a moan and looked back to find Ethan staring at his ass.

"Hmm, maybe branding your ass isn't a bad idea, after all."

Jamie grinned and wiggled his butt. "Yeah? You think the Tin Star brand would look good on my ass?"

Ethan nodded. "Yeah, but *Property of Ethan Whitehall* would look even better."

They ended up showering together.

* * *

Later that day, after working out in the south pasture, Jamie came in to find Bill sound asleep on the couch, his foot on a pillow and an ice pack on his foot.

"He got caught in the fence rung trying to climb over the corral gate. Ankle swelled up. I took him into the clinic in town to have it X-rayed. It's just a bad sprain." Ethan was lounging against the kitchen door with a glass of tea in hand.

Jamie whistled. "Ouch!"

Ethan nodded. "Yeah, I think it hurt his pride more than anything. Damned old fool. Can't seem to get it through his head that he can't do the shit he used to do."

"Climbing over the fence shouldn't be that big a deal."

"It is when you have a saddle slung over your shoulder."

"Ah!"

"How are you feeling? You want some tea?"

Jamie walked to him, grabbed the glass and took a swig. "Thanks."

Ethan snatched it back with a grin. "This is mine! I meant that I'd get you one."

Jamie chuckled and snatched it back, "No, I want this one!"

Ethan gave him a quick kiss, then shook his head and walked into the kitchen. "Spoiled brat!"

"Yeah, but what can you do?" He sat down at the table while Ethan made himself another glass of tea.

Fred was lying on the kitchen floor on her back and completely surrounded by her toys. Jamie chuckled. "So that's where she went. She was with me all day, then about an hour ago she split."

Ethan pulled a chair out and sat down. "Yeah, she came to the back door asking to be let in. When I did, she gathered every one of her toys. Should have seen her trying to put them in her mouth all at once. Crazy dog." He reached down to stroke Fred's belly.

Jamie took a sip of tea and watched Ethan. Damn, the man was gorgeous. And he loved the smile Ethan always wore when he talked about Fred.

"Listen, Jamie, I've been thinking. I think you should take over Bill's job."

"What? Damn, Ethan, the man just got hurt, he's not incompetent. Besides, Ed and Hayden have been here longer than I have."

"Just listen. Bill and I discussed this before, and after today...I think this will work out better for everyone."

Yeah, right! What was Ethan up to? "All right, I'm listening."

"Bill is going to take over some of my work—God knows I'm tired of sitting in front of a computer so much—and the work around the house. He'll still putter with the machinery, but you can take over the cattle and other livestock, the usual foreman responsibilities. Ed and Hayden will answer directly to you and you can hire some more hands. Hell, with Bill doing some of my paperwork, I'll be able to get more done, too. We'll probably move him in the house, 'cause eventually we'll need more room in the bunkhouse as well."

Jamie opened his mouth to protest, but Ethan continued. "I want to buy a couple more head of cattle, and I've been thinking about breeding horses. I want to expand the operation. Been wanting to for years, but Bill wasn't up to it. You are. Bill isn't going to be able to handle that many longhorns. And he damn sure can't break horses anymore...not without killing himself."

"Bill is okay with this? He's becoming, like, what? A glorified housekeeper?"

Ethan snorted. "Good lord, don't let him hear you say that! Yes, he's fine with it. He said he'd even take up the cooking if you want. He's going to basically trade jobs with you, except you'll still be doing all the stuff outside. You just won't have to do any of the housework or cooking."

Jamie groaned. "Do you really think this is going to work? I'm picky about how my food is cooked and how my house is cleaned. Do you honestly think I'm going to be happy with someone else doing it?" Not to mention he was scared to death to make things truly his, run things like he wanted to run them.

Ethan gave him a sharp look, almost like he'd seen that thought in his face. Then sighed and leaned forward. "Jamie, if you are going to get on with your life, this is the next step. You can train Bill to do everything to your liking."

"So what is this? Therapy?"

"No, that's not what this is about. You fucking work too hard! You already do Bill's job, and you do all the house stuff, too. I'm just asking you to let Bill help out with the house. He said he trusts your judgment and that you'd make a fine foreman."

Jamie shook his head. "I just can't believe Bill would be willing to give up working outside."

"He's not going to. He's just going to let you call the shots and make the major decisions. He's tired, Jamie. He's sixty-two years old and has lived a hard life. He wants to take it easy, but he can't just retire. Says he's worse than useless if he doesn't do something. You can handle this, more than handle it, and help me build this place up like I've always wanted to do."

"But what about Ed and Hayden? They've got seniority. It's hardly fair for me to take over Bill's job."

"They won't have a problem with it. Bill suggested you. He says you know more than they do, and you are definitely better at running things and taking charge."

"What happened to you not wanting me too far away from the house?"

"You won't be, not until we get this shit straightened out and find out who the hell is trying to hurt your fine ass. That's one of the reasons we're hiring more hands."

Jamie sighed. "Great!" He put as much sarcasm into the word as possible. "So it amounts to Jamie not doing shit, too!"

"No, it doesn't! I've been wanting to expand the Tin Star for a long time. With you managing things and taking over for Bill, I can finally do that."

"They'll—Hayden and Ed—they'll think I landed the job 'cause I'm fuckin' the boss!"

Ethan laughed. "You are fucking me. Is that what's bothering you?"

"They know."

"They do?"

"Yeah."

Ethan shrugged. "Well, there you go! They will *know* you got the job by fuckin' the boss!" Ethan's lips twitched.

Jamie rolled his eyes and stood up. "Ha ha!" He walked out of the kitchen. He needed to think about this. It smacked of a handout! Of Ethan trying to fix things for him, make him feel better. What the hell could Bill possibly be gaining from this? Damn it!

He wasn't ready for this responsibility. He was afraid to let the Tin Star mean something to him. To actually make it his, or leastways partly his. What if Ethan decided he didn't want him anymore? Not that he'd give up Ethan that easily, but the ranch wasn't his, it was Ethan's.

Bill sat up on the couch as he walked through the living room. "Hey, kid! Where you going in such a hellfire hurry?"

Jamie stopped. "Oh, hey, Bill! How's the ankle?"

"Not too bad, considering. Ethan tell you what happened?" Bill looked kind of pink in the cheeks.

"Yeah." He sat down in the chair across from the couch. "You really wanting to hang out here at the house, doing chores and such?"

Bill chuckled. "So that's what's botherin' ya. Told Ethan it would. Actually, kid, I think it'd be nice. Besides, it's time I did something else. Been a cowboy for damned near forty years."

Jamie shook his head. "I'm not buying it, Bill."

Bill sighed. "I'm getting too damn old to do the things I used to. I know that. Don't like to admit it, but I know it. With Ethan buying more stock…" He shook his head. "It's a job better suited to you than me. Frankly, kid, I don't want the headaches. Not that I'd admit that to too many people, but you ain't just anybody."

Jamie took his hat off and tossed it onto the coffee table and ran his hands through his hair. "Why me?"

"Why not? Son, you were born to this job and you do it well. You're better at giving orders than I ever was. Hell, I was impressed as shit when you realized that Betty Lou was foundering. I'd've never picked up on it that soon. And I've never been able to make cowboys work as hard as you do! There is just something about you that makes 'em want to do their best for ya. Don't sell yerself short, Jamie. Hank trained you well. Ya might have gotten the job over at the Quad J 'cause you're family, but ya kept it for as long as ya did 'cause yer good at it."

Jamie tried not to blush, but holy shit! It was nice to be appreciated. "What about the other two? Won't it just chap their hides that I got the job over them?"

Bill smiled and shook his head. "They ain't either one like that and you know it. They're good men. And they are sure as hell impressed with you. They've both informed me of yer finer qualities. They got a lot of respect for you, kid. And they ain't the only ones." Bill gave a sharp nod.

Jamie almost felt like someone knocked the wind out of him. "Thanks, Bill. That means a lot to me."

"Yer welcome. Besides, the place is yer home now, too. Yer gonna be here long after I'm gone, kid."

God, I hope so.

Chapter Fifteen

It was Thanksgiving morning and things were shaping up to be a pretty darn good day. Jamie had gotten the turkey into the oven and gotten Bill to work on the other fixin's. Despite all the problems over the last couple of months, Jamie had a whole lot to be thankful for.

Bill was getting quite adept in the kitchen, and he wasn't shaping up too badly on housework, either. In fact, he and Bill were both settling into their new jobs nicely. Ethan had bought four new horses, and they were set to go to a big cattle auction in a couple of weeks, so he was staying busy with ranch work. He had been interviewing for more ranch hands all week and was thinking he'd finally found one. Slowly, but surely, the Tin Star was becoming his, too, and it felt…right. It was still a little scary, but right.

There hadn't been any more acts of vandalism. The sheriff wasn't any closer to finding out who had done it, but at least there weren't any new incidents. His dad hadn't called or carried out his threats…yet. Ethan still had his lawyers checking into the money situation, but he really didn't care too much. It wasn't money he was really counting on other than to buy into the steakhouse deal, but Ethan was fronting him the money and had said he could pay it back from the profits they made.

Nope, his life wasn't bad at all. He had just about everything he could want: a great job, food in his stomach, a better relationship than he'd ever dreamed possible and a family—one he really fit into. *Yup, pretty damned good.*

"What are you smilin' at, boy?"

Jamie started and looked at Bill. "Just thinking I've got a lot to be thankful for."

Bill smiled. "We all do. Have ya heard from Margaret this mornin'? Did she say what time she was gonna come over and help with supper?"

Jamie laughed. "Oh, lord! You've got it bad! You old dog!"

Bill clutched the batter-covered spoon he was using to stir the cornbread mix to his chest. "Me? An old dog?"

"Yes, you! You might fool Ethan, but I know darned well you have something going with Margie."

Bill's face went blank.

"Bill, I think it's great. I adore Margie, and I want her to be happy. I've seen how you two look at each other. Go for it, is all I'm saying."

The old man's face lit up, then he cocked a brow. "What's Ethan say?"

Jamie quirked a brow back. "Does it matter?"

"Yup, it does."

"Ethan says it's just my wishful thinking. He's fine with it, just thinks I'm seeing things that aren't there. I'm not, am I?"

Bill shook his head. "Nah, you're seein' right. Just like I know 'm seein' right, even though Margaret won' confirm it."

Uh oh! Yeah, Jamie had suspected the old ranch hand knew about him and Ethan, just like the other men, but how did he feel about it? And why did it matter to him? It shouldn't, but it did. He liked Bill. And there was the fact that Bill was sort of a father figure for Ethan. "Confirm what?"

Bill laughed. "Turned da tables on you, didn' I, boy? I mean you and Ethan, of course. Don't play dense."

"Why not? You played dense when I mentioned you and Margie."

"Oho! Gettin' sassy, are ya?" Bill wasn't able to hide the grin tugging at his lips.

He laughed at the mock sternness Bill was trying to pull off, but in all honesty, he was slightly nervous about what Bill thought.

Finally, Bill smiled, not trying to hide it. "Relax. 'M glad Ethan found ya. I always did like you. Always thought you'd be a good match for m' boy."

"What?"

"Don't act so surprised. I've always known. Hell, how could I help but know? I helped raise 'im from the time he was four. I'm pretty sure his daddy knew, too. We never discussed it, but, well..." Bill nodded, decisively. "He knew. And he didn't give a damn! Unlike that bastard that sired ya." Bill turned back to stirring the batter.

When he spoke again it was soft, apologetic. "I'm sorry, Jamie. I'll never understand how a man like that managed to bring up three such fine children." He shook his head. "I think you and Ethan'll do all right."

Jamie blinked. Good grief! Talk about revelations! He was stunned. Before he could say anything, Ethan's voice came from the doorway.

"So you think he knew?"

Bill and Jamie both jerked their attention to Ethan, who was leaning against the kitchen doorway in a pair of faded jeans and pullover shirt and socked feet. He looked for all the world like the answer to his question wasn't important, but Jamie knew damned well it was.

"Yeah, he knew. And he didn't care, just like I don'. Don' get me wrong, I'm sure he'd 'ave rathered it be otherwise, but he didn't love ya any less."

A small grin flitted across Ethan's lips, one so quick that if he hadn't been staring at the man's mouth, Jamie might have missed it. Ethan shoved away from the entrance and entered the kitchen. He patted Bill on the shoulder.

Bill patted him back, then hauled him into a quick hug. He let go and went back to the cornbread, pouring it into a pan. "You two get yourselves outta here, so I can get to finishin' this. We gonna have supper at midnight at this rate."

Jamie grinned and shook his head. "Ya old fart!"

Bill growled at him.

Ethan laughed and hugged Jamie. "Happy Thanksgiving."

"Happy Thanksgiving to you, too. I was just thinking how many great things I have to be thankful for."

"Yeah?" Ethan grinned down at him.

"Yeah." He kissed Ethan. Then nibbled for a few seconds.

"All right, cut that out! I'm tryin' to cook in here! I may know about it. I may even be glad, but I damn sure don' wanna see it!"

He and Ethan laughed, squeezing each other tighter.

Ethan stepped away and headed for the door. "Well, fine. I won't argue. If I stay, I'm liable to be put to work cooking. Grab us some beers, Jamie, and come on into the living room. We can make out in there."

Bill pointed his spoon at him. "Now, don' make me put my boot to yer ass, boy!"

Ethan chuckled and left.

Jamie laughed, too, and went to the refrigerator. "Well, shit! We're outta beer." He turned toward Bill and sighed. "And I was really looking forward to necking on the couch."

Bill groaned. "Don' think I won' kick your ass, too, kid!"

Jamie came out of the store with a case of beer in each hand and one under each arm. Thank God for gas stations with convenience stores. He hadn't even considered that everything would be closed when he'd headed out after more beer, just that they were going to have a houseful of people all wanting alcohol for the Cowboys' game later that night.

"Hey, faggot!"

Aw, shit! Not now, dammit! He had his hands full. Jamie kept walking, ignoring the taunts that came from behind him.

"Hey, queer, I'm talking to you!"

Jamie groaned, still heading toward the car. A shove from behind forced him to stumble into the front of his and Ethan's Mustang. "Motherfucker!" He set the beers down and turned.

Tom Cooke and Carl. Great.

Tom smiled. "Come on. You might have gotten the best of Carl here and Jeff." He looked around. "But I don't see Whitehall and his foreman to bail you out now."

Jamie sighed. He really didn't want to get into it with them. He knew he could give a good accounting of himself, and he did have the gun under his jacket, but he really didn't want to hassle with them.

Carl and Tom suddenly looked past Jamie as a smooth, deep voice said, "I don't know who the hell you are. But, Carl, if you want to continue to work for the Quad J, you'd best be on your way."

What the...? Who was that? Jamie didn't recognize the voice but it was somewhere behind him. He could feel the man's presence. Jamie didn't like having someone at his back that he didn't know, but he sensed more trouble from in front of him than behind. So he kept his eyes on the known threats.

Carl scowled at the man behind Jamie. "You can't fire me! Killian hired me and Jeff. You and his damn boy ain't got nothing to say about it."

The man behind him chuckled, but without any evidence of humor. "Oh, I reckon John will have plenty to say about it. Killian may have hired you but, make no mistake, John runs the place and he gave me the authority to hire and fire whom I see fit. And I don't think he'll take too kindly to you harassing his brother."

Carl spat on the ground, pivoted, then walked off.

Tom looked at Jamie, then over his shoulder at Carl's back, apparently weighing his chances, before he, too, turned and stalked away.

Jamie turned and came face to face with one of the most striking men he'd ever seen. He was as conventionally handsome as Ethan or even Jamie himself, but this man oozed masculinity. He had a small, crescent-shaped scar at the edge of his right eyebrow and his smoky gray eyes sparkled with good humor. The man wore a tan felt cowboy hat over light-brown hair and had a day's growth of beard. Though his eyes were smiling at Jamie, his lips were not. He wasn't as big as Ethan, but he looked tough as hell. The man wore a look that clearly said anyone who messed with him would get his ass kicked. This was not someone you wanted to get on the wrong side of.

Jamie held out his hand to the man. "James Killian. But then you apparently know that."

The man chuckled, a rough sound that held humor this time, then shook Jamie's hand. "Royal McCabe. I'm the new foreman at the Quad J."

"Pleasure to meet you. Thanks for the assist."

McCabe dipped his head. "You're welcome. Your brother speaks very highly of you. And judging from the looks of things when I took over, I'd say he speaks the truth. Nice to finally meet you."

"Did I hear you right? Carl and Jeff work for the Quad J now?"

McCabe sighed. "I'm afraid so. Your father hired them last week. Haven't gotten around to discussing it with your brother yet. I doubt he even knows."

Well, son of a bitch. He was pretty sure John didn't know. He would have told Jamie something like that, so what would he say when he found out?

"Well, I better get back to the Tin Star. I imagine everyone has discovered we're out of beer by now. Thanks, again."

"Welcome. Have a nice Thanksgiving." McCabe gave a quick nod and left.

"You, too," Jamie called over his shoulder. He worried over Carl and Jeff all the way back to the ranch. He felt betrayed. Not that it was his brother's fault, but John should be keeping better tabs on his people, damn it! Jamie was going to have to talk to him about that.

Jamie pulled up the driveway. Ethan and Fred met him as soon as he stepped out of the car.

"Need some help?" Ethan's grin faded as soon as he caught look on Jamie's face. "What happened?"

"I met the Quad J's new foreman."

"Yeah?"

Jamie nodded. "Says that Jeff and Carl are working at the Quad J."

"Son of a bitch! What the hell is John thinking?"

"Don't think he knows. McCabe says he hasn't seen him long enough to tell him. Apparently my dad hired them."

"McCabe told you this?

Jamie nodded and handed Ethan two packs of beer. "I had a run-in with Carl and Tom Cooke. McCabe stepped up behind me and let them know it wasn't going to be just me if they decided to start something."

"No shit?" Ethan's face had tightened at first but relaxed a little toward the end of his recitation.

"No shit." Jamie grabbed the remaining two packs and followed Ethan into the house.

"You ready to let me have a heart-to-heart with John now?"

"Yup, as long as you let me add my two cents."

The house was chaos. Margie was in the kitchen directing Bill and John. John was whining about how he was a guest and not supposed to cook. Margie was threatening to beat him over the head with a ladle. Bill was laughing and having a grand ole time.

Julia was in the dining room directing Ed and Hayden on how to set the table. She was her usual chatty self. Jamie felt sorry for the two men.

Jamie looked at Ethan. "No wonder you came running out to help bring the beer in."

Ethan chuckled. "Yeah, Julia has been giving out orders since she got here. Oddly enough, Ed and Hayden don't seem to be minding it all that much."

"Poor things. Can't imagine allowing someone whom I'm not employed by to boss me around."

"You let me boss you around."

Jamie raised an eyebrow. "Maybe because you're my boss?"

"Am I?"

"Aren't you?"

Ethan shrugged. "Maybe at first. You're more like a partner now."

Jamie grinned. "You know, I'm beginning to feel like it. Seeing McCabe didn't really bother me all that much."

Ethan smiled and kissed his cheek. "Good."

Julia looked up, spotted them, and smiled.

Ethan leaned in and whispered in his ear. "Run! I'll head out the back. You head out the front. Maybe we can confuse her enough that she won't follow. Oh, shit! Too late."

"What are you grinning at, Jamie?" Julia stepped right up in front of them, blocking their exit.

"Nothing. How are you doing?" He hugged her.

"Do you really want me to answer that?"

Ethan shook his head. "No, he just wants you to say, 'Fine. Happy Thanksgiving.'"

She swatted Ethan. "I'm tired. My back hurts. My feet hurt. They've been working my ass off at the hospital. I need a vacation!"

Ethan shrugged and mouthed, *I tried.*

Jamie grinned. "Man, that sucks!"

"Yes, it does." She nodded. "How are you? Are you okay?"

"I'm great." And it was true. He belonged here. Now if he could only figure out what was going on with his brother, everything would be perfect.

"Good. So tell me about Hayden." She waggled her eyebrows.

Jamie groaned. "Ethan's known him longer than I have. You should— Don't even think about it, Cowboy! Get back here— ask him." Jamie rolled his eyes. The man had actually tried to make a break for it, as if Jamie would allow that.

Ethan raised a brow.

Jamie crossed his arms over his chest.

Ethan did the same and cocked his head.

Julia huffed. "Well?"

Jamie should have seen it coming by the twinkle in his cowboy's eyes.

"Sorry, Jules." Ethan managed to keep a straight face. "He's gay."

Jules snapped her fingers. "Damn! How about Ed?"

"Gay, too." He didn't even crack a smile.

Jamie threw his head back and laughed. Even he wasn't willing to go that far to keep Julia away from the men. Oh, brother! "You better tell Hayden and Ed. I don't think they know."

Jules groaned, put her hands on her hips, then threw them in the air. "Fine! I'll find out myself." She glared at them both.

"Thank God!" Ethan laughed.

Jamie shook his head. "You hit an all-time low with that one."

"Give me a break, I was desperate. I almost told her Hayden was married. Given the lack of a wife, I don't think that one would have held water."

"I got news for you. The gay thing didn't hold any water, either."

Ethan shrugged. "Made her leave us alone, didn't it?"

Jamie chuckled. "Yeah, I guess it did. You ready to abuse the rest of my family? Or you wanna wait till after supper?"

"Up to you. I'm keeping quiet."

"Why are you keeping quiet? He's your best friend."

Ethan raised a brow. "Oh?"

Jamie's heart nearly stuttered. *Damn!* There was no mistaking what Ethan meant by that. His loyalties lay with Jamie first...not John. He grinned, then threw his arms around Ethan's neck and kissed him.

As kisses went it wasn't the most graceful or even the most romantic. How could it be with the chorus of critics? There was everything from "Eww," to "Take it upstairs," to "Someone get a hose."

Jamie smiled against Ethan's lips but didn't let go of him. "After supper?"

"Yeah, after supper." Ethan gave him a quick peck, then pulled away to glare at the trio in the dining room. "Y'all shut the hell up!"

Jules, Hayden, and Ed all broke into peals of laughter. Jamie couldn't help but join them.

* * *

Ethan sat across from his best friend of twenty-six years and his lover of three months, and there was not the slightest bit of regret in him. He knew where he stood. John was like a brother to him, but he cared about Jamie more. There was no question of whose side he was on...not that they were picking sides or anything. They were there to inform John that his daddy had hired men behind his back. If John didn't already know, then he needed to pay better attention to what his daddy was doing. He was staying on to keep from putting good, hard-working people out of work, and if Jacob was trying to take over again by dealing behind his eldest son's back...well, it didn't look too good.

Ethan was letting Jamie do the talking, and thinking that maybe he shouldn't have.

"What do you want me to do, Jamie?" John jumped up and began to pace.

Jamie leaned back against Ethan's desk and crossed his feet. "I want you to stop ignoring the problem. Whose side are you on?"

"How can you ask me that?"

Ethan sighed. This was going to be a long conversation if they kept going around and around. They'd had this conversation already.

"Because you can't sit in the middle anymore. Pick a side of the fence. Either you support me or you don't. Supporting me to everyone but Dad doesn't cut it. And you aren't doing yourself any favors by ignoring Dad's actions."

John stopped and looked at him. His mouth dropped open, then he snapped it shut.

"What?" Ethan got up and walked around the desk to lean against it next to Jamie.

John glared at Jamie. "Are you threatening me?"

What? Where had that come from? What the hell was he talking about? Ethan turned to Jamie.

Jamie glanced at him, startled, then frowned and looked back to John. "That depends. You done something we should know about? Are you an accessory?"

Oh, shit! This was going downhill fast! Ethan hadn't even drawn that conclusion. He was pretty sure John hadn't meant it that way either. But before he could try to salvage the situation John was already responding. "Fuck you!"

Jamie straightened from the desk. "No, fuck you! You turncoat! Why don't you go kiss Daddy's ass! Maybe you can share a jail cell!"

John gave one last grim look at Ethan, then turned and stormed out.

Ethan looked at Jamie. "Was that really necessary?"

"He looked guilty."

Oh, good lord! *Siblings!* "He looked guilty because he wants to tell your dad to take a flying leap, he knows deep down he should, but he can't. It doesn't mean he was in on anything your father might have done. Hell, we brought him in here to tell him about your dad hiring Carl and Jeff behind his back. Damn, you have a temper! Remind me not to piss you off."

Jamie scoffed. "He started it!"

Ethan shook his head, suddenly seeing the situation from a different perspective. "Your daddy started it. This is probably what he wants, you and John at each other's throats. Your brother might not be handling this the way we want him to, but he's always supported you otherwise and he doesn't deserve being called a turncoat. You gonna let your daddy win?"

"Fuck!" Jamie ran out of the room.

Ethan followed at a more leisurely pace. Walked through the living room where everyone else was watching the football game. No one but Julia seemed to notice the upheaval. She was looking toward the kitchen where Jamie and John had gone. She caught Ethan's gaze and stood up.

Ethan shook his head and held up his hand, silently reassuring her that he had it covered.

She bit her lip, her attention darting back to the kitchen, but she sat back down.

He walked into the kitchen to find John standing at the door and Jamie in front of it, blocking his brother's exit. "I'm sorry. I'm just a little... I finally realized that he isn't going to let me go home, that it's irrevocable."

John sighed and grabbed Jamie, hugging him. "I'm sorry, too."

Ethan started a pot of coffee, then leaned against the counter. "Have you seen any proof of him having Jamie drugged? Or being involved in the damage to Jamie's truck or the fence?"

John shook his head. "That's just it. I can't find any evidence of it. I don't want to believe him capable of it, but at the same time, I've been looking. I have to know for sure. I didn't find out about Jeff and Carl hiring on at the Quad J until yesterday."

Ethan nodded. He'd had a feeling that John had known.

"You knew?" Jamie blurted out.

Damn, Jamie was on a roll today. He wasn't usually so quick to jump to conclusions, but apparently the strain of the situation was getting to him. Ethan gave him the don't-start-any-more-shit-look and got lucky. Apparently, Mr. Hothead was going to pay attention to the warning.

Jamie sighed and lowered his voice. "Couldn't you have called and said something?"

John dropped his head. "That's just it, Jamie. I didn't know how to tell you. I didn't want to upset you."

Ethan reached for three cups. He was beginning to see part of the problem.

Apparently, Jamie did, too. He smiled at his brother. "I'm a big boy. I really can take care of myself. I don't need you..." He glanced over his shoulder at Ethan. "...or anyone else to shield me from things. You aren't helping me by keeping me ignorant of what's going on. I know he doesn't give a rat's ass about me, John. He never has. It hurts but it's okay. I can't make him care, never could, so he did me a favor by kicking me out. It's turned out to be the best thing ever to happen to me." Jamie looked at Ethan again and smiled.

Ethan smiled back. Jamie was finally getting it.

Chapter Sixteen

Jamie was bent over picking up tack in the stables when Ethan snuck up behind him and pressed his hips against Jamie's butt. He couldn't see Ethan, but he knew it was his cowboy. No one else would dare or even think about touching him like that. He chuckled and straightened. "You want something, Cowboy?"

Ethan's hands landed on his hips and pulled his back flush to Ethan's chest. Warm breath tickled his ear. "Umm, how did you know?"

Jamie reached behind him and grasped the hard prick pressing against his ass. "Lucky guess." He spun around and put his hands on his cowboy's shoulders.

Ethan was in a pair of sweatpants, a tee-shirt, and sneakers. His hair was tousled and he looked like he'd just gotten out of bed. Which was entirely possible, because that's where Jamie had left him when he'd gotten up and dressed earlier. "You just get outta bed?"

"Nope. Just haven't gotten dressed yet." He leaned in and kissed Jamie, his tongue probing.

Jamie grinned and opened for him.

Ethan wasn't playing around; he devoured his mouth and pressed himself against Jamie, his hips rocking side to side, his cock rubbing against Jamie's. It didn't take long for Jamie's own cock to swell. Damn, somebody was horny this morning. He chuckled and reached into Ethan's sweats, gripping that sweet prick.

Ethan groaned and bucked into his hand, coming up for air. "Where is everyone?"

Jamie squeezed his cock, watching his lover writhe and moan. Oh, geez, the sight was unbelievably arousing.

"Bill went to Margie's, and Hayden and Ed are out fixing the gate between the north pasture and the road. And our new hand doesn't start until next week. Just me and you here."

Ethan tugged and maneuvered Jamie until they were in the stall that held all the hay. The backs of Jamie's legs hit a bale and he nearly went head over heels. Ethan steadied him, then pushed on his shoulders, making him sit. The next thing Jamie knew, there was a hot, hard dick nudging his lips. He smiled and pulled his hat off, handing it up to Ethan, who set it on his own head. Looked like his cowboy was in a hurry.

He flicked the jutting organ with his tongue, then licked up its length, one hand holding the base, the other on Ethan's hip. He glanced up at Ethan's gasp. His heart clenched at the picture his cowboy made. Ethan's face was a study in bliss. Underneath Jamie's hat, Ethan's eyes were closed, his mouth pursed. Jamie briefly wondered how long it would take for him to throw his head back and lose Jamie's hat in the hay. From the looks of it, not long at all. He focused back on the thick cock in front of him and took the crown into his mouth, sucking lightly.

"Oh, fuck!" Ethan arched, grabbed Jamie's head, and the hat dropped on the floor behind him.

Jamie grinned around the throbbing cock in his mouth and engulfed it all the way, burying his nose in the curls above.

God, he loved this! He couldn't decide if it was the feel of the thick, hard penis sliding through his lips and over his tongue, or if it was the complete and utter enjoyment that Ethan got out of having his dick swallowed. The man was sexy as hell. Whatever the reason, Jamie couldn't think of anything he'd rather be doing. Well, that wasn't exactly true; he'd rather be getting fucked, but this was a close second. And damned if he wasn't getting good at it. He already had Ethan panting and thrusting into his mouth.

His lover reached down and grabbed Jamie's hand from his hip and slid it back to his ass. Jamie squeezed and eagerly moved his hand, intent on teasing that tight little hole. His fingers ran into something. His eyes widened in surprise. Oh, fuck! Ethan had one of Jamie's plugs in. His cock jerked, and he groaned, the fat prick in his mouth jerking in response. Tugging on the end of Ethan's plug, he jostled it around a bit. Oh, Ethan was going to get it but good! Jamie was so freakin' turned on his balls ached. As soon as Ethan came…

It wouldn't be long now. His cowboy's fingers were wrapped tightly in his hair now, his hips thrusting hard into Jamie's face.

Jamie moved the plug again.

"Oh, shit, yeah! Oh, fuck! Jamie!"

He did it again.

Ethan's cock spasmed in his mouth.

Oh, yeah, Jamie had him now. He pulled the plug out.

Ethan threw his head back and let out a long, ragged groan. His belly pressed into Jamie's face, and he came down the back of his throat.

Jamie swallowed the tangy flavor down, pleased as punch. Mmm, yeah, just what he'd wanted. He continued to lick and suck until Ethan relaxed. Then Jamie stood up and pushed him against the wall, face front, dropping the plug by his hat. He had his jeans undone in record time and flattened himself against Ethan. He licked up his neck.

Ethan shivered. "Guess this means you liked my surprise?"

"Oh, yeah. You're about to find out how much." He moistened his fingers with his saliva, smoothed his fingers down his own cock, then spread the tight, lubed little hole with his fingers and pressed his dick in. Oh, damn, that felt good. He sighed, dropping his forehead to Ethan's shoulder.

Ethan chuckled and moved his hips back, undulating in a circular motion.

Jamie's breath hissed out. The sensations were too much. He didn't want to come yet, but if the man didn't stop his motions... He grabbed Ethan's hips, stilling them. "Ah, man! Give me a minute, Cowboy."

"Yeah, well, don't take too long." Ethan grabbed his hand and brought it around to his erection. "Damn, that feels incredible."

Jamie groaned. "Can't believe you're hard again."

"Never went soft."

Oh, God! Jamie bit Ethan's shoulder and thrust, squeezing the hot prick in his hand as he did. At this rate, Jamie knew he was never going to last. His cowboy felt too damned wonderful and had him too damned turned on. And if the man didn't quit clamping his ass muscles on his cock like that...

"Oh! Yeah, good! Real good!" He couldn't stop himself now even if he wanted to. He plunged hard into Ethan again and again, still pumping Ethan's cock.

His lover took it all, propelling against him and giving as good as he got. "Oh, yeah, fuck me, Blue Eyes!"

That raw, needy voice was all it took to push Jamie over the edge. He slammed his hips forward, stiffened, and came with a hoarse grunt. He stayed where he was for several moments afterward, then realized that he still had Ethan's dick in his hand and that he hadn't come. In fact, Ethan was squirming around, trying to force him to move his hand. Jamie chuckled and obliged.

He tugged on his cowboy's rod, twisting and compressing, whispered encouragement into his ear. It wasn't long before Ethan was gasping for breath again and his thick cock was pulsing in Jamie's fist, spurting. The muscles around Jamie's cock where he was still embedded tightened as Ethan came, making him groan as well.

"Damn, Cowboy! You trying to kill me?"

Ethan's head flopped back on his shoulder. "Me, kill *you*? I think you have that backward. I'm the one that just came twice. My freakin' balls are already protesting."

Jamie chuckled, pulled out, and slapped him on the ass. "Serves you right, coming out here with a plug in. Geez! You could have warned me at least." He yanked his pants back up, then picked up his hat and the plug. "Fuck, that was amazing!"

Ethan turned around and frowned. "Apparently, I didn't plan as well as I thought. I need a rag."

"No, you don't. You aren't even dressed yet. Just use your shirt or something."

Ethan rolled his eyes. "It's cold out there."

"Apparently, it's not too cold since you're wearing a tee-shirt. Here, let me help." He grabbed Ethan's sweats and pulled them up.

Ethan groaned. "Butthead!"

Jamie laughed and gave him a quick kiss. "What are you doing today?"

"Just finished the herd records. So, nothing. I came out here to see if you needed help."

"Good! You can come with me to town. Melissa just called and our order is ready at Hatchers." He patted Ethan's butt again. "Go get dressed. Here." He handed him the plug. "Take this. Don't forget to clean it."

"Damned bossy foreman!"

He watched Ethan walk out of the stables with a grin. "Damned sexy cowboy."

Jamie pulled up at Hatcher's Feed and got out. He'd been driving the Mustang while his truck was in the shop, but getting all their supplies into the trunk of the car was not going to happen, so they'd taken Ethan's truck.

Ethan came out of the passenger side, shut the door, and joined him on the sidewalk. "How 'bout after we pay Melissa, we go get a bite to eat, then come back and load the stuff up? I'm starving."

Jamie nodded. "Sounds like a plan. We'll have to drive around back to load up anyway. I doubt that—"

"Well, well, if it isn't my faggot son and his lover." Jacob stepped in front of the door, blocking their entrance. There were three Quad J workers behind him, one of whom was Jeff.

Jamie sneered. "Well, well, if it isn't my asshole father."

Ethan chuckled.

Jamie couldn't see him because there was no way he was going to take his eyes off the four men in front of him, but he was pretty sure Ethan had dipped his head in greeting before he said, "Jacob. Can't say it's nice to see you."

Jeff reached around Jacob to push Ethan's shoulder.

Jamie made a grab for the man, but Ethan pulled him back.

His father chuckled. "Ah, come on, Whitehall. If he wants to fight, I'm sure my boys will oblige him."

Jeff spat on the ground close to Ethan's boot. "What, Whitehall, you got nothin' to say about what the boss said? You a fag now, too?"

Jamie tensed, ready to pounce.

Ethan squeezed his shoulder a little, trying to calm him, he supposed. Cool as you please, his lover responded to Jeff. "Jamie doesn't need to prove anything. He's already stomped your ass once." Jamie looked up in time to see Ethan bare his teeth. "You touch me again, I'm going to break you in two. Now, we have business to attend to." He steered Jamie between the men and past the door.

His father simply walked off. His men, on the other hand, yelled all sorts of slurs at the two of them.

Jamie was seething. He turned on Ethan.

Ethan held up a hand. "Don't! Just don't."

Damn it! He knew Ethan was right, but he was pissed. Just itching for a fight, but clearly he wasn't going to get one if his cowboy had his way. He sighed, took several deep breaths, a few turns around the room, then walked back to the counter.

"They were asking for it."

"Yeah, they were. And I bet it pissed them off that they didn't get it. Besides, I doubt Melissa wants blood in front of her store."

Melissa chuckled as she came out from the storeroom. "Actually, Ethan, I'd just hose it off. You should have let Jamie have them." She looked past them toward the door. "Guess they got the picture and left, but you two be careful when you leave here. Watch yourselves."

She glanced back at them, then leaned on the counter, motioning them forward. She lowered her voice. "I don't like this one bit. Those men are no good. They aren't any better than Killian himself. I overheard Carl Blake and Jeff-what's-his-name talking to Tom the other day. Said he'd gotten himself a new rifle and that it was going to come in handy for huntin' fairies— no offense, Jamie; just repeating what he said. He also said how the 'damned fag's boyfriend' wasn't going to come to his aid next time."

Jamie saw his cowboy stiffen, but Ethan didn't say anything.

Melissa shook her head and looked at Ethan. "Killian himself has been stirring up trouble. He's trying to get the town council to change the zoning laws. The man has it in for you, Ethan, as much as he does for Jamie."

Ethan shrugged. "Well, I can't say he's my favorite person, either. What's up with the zoning laws? How's that going to affect me?"

"Not you directly, darlin', your Aunt Margaret. Heard Jeff telling Tom that Killian was trying to get the council to change the laws so your aunt couldn't run her business out of her home anymore."

Jamie gasped. *That son of a bitch!* It was one thing to try and run him out of town; it was another one entirely to try and hurt Margie and Ethan to get to him. "Damn it!" Maybe it would just be best if he left. He didn't want to hurt any of them.

"No!" Ethan grabbed his shoulder.

"Huh?"

"I know damned well what you're thinking; I can see it on your face. You are not leaving. We'll fight this. He's not going to win!"

"I don't know, Ethan. I mean, I'd hate to see Jamie leave, too, but it might be for the best, at least for a short period." Melissa gave him an apologetic smile. "Things will calm down after a while and people will stop talking."

Ethan raised a brow. "Talking?"

Melissa cleared her throat. Her gaze darted back and forth between them. "You know, saying you're gay, too, and how you and Jamie are together."

Ethan faced her squarely. "I really don't give a shit what everyone thinks. Fuck 'em! Maybe Jamie was right in the first place, maybe hiding isn't the answer. They don't have to like me, but I'll be damned if they run me and the people I care about out of town. We have as much right to be here as they do." He pulled his wallet out and tossed it to Jamie. "Pay Melissa. I'm going next door to get a bite to eat. I can't think on an empty stomach." He turned and stalked out, leaving Jamie and Melissa speechless.

Melissa watched him leave, then her shocked gaze snapped back to Jamie. "Oh, my God! It's true? Y'all are lovers?"

Jamie shrugged. How the hell was he supposed to answer that?

"Damn! Another good one lost. I swear! It *is* true! Y'all are either married or gay!"

Jamie laughed. "My sister says the same thing. I'll tell you just like I tell her: you'll find a good man one of these days."

She grinned and patted his hand. "Maybe. I'm beginning to give up hope. You wanna come back and pick up your order after y'all eat?"

"Yeah. I better pay you and find him." He handed her Ethan's credit card, signed for it, then put Ethan's wallet in his shirt pocket. "Thanks, Melissa. We'll meet you at the ramp 'round back in about half an hour?"

"That'd be fine, darlin'. Take your time."

He nodded and turned to leave.

"Jamie?"

He reversed.

"Be careful. I don't think you and Ethan should leave town either...not really. Y'all do have as much right to live here as anyone, but please be careful! I don't trust your daddy or those men he's got working for him. Not one bit."

He tipped his hat in thanks for her concern. "I don't either, Melissa. I don't either."

Chapter Seventeen

Jamie walked into the little restaurant across the street from the feed store. Ethan was sitting at the booth in the back corner, frowning at his salad and stabbing pieces of it with his fork.

Jamie tossed Ethan's wallet onto the table and slid into the booth across from him. "Geez, what did that salad do to piss you off?"

His cowboy looked up, brown eyes flashing from under his black hat. "The salad didn't piss me off, you did."

Huh. He hadn't expected that. He'd thought Ethan was pissed about Jacob trying to cause more problems.

"Goddammit, Jamie, if you want to leave so fuckin' bad, then go! You're the one who convinced me that we have to fight this. That we need to make people accept us, not stick our heads in the sand and pretend to be like everyone else so that their delicate sensibilities aren't disturbed."

Aha! Jamie grinned.

Ethan glared.

"I'm not going anywhere, Cowboy. Not unless you come with me." And he meant it. He wasn't leaving unless Ethan wanted him to. He was finally making a place for himself and he'd be damned if he'd toss it all aside the way he'd been tossed. He'd fight as long as Ethan would fight with him, as long as there was something worth fighting for.

Ethan sighed, his face relaxing. The anger disappeared.

Under the table, he ran his booted foot up the side of Ethan's leg. "I can't say I'm thrilled about causing you problems. I never meant to do that. And I damn sure don't like causing Margie grief, but I'm not going anywhere, Ethan. It was just a fleeting thought." He stared into those brown eyes, begging the man behind them to understand, willing him to see everything he felt inside. Everything he was afraid to say out loud for fear that he'd somehow jinx it.

"I won't leave unless you tell me to. If I run now, I'll always be running." He winked. "Unless I run off to California to be with all the other oddballs."

"Well, now, that's just stereotyping...prejudiced, even. I went to school with a guy from California. He was a good man."

Jamie raised a brow, staring into his cowboy's suddenly twinkling eyes. "Yeah? I guess you're right. It is stereotyping, isn't it? The old, 'in Texas, men are men, steers are steers, and queers should all move to San Francisco' mentality. I'm sorry."

Ethan smiled. "'S okay; that guy was weirder than hell."

Jamie laughed. "We all right now?"

"We're good. I just...I don't want you to be anywhere but here, Jamie. We'll handle it. I can guarantee you that Aunt Margaret won't want you gone, either."

Jamie blinked. His damn eyes were all watery. He grabbed Ethan's tea glass for something to do, and took a drink as the waitress came over and set another glass down in front of him.

"Here ya go. You want your salad now? Y'all's chicken fried steaks will be out in a minute."

Jamie looked up at the waitress and smiled, and gave Ethan his tea back. "Sure. Thank you."

"Welcome, hon." She winked and left.

"Hope the order's okay with you."

Jamie smiled. "What if I didn't want chicken fried steak?"

Ethan nudged him under the table with his foot, not quite a kick. "Don't be difficult."

"When am I ever difficult?"

"You're always difficult, or you'd have gotten it through your thick skull a long time ago that I want you here."

Jamie sat quietly for several minutes. Then, "I've got it, Cowboy. I'm staying and I won't ever doubt you or that I belong here again."

Ethan nodded. "Good."

"We're going to need to sit in on the town council meetings to find out what the hell is going on."

"Yeah. I already asked around; they have one this next Friday. Already called Hunter to tell him about what Melissa overheard, including the rifle comment."

Jamie nodded. That was his cowboy, already looking ahead.

Their lunch arrived and they finished their meal with talk about the ranch and the upcoming holidays. Jamie thought both of them were more at ease with each other now.

* * *

Ethan pulled the last bag of feed off the truck, threw it over his shoulder and headed toward the barn.

Jamie came out just as he was going in. "That it?"

He dropped the bag on top of the others. "Yeah. What now?" A hand cupped his ass.

"I can think of a few things."

Ethan chuckled as his cock perked up. "I bet you can." He leaned in for a quick kiss.

Jamie's hands, as usual, began roaming everywhere at once. His sweet little moans weren't long in following.

Ethan pulled back, his prick throbbing, and stilled those octopus hands. "Good thing Bill's out with the boys. Inside, Blue Eyes."

Jamie whimpered, but followed him outside and across the way into the house.

No sooner did the door shut behind them than Jamie was all over Ethan. Pushing him against the wall, kissing the living daylights out of him. He could barely catch his breath. Before he knew what hit him, Jamie had his jeans open and was kneeling in front of him, sliding that hot, incredible mouth over his cock. "Oh, damn! Jamie!"

Jamie suckled the head for a few luscious seconds, then that greedy mouth was sliding down his shaft, taking him deep. Those whimpers, sexy as hell, filled the air as his Blue Eyes swallowed his cock, sucking and licking like his life depended on it.

Pale blue eyes peered up at him, Jamie's gray hat tumbling to the floor as his swollen lips and one hand worked Ethan's prick. Fuck! The sensations were indescribable. His balls pulled up, his cock jerked. Damn, Jamie had become an expert at blowjobs, all right!

Jamie's other hand found his balls, fondling and teasing. His cheeks hollowed out every time he pulled up.

Ethan grabbed that dark head, sliding his fingers into the thick black hair, gripping fiercely. He tried not to thrust, to be still, but he was failing miserably. That hot mouth on his cock— it was like a fucking work of art. He groaned in time with Jamie's little mewling noises.

Jamie seemed to be enjoying it as much as he was. His other hand slid around to Ethan's ass, pulling him closer, encouraging him. All the while those blue eyes peered up at him.

"Oh, fuck, baby!" Ethan thrust, fucking that tender mouth. Jamie accepted it, tugging him closer, his other hand still working Ethan's balls. His eyes closed and he moaned, stiffening a little, but continued to suck Ethan's dick.

The knowledge that Jamie had just come in his jeans from sucking him off was exhilarating and pushed Ethan to orgasm. He hardened still more, held that beautiful face to his groin as he came down the back of Jamie's throat with a hoarse groan.

Jamie sucked and laved him even as Ethan's cock softened. He finally pulled away and kissed Ethan's hip, then nuzzled his face in the crease of Ethan's thigh. Ethan's fingers released Jamie's hair. He sighed, stroking the black strands out of Jamie's face.

Jamie gave him one last kiss and smiled up at him. "Damn, it's good to be home."

Ethan smiled back, feeling a stab of relief. *Home.* His and Jamie's. Jamie was here to stay.

"Where the fuck did my hat go?"

Ethan laughed. So much for romance.

* * *

When he woke up, it was almost dark and Ethan was not in bed. He lifted his head and looked around. Hmm, didn't look like he was anywhere in the room. Jamie sat up and stretched. Where the hell had his lover gone? How was he supposed to wake his cowboy up with a kiss if he wasn't there? Guess they weren't going to have another round of fucking.

Jamie got out of bed and pulled on a clean pair of jeans and the shirt he'd worn earlier. Ethan was probably downstairs. Maybe even fixing supper, if he was lucky. That would be nice. It would save him the hassle of cooking. Of course, if Ethan was taking care of their meal, it was TV-supper night, but that was okay, too.

He got into the kitchen only to find it empty. There was a note on the counter, however.

Went to town to pick up supper. Be back soon. Love, E.

He touched the last two words gently.

"Hmm, wonder where he went to get supper." He looked out the back window and saw Bill walking toward the bunkhouse. He opened the door. "Hey, Bill! You know where Ethan went?"

Bill grinned and ambled on over. "Yep." He smiled.

"Well?"

"If ya wait just a little longer, you'll find out." He grinned and headed back to the bunkhouse.

Okay, that was weird. Damn, he hated secrets. The sound of a vehicle pulling up cut off any further thoughts. From the corner of his eye, he saw something red. He turned his head and saw Ethan come to a stop in Jamie's truck.

Jamie felt a huge smile beaming from his face. Wow, Ethan had gone and gotten his truck from the body shop! He hadn't even known that it was ready. After a week of messing with the insurance company and another two weeks in the shop, he had begun to give up hope that he'd ever get it back. The Mustang was great, but he'd missed his truck. Ethan was going to get the biggest kiss of his life for this.

Jamie started down the steps to meet his cowboy. Ouch! He should have put his boots on. Oh, well, he'd tough it out. He wanted to see his truck—and the man who'd driven it back.

Ethan stepped out of the truck, grinning at Jamie. He opened his mouth to say something, but a shot rang out.

"Shit!" Jamie looked around real quick, but didn't see anybody. He turned back to Ethan to question him before he noticed the look of shock on his cowboy's face. Then a red stain appeared on the front of his light blue shirt.

"Fuck! Ethan!" Jamie took off running toward his lover. The only thought in his head was that he had to get to Ethan. Everything felt like it was in slow motion. He could see Ethan begin to fall. From a distance, Bill was yelling for him to get down.

He ran, his bare feet barely registering the sharp gravel on the driveway. He reached Ethan seconds after he hit the ground belly first, his cowboy hat rolling past Jamie's foot.

"Ethan!" He landed on his knees, sliding into Ethan, one leg hitting a muscular shoulder. Jamie rolled Ethan over and shielded him with his own body. Ethan's eyes were closed, his face pinched, rapid, shallow pants bursting from his lips. "Fuck! Bill! Call 9-1-1! Get us a helicopter here now! And call Sheriff Hunter!"

He barely heard Bill's quick acknowledgment before Ethan gasped something and pulled him down.

He leaned down to hear. "What?"

Pain-filled brown eyes looked up at him savagely. "I said, get your ass down! Before they decide to shoot you, too."

"I'm okay, Cowboy. You hang on." Blood was saturating Ethan's shirt. "Fuck! Ethan you're bleeding bad. We have to get this shirt off so we can see how bad it is."

"Went all the way through." Ethan's voice was very soft and shaky.

Jamie was grateful there wasn't a bullet ricocheting around in Ethan doing more damage.

Ethan closed his eyes again, his face suddenly paler.

"Ethan!" Jamie immediately felt for his pulse. It was weak, but there, thank God. He ripped Ethan's shirt open, looking for the wound, which was raw and ugly, high up on the right side, not too far below the collarbone, then gingerly felt beneath Ethan, to his back for where the bullet had entered. Both wounds were bleeding heavily. He rapidly tore strips off part of Ethan's shirt and tried to roll Ethan onto his side while keeping pressure on both wounds. "Ethan! Talk to me."

"'M here." Brown eyes blinked open, then shut again.

"I'm going to put you on your side to try and stop this bleeding. I want you to let me and Bill do all the work, okay? You stay still."

Between Bill and him, they managed to maintain pressure on the injured areas and get Ethan lying on his side. Still, there was blood everywhere.

Jamie quickly stripped off his own shirt and tore off two sections to create pads. Bill held one pad to each wound and pressed while Jamie used strips from Ethan's shirt to tie them in place. He nodded to Bill to indicate he was done. Then they gently laid Ethan down on Jamie's leg, centering the pad that was on Ethan's back over Jamie's thick thigh muscles, and supporting his head with an arm. Jamie kept pressure on Ethan's chest over the front wound.

"Don't feel so good. Hurts where you're pushin'."

"I know it does, but it'll help to stop bleeding. Keep talking to me, Cowboy."

Ethan barely nodded, and didn't say anything. His dark hair was in his eyes. It was getting long, needed to be cut. Jamie would have brushed it out of Ethan's face, but he was afraid to let up the pressure on the wounds. Ethan had lost a lot of blood.

Ed and Hayden were suddenly there, smelling of sweat, horse, and dirt. So was Fred; she took up residence at Ethan's feet, growling at anyone that got near him.

Jamie was hardly aware of them; everything was just background noise. His focus was where it needed to be: completely centered on Ethan. His cowboy was so pale, the blood soaking through his fingers despite the pads and the force he was exerting. He pushed harder.

He thought he could hear the helicopter now. He could even see it. Feel the dirt that it stirred up hitting his face. He leaned over, trying to keep the dirt and gravel from hitting Ethan.

"Jamie, call Fred off, so we can get Ethan to the helicopter. We have to get him out of here. Jamie!"

Jamie glanced up at Hayden, then his dog. "Fred, sit!"

She dropped immediately.

The sheriff's car came screaming up the drive.

Jamie lifted Ethan's head into his lap as Hayden helped push down on Ethan's wounds.

Gray Hunter jumped out of his vehicle while talking on his radio. The helicopter was louder now, making it impossible to hear the sheriff.

"You still with me, Cowboy?"

There was no answer.

"Ethan?" *Fuck!* "Tell them to hurry!"

Gray was saying something to him.

"Huh?"

"Jamie, the helicopter is landing. You go with Ethan to the hospital and I'll meet you there. My deputies are looking around the ranch. Bill will follow you to the hospital after he picks up Ethan's aunt. Do you need me to call anyone?"

"Call my brother and tell him to get a hold of my sister."

"Will do. Here they come." He signaled to the pilot to land in the wide area between the barn and the corral.

Two men slid out and rushed over with a gurney and took Ethan from his arms. Hayden pulled him out of the way as the two men maneuvered Ethan onto the stretcher, immediately started an IV, strapped his wounds more tightly, then raced to the helicopter. Jamie looked down at his blood-soaked hands, his stained chest, then sprinted after the men. One of them looked at Jamie as he skidded to a halt beside Ethan. "You going, too?"

Jamie nodded.

The man pointed to the front of the chopper. "Up there. We need room to work back here."

Jamie nodded again, ran around the other side of the aircraft and jumped in, shutting the door behind him. The pilot handed him a set of headphones, which he put on, then looked back over his shoulder to where the paramedics were working on Ethan. His cowboy was so pale. *God, please....*

Jamie didn't remember anything of the flight. It seemed to be bare moments before they were landing on the roof of the hospital Julia worked at.

Jamie got out and was right behind Ethan and the paramedics as they rushed inside, where he was hit with a barrage of questions and Ethan was wheeled rapidly away from him. He desperately wanted to follow his cowboy but answered everyone as quickly and as best he could. Eventually, he was led to a waiting area.

It seemed like hours before a hot cup of coffee was pressed into his hands. He looked up into Julia's worried blue eyes.

"Hey. We really gotta stop meeting in hospitals."

He dredged up a weak grin from somewhere. "Hey. You find out anything?"

"I just got here. He's still in surgery, but they've got him stabilized. That was all I found out before I came to find you. I'm headed down to the OR now. John, Margie, and Bill are on their way."

Jamie nodded. "'Kay. Go check on him, Jules."

She nodded, then bent and kissed his forehead. "I will, baby. I'll let you know as soon as I find out more. You gonna be all right?"

"I'll be fine. Just go check on Ethan for me, please."

He had to be okay; he just had to. Things had been going so well. They'd gotten things worked out between them. Started planning for the future, more or less. And now this. It was like some bad dream; it almost didn't seem real, except Ethan wasn't there beside him, making him feel better, telling him everything would work out.

Jamie took a deep breath, blinking back tears. He drank his coffee and tried to keep from playing the "what if" game. It wouldn't do him or Ethan any good. And Jules had said he was stabilized, hadn't she?

Jamie dropped his head in his hands, trying desperately not to cry. *Huh! Imagine that. I'm still barefoot.*

An hour later, John, Bill, and Margie came in, demanding answers that Jamie couldn't give them. They were all mad, scared and none too quiet about it all. Margie was crying, Bill was crying and John's eyes were suspiciously shiny and red-rimmed.

Jamie finally got everyone calmed down and kept them busy. He'd sent Bill and Margie after more coffee and John to find him some sort of footwear and a shirt.

He went to the hospital entrance and got on the phone with Hayden, trying to find out whether Hunter and his men had discovered anything. Unfortunately, he wasn't getting anywhere except more and more pissed, but that was okay, because being pissed and looking for answers kept worry in the back of his head.

He paced. It seemed to make him feel better. Sitting only made him feel more helpless.

Sometime during his quest for answers, someone pushed another cup of coffee into his hands, as well as a pair of the foam slippers patients were often given and a hospital gown, both of which he put on. Hayden called him back and said that the deputies had found a shell casing about thirty yards from where Ethan was shot, in the wooded area across from the drive. The sheriff was on his way to the hospital and his deputies were still searching the ranch. Hunter was on Hayden's other line and would call Jamie or let him know what was going on after he reached the hospital.

Ten minutes after he got off the phone, Julia and the others found him again. He ran to her.

"He's out of surgery and in the recovery room. Once the surgeon and anesthesiologist give the okay, they'll move him to the ICU. He was really lucky; the bullet went right through, so there wasn't as much damage as there could have been." She paused. "He had a lot of blood loss, as you know, so they had to transfuse some units of blood into him. Fortunately, the bullet went in at an angle between his spine and shoulder blade and came out just below his collar, just nicking his lung, which didn't collapse, thank God, so they didn't have to put a chest tube in. They're going to monitor that and make sure his lung stays inflated. There's some damage to the muscles in his chest and back, which will heal in time, but none of the bones or major blood vessels were injured."

"When can I see him?"

"Come on, let's get you cleaned up; then it's possible I can get you in there, before they move him." She smiled at him. "Being my brother does have some advantages. I've already been in to see him."

John gripped his shoulder but didn't say anything. Margie started to protest, but Bill put a hand on her arm, quieting her. Jamie mouthed "Thanks" to Bill, then followed Julia.

* * *

He became aware of a hand squeezing his, and several beeps and other assorted noises. Where the hell was he? Damn, his chest hurt, and he felt sore everywhere.

Oh, yeah. He'd gone to get Jamie's truck and...

"...love you, Cowboy."

Jamie? He tried to clear his thoughts.

Jamie had never told him he loved him. Sure he knew, just like Jamie knew he loved him, too, but they'd never said it aloud. He cracked his eyes open.

Jamie was sitting beside him, gripping his hand tightly. His dark head rested on the bed beside their entwined hands.

"Love you, too, Blue Eyes." Damn, it was hard to talk. His throat was scratchy, dry.

Jamie's head popped up, eyes wide, tired, hopeful. "Ethan?"

"Water?"

Jamie smiled, tears brimming. "Let me ask." He got up and left.

Ethan must have dozed because the next thing he knew there was a nurse checking him over. Then she was instructing Jamie to only give him ice chips first, then small sips of water with a straw if his stomach was able to handle the ice chips. Jamie obeyed her to the letter, much to Ethan's annoyance.

Jamie gave him some ice chips, then set the cup on the nightstand and grabbed his hand. He blinked those big blue eyes at him, then closed them and tilted his head toward the ceiling.

Ah, Blue Eyes, don't cry. It'll be all right. He squeezed Jamie's hand with a surprising lack of strength.

When Jamie looked at him again, tears were dripping down his cheeks. "Thought I'd lost you."

"No, baby, I'm here. Too stubborn to die."

"We can't stay here anymore, Ethan. This has gone beyond serious."

Ethan released Jamie's hand, reached up, brushed a tear away. He had to make his Jamie feel better, had to make him understand. "We're not back to this, are we?" He blinked. Jamie's face wavered before him. Damn! He was so tired. How long had he been here?

"Jamie, you were right. People will never accept us unless we make them. We are not going to let them force us out."

"But—"

He shook his head softly, his eyelids falling. Really tired. Someone—Jamie—gripped his hand. He opened his eyes again. "No buts, Blue Eyes. As you said, if we run now, we'll always be running."

Jamie shook his head as well. "You yourself told me that the Tin Star is just a place, not worth our lives."

"Different, Jamie. 'S different. You want to leave, won't stop you, but I can't go. Wouldn't be able to live with myself."

Jamie nodded and gave him a wobbly grin through his tears. "Stubborn bastard."

Ethan smiled, or tried to. It was a little difficult under the circumstances. "Already told you that. Too stubborn..." He swallowed, trying to moisten his throat. "...to die and too stubborn to run."

Jamie grabbed the cup of ice chips and tipped it to his mouth again.

"Thanks."

Jamie nodded and replaced the cup. "Welcome." He sat silently for several minutes, still holding his hand, dropping kisses on his knuckles every now and again. Then he whispered. "I'm scared, Ethan."

His eyelids were so heavy they hurt. "I am, too, baby," he whispered back, closing his eyes, then blinking them back open, struggling to stay awake a little longer.

Those pretty blue eyes looked back at him, bloodshot and wet. "I'm staying and fighting, too, or I'll die trying."

Ethan shut his eyes on a nod, hoping like hell that that wasn't going to be necessary.

Chapter Eighteen

"Sheriff Hunter, please." Jamie looked from his rearview mirror back to the road, scanning it on each side as he drove. Since Ethan had been shot two weeks ago, he'd become very diligent about staying alert, paying close attention to his surroundings. Unfortunately, it was dark out and he couldn't see much beyond his headlights.

The sheriff had discovered where the shooter had been hiding. Even better, he'd found the bullet, too. Now they were waiting for the forensics results on it to come back.

"Hunter."

Jamie blinked, so focused on his surveillance that he'd momentarily forgotten the phone. "Gray. Hi. It's Jamie. You got any more news for me?"

The sheriff heaved a heavy sigh over the phone. "No. I wish I did, Jamie. I'm still looking. I'm checking out several leads, including the ones you gave me. So far, everyone has an alibi and I'm waiting on the ballistics report. Those assholes at the lab keep giving me the same ole song and dance; they take their own sweet little time." He sighed again, more quietly this time. "How's Ethan?"

Damn it!

Jamie checked the rearview again, trying not to let the lack of information get to him. "He's fine. Sleeping a lot. Walking around his room when he wakes up. I've been so busy I haven't seem much of him."

"Yeah, I can imagine. Listen, don't get so caught up in stuff that you drop your guard. I understand you not wanting to leave—hell, I wouldn't either—but you pay attention to everything around you, you got that?"

Jamie automatically glanced from the rearview mirror, then to the front and side to side. "I am, Gray. Trust me, I'm taking it very seriously. How can I not?"

"I know you are. Just don't want you to forget, especially when you're involved in taking care of business. I've still got my deputies going out by y'all's place four and five times a night, just looking around, making sure everything is as it should be."

"Yeah, I know, I've seen them. I really appreciate that, Gray." Jamie was getting close to the ranch and didn't want to be on the phone when he pulled up. He'd gotten into the habit out of getting out of the truck and into the house immediately after he parked. He wasn't going to chance sitting or standing long enough in one spot in the open to become an easy mark. A moving target was much harder to hit. "Listen, Gray, I'm almost home. Just wanted to call and touch base with you."

"I'll let you know as soon as I find out anything, Jamie. You take care."

"Will do. Thanks."

"Welcome. Later."

Jamie hung up as he turned up the drive. As soon as the truck came to a stop, he turned off the headlights, parked it, and got out. He didn't run to the house, but he sure didn't let any grass grow under his feet, either. He opened the back door and locked it behind him.

Damn, he was tired! He felt like something the dog had dragged in. Jamie blinked down at his watch. 9:52. A hell of a lot earlier than he'd been getting in lately. He was worn to the bone and missed his cowboy. Maybe Ethan would be still be awake tonight.

Ethan had stayed in the hospital for a week and wasn't yet up to full strength at home. Luckily, Jules had taken time off to help with Ethan, whom she was having a hard time preventing from overexerting himself, and Bill had been here to cook. Jamie grinned. Julia's cooking had been Ethan's biggest concern when he'd learned that Julia was coming home with them.

Cooking or no, she'd been a huge help. The Tin Star couldn't manage itself, and Julia being here for Ethan took a lot of worry off Jamie's mind. Jamie had to handle not only his work but Ethan's, too, not to mention attending the town council meetings to try and find out what his dad was up to, and keeping an eye on the steakhouse deal Ethan had been working on. And, of course, there was the ongoing investigation into the shooting.

Jamie leaned against the kitchen door as he closed it, just resting for a second and thinking about the council meeting in town tonight. He grinned abruptly. Man, had his daddy been pissed when the vote to change the zoning laws had not passed.

Jamie was relieved. He'd worked his ass off talking to council members and fighting to keep that vote from going through. Frankly, he could only be grateful that there hadn't been much of a fight. Even without his input, the law probably wouldn't have passed anyway.

Apparently, his daddy and his cronies hadn't thought it out very clearly when they'd decided to put the decision to a vote. If the law had passed, it would have adversely affected at least three of the council members either directly or indirectly, so there had been a landslide defeat. Hoo boy, had it chapped his dad's ass to see Jamie up there, rubbing elbows with the council members and the town political heads. In fact, it had upset his father so much that Jamie had considered running for a council seat next year just to piss off his old man. But he hated all the double-dealing in politics, and he didn't think they'd take too kindly to having to deal with a gay man on a regular basis. Still, he'd been somewhat surprised at the relatively warm welcome he'd received. It seemed that quite a few residents disagreed with his daddy's treatment of him.

Jamie chuckled again at the memory of his father's red face when the vote had been read.

He pushed away from the door. Bed. He needed his bed right now. He was exhausted down to the bone. Maybe he could stay home with Ethan this week, now that the steakhouse deal was wrapped up, and the zoning laws weren't changing any time soon. Hell, he'd settle for just thirty minutes alone with Ethan. He hadn't seen his cowboy except when he crawled into bed at night and, by then, Ethan was already asleep.

"Fuck off!" Ethan's bellow came from the direction of the office.

"Fine! Be that way, but if you wear yourself out and take a turn for the worse, I'll shoot you myself. And I know exactly where to aim!" Jules stomped into the kitchen. Her face lit up on seeing Jamie.

"Hi, baby boy. How are you?" She hugged him.

Jamie smiled and returned her hug. "I'm good. Better than you, it appears. What was that about?"

Jules pulled back with a groan. "The stubborn bastard won't listen to me. He needs to watch how much he does, but noooo, he's bored."

Jamie chuckled. "When did all this start?"

"A few days ago. He's feeling much better and taking less of his pain meds, so he's awake more and getting around more. I swear if I hear one more complaint about what's on TV, I'm going to strangle him. Go see if you can get him in bed. He's been down here a few hours."

"All right, I'll try. Guess what?"

Her face lit up again. "They found out who shot Ethan?"

Jamie sighed and shook his head. He wished. He was tired of worrying about it, tired of looking over his shoulder every five minutes. Just plain tired. "No, not yet. But the town council voted down the zoning change."

"That's awesome! I know you were anxious about it. But I wish that they'd find the shooter already. How long are they going to mess around? What if it happens again? What if it's Daddy, Jamie?"

"Don't know, Jules. But I will say that so far they don't think it was him. He doesn't own a rifle of the caliber of bullets that hit my truck and Ethan. And John is his alibi for the night that Ethan was shot. He didn't do it, Julia. Maybe he had someone take care of it, but he didn't do it himself. They're checking out Carl, too, since he was bragging about a gun, but so far his alibi is solid, too."

Jamie closed his eyes. He wanted so badly to take Ethan and just get the hell outta Dodge, but Ethan had made it clear in no uncertain terms when he'd woken up in the ICU that they were staying. And Jamie agreed with him, he did, but he couldn't help but be terrified for Ethan, himself, and their loved ones.

Julia nudged his arm. Have you eaten?"

"I'm good. I ate at Margie's when I went to tell her the good news."

"All right, then. Go on. Get him in bed. I'm off duty and headed there myself; the stubborn jackass is all yours." She came up on her toes and kissed him on the cheek, then walked off. "Love you. Night."

He grinned at the fondness in her voice when she'd said "jackass." She might be frustrated with Ethan, but she understood why he was being so cantankerous. The man just wasn't used to not getting around easily or quickly, and not doing much of anything.

"Love you, too. Night."

When Jamie got to the office door, he leaned against the frame and watched Ethan for a few minutes, unnoticed. Damn, the man was still sexy as hell, even if he wasn't yet recovered. Jamie's cock noticed, reminding him that it had been two weeks since they'd had sex. Two long weeks since he'd been able to hold Ethan in his arms, get close to him.

Ethan's hair was all over the place. He had on a tee-shirt and a pair of sweatpants, and was clicking away on his computer keyboard with one hand, while the other was idly petting Fred, who had her chin resting on his thigh.

Fred looked over at him and barked. She ran toward him, her tail wagging.

"Hey, pretty girl! You watching over our cowboy?" He pet Fred, lavishing endearments and strokes on her before he looked back at Ethan.

Ethan smiled, then raised an eyebrow. "Are you going to bitch at me, too?"

Jamie held up his hands. "I'm too damned tired. Besides, as long as you aren't trying to break horses or brand cattle or anything like that yet, I don't guess you'll hurt yourself."

Ethan nodded, then his gazed raked over Jamie from head to toe.

Jamie's cock noticed that, too.

"You look fuckin' edible."

So do you! Jamie looked down at the gray suit he was wearing. He'd found it in Ethan's closet this morning. "Yours. Hope you don't mind."

"Never looked that good on me. Come here."

Jamie went to him. Ethan scooted back to make room, so he leaned on the desk, looking down at his lover.

Ethan's hand brushed over his thigh, then he looked up, meeting his gaze. "Damn, you look like hammered shit."

He chuckled and grabbed Ethan's hand, not really wanting to stop its upward progress, but needing to. There was no sense starting in something Ethan couldn't finish. "Well, which is it? Hammered shit or fuckin' edible?"

"Both. What have you been doing?" Ethan stood up slowly and cupped his face, tilting it up, so the light shined into his face, under the brim of his hat. "When is the last time you slept, and I don't mean that damned catnap you barely caught. I know damned well you didn't get into bed until four this morning, then you were gone again at six."

He smiled at his cowboy's concern. "I'm supposed to be worrying about you, not the other way around."

Ethan leaned forward, easing his head under the brim of Jamie's hat, and kissed him. "What have you been up to, Blue Eyes? You've been running yourself ragged, haven't you? I saw the purchase orders for the new horses and bull. We also got an invitation in the mail for the grand opening of the steakhouse. What else have you been doing, and why the hell haven't you been getting enough sleep?"

"Because this place won't run itself."

"Man, Jamie, I hate...this sucks."

Jamie nodded, feeling sympathy for his lover. "I bet. Knew it wouldn't take long for you to get bored."

"It's not that. I mean I *am* bored, but... You're being careful, right?"

Damn! There he went again with the concern. It felt so good to be fussed over, made him feel loved, but he didn't want his cowboy concentrating on him when he should be focusing his efforts on getting better. "Yeah, I'm being careful."

"I don't want to...won't...leave, but then I get to thinking. If anything more were to happen to you, would I have made the right choice? Am I letting my pride get in the way?" Those brown eyes were serious.

Jamie heard all the words that had not been said. Ethan was second-guessing their decision to stay. He reached up and cupped Ethan's cheek, running his thumb over it in a tender caress. "I'm fine, Cowboy. Watching my back. And I don't want to leave, either. We can't run from this."

Ethan nodded. "Yeah. Just...be careful, baby. I don't like you out there running around all over the place, even if it is for business."

"Promise." Before Ethan could demand a blood oath, he kissed him. "Besides, I can't be here with you and not want to touch you. So it works out for the best."

"Who says you can't touch me?"

He snorted. "Do you really think you're up to what I've got in mind?"

Ethan grinned and raised an eyebrow. "Oh, yeah." He waggled his eyebrows and glanced down meaningfully.

Jamie, peeked, too, and wished he hadn't. He groaned. Ethan was every bit as hard as he was. His sweats were tented, his cock just begging for Jamie's attention. Jamie looked back up and quickly tried to regroup. "The council voted against the zoning change."

"Really? That's great. Now, quit changing the subject." Ethan leaned into Jamie, kissing him again. This time his tongue flicked across Jamie's lips, seeking entrance.

Jamie groaned. He was a goner, and he knew it. He was just too drained and yet too turned on to fight it. So what if he had to use his own hand to get off? At least Ethan would be there with him.

He angled his head and opened his mouth, finding Ethan's tongue with his own. After a few minutes, he pulled back. "It's too soon. Don't want to hurt you."

Ethan nipped his bottom lip. "No, it's not. God, need you bad, Jamie. Just relax and go with it. You won't hurt me, I swear."

"You better be right." He took one more long, lazy kiss from his cowboy, then led him upstairs.

He pulled his clothes off, then undressed Ethan carefully, starting with his shirt. He pulled the baggy tee off gently, kissing every inch of skin he uncovered, especially around the stitches from the bullet wounds on that tanned, muscled chest and broad back.

God, he'd been so close to losing all this, losing Ethan. This wasn't the time to let himself dwell on it, though. If he started thinking about it too much, he'd break down again. And he was so darn weary that once he started, he would probably end up bawling like a damned baby. So he stopped himself with one last kiss to the ugly scar on his lover's chest and went down on his knees.

Ethan's hands combed through his hair. He thought he heard Ethan whisper, "Love you, Jamie," but he wasn't sure. He slid his hands inside the waistband of Ethan's sweats and slid them slowly down his legs.

That luscious, thick cock bounced free, hitting his cheek. He closed his eyes, nestling his face against it. Ethan smelled wonderful. Jamie inhaled deeply, taking in more of his scent. Damn, he'd missed this.

He turned his head, catching Ethan's shaft in his lips. He licked up, then down, taking his time, savoring, feeling the velvety soft skin of his man against his lips. "Taste so good."

"Mmm, feels so good."

"What a coincidence. It's supposed to."

Ethan's hand caressed his cheek. His voice was a soft caress, "Ahh, more action, less talk… Tease."

Jamie chuckled, loving their easy, playful banter. Taking one last taste, he stood up and moved to the bed. He held open the covers for Ethan. "C'm'ere, Cowboy."

Ethan walked toward him, wincing a little when Jamie helped him slide into the bed beneath the sheets.

Damn! "Careful, Cowboy. No pain, remember?" Jamie got in next to him and gently pulled Ethan close so that their cocks touched. *Oh, yeah!* His dick was practically ecstatic at the contact. Jamie nuzzled Ethan's neck.

"Umm. Nothing wrong with pain, as long as I have you to kiss it better." Ethan's voice sounded a little strained.

Jamie leaned back, checking his face, trying to decide if Ethan felt good or if being on his side was pulling on his wounds. His lover's face was a little pale.

"Where's it hurt? Can't kiss it better if I don't know where you ache."

Ethan smiled, his face slightly pinched. "Sorry. I need to lay on my back, I think."

"Then do it." He pushed Ethan down gently, then leaned over, trailing kisses down that beautifully masculine face. "Tell me what you need, Cowboy."

"Ride me?"

Jamie groaned, his cock jerking. "I can definitely do that. Love riding my cowboy." He stole another kiss before straddling Ethan's hips and reaching for the lube in the nightstand drawer.

He slicked up both of them, then slowly sank down onto Ethan's thick cock. "Fuck, yes! Love this!"

Ethan gasped, nodding slightly. His eyes were closed. "Oh, yeah!"

"You good? No pain?"

That brown gaze bored into his, full of passion. "No, no pain. Not from the wounds, anyway. But it sure hurts like hell to not move."

"Then by all means let me fix that for you." Jamie impaled himself on Ethan's cock over and over again. It felt wonderful and he was soon on the edge. After having had nothing but his hand for a couple of weeks, it wouldn't take much to send him over. The only reason he hadn't lost control already was the niggling concern at the back of his mind about Ethan's health. Although, judging from the sounds below him, Ethan was doing just fine.

Ethan's stomach muscles tightened, then his features grew taut.

Shit! He hadn't even thought about how tensing up at the pleasure might hurt Ethan. He'd just figured if they took things slow, everything would be fine. And it sure felt more than okay, but he knew damn well how hard it was not to stiffen up as you came.

"Relax."

"I'm trying. Just feels so good."

Jamie rubbed his hands lightly over Ethan's chest and belly, wishing like hell he could bend down and kiss him. But no way was he going to risk putting any pressure on Ethan's chest. So, he continued to caress his lover's skin as he leisurely rode the cock inside him. After a few minutes, Ethan felt almost boneless beneath him. Now if he could just figure out how to keep his cowboy relaxed as he peaked. He was ready to come and knew that Ethan had to be, too. He caught Ethan's gaze. "Close, Cowboy."

"Yeah, me, too."

"You have to stay loose." Even as he said it, he felt Ethan tense. Ethan cried out, and Jamie felt heat fill him.

"Oh, fuck!" Too late now. Jamie followed Ethan into his own climax. His come spilled onto Ethan's stomach as he grabbed hold of his wayward cock, trying to avoid splashing Ethan's healing scar.

He kept still for several moments, trying to gauge how Ethan felt. Finally, those brown eyes blinked open and smiled up at him. "I needed that."

Jamie let loose a breath he hadn't realized he was holding, then slid off Ethan and the bed. "Me, too." He bent over and kissed Ethan's forehead before he went to the bathroom to get a towel. "You need any pain pills or anything?"

Ethan shook his head, his eyes closing again.

By the time Jamie came back to clean him up, his cowboy was sound asleep. He wiped them both down, then returned the towel back to the bathroom. Finally, he slipped into bed and stayed there.

He lay thinking for the longest time, trying to figure out how to hold his lover without hurting him when Ethan, still sound asleep, slid his hand into Jamie's.

Chapter Nineteen

Jamie looked over his shoulder for the fiftieth time in the last ten minutes. This was the first time Ethan had been out of the house in over three weeks. He wasn't paranoid, exactly, but he would be damned if he'd let something happen to his cowboy while they were out and about. Ethan seemed to be enjoying himself and Jamie wasn't about to allow anything interfere with his pleasure. So, if he was a little extra wary and tense, it was still well worth it.

"This is it! What do you think?"

Jamie glanced at Ethan, and saw him checking out the others wandering around the Christmas tree lot. Good, his cowboy was paying attention, too. It was nice to know that he could have a good time without letting his guard down. Jamie wished he could do the same.

Ethan looked back at him. "Well? What do you think?"

Jamie stared at the tree his lover was pointing at. Hmm. Maybe Ethan had been paying too much attention to the crowd and not enough to the trees. "That is the saddest excuse for a Christmas tree I've ever seen. I can't believe they are even trying to sell this thing!"

Ethan snorted and glanced around again. "It only needs a little love."

Yup, he was definitely not paying as much attention to picking out a tree as he was to what was going on around him. That was good, but one of them was going to have to look for a decent tree.

"What it needs is a shredder!" He leaned in and whispered to Ethan. "I'm watching our backs; you look for our tree."

Ethan elbowed him. "I can do both. Have been doing both, in fact. I want this one."

Jamie looked back at the pathetic thing. It was big and ugly, and bare in spots, but if it made Ethan happy... He groaned. "Fine. We'll get this tree."

An hour later, Jamie was lying in the floor, sorting Christmas decorations, and Fred wasn't helping any. She thought he was trying to play and that the ornaments were her toys, so she kept stealing them. "Cut it out, mutt!"

Ethan chuckled and hung another ball on the tree. "Put her to work. Have her bring them to me."

"You think that'll work? I don't think we can get her to do that without her taking off with them."

Ethan turned to look at him, "Sure we can. Give it to her and tell her to 'Take it to Ethan.'"

Jamie shrugged. It might be worth a shot. He was sick of chasing her down to get the ornaments away from her. And he hadn't even started going through the box marked "breakable" yet. *That* was a nightmare just waiting to happen. Jamie held out a plastic angel to Fred. "Take this to Ethan." She grabbed it with her mouth.

Ethan bent down immediately and stuck his hand out. "Fetch."

Fred looked at him, then at Jamie before she trotted over and dropped the angel into Ethan's hand.

Well, son of a gun! He'd known she was smart, but this! He dug out another ornament and held it. "Fred. Take this to Ethan."

She bounded over, snatched the plastic Santa out of his hand.

Ethan grinned at him and winked, then repeated, "Fetch."

She took the Santa to Ethan and ran back to Jamie, waiting for yet another decoration. Within a few minutes, they had her picking up the tree accessories on her own as Jamie laid them out and taking them to Ethan without being told to. Ethan didn't even have to say "fetch" to get her to bring it to him. Pretty freakin' cool!

Jamie lined up a dozen or so more for her, then stood up and stretched. He could really use some hot chocolate. He walked over to Ethan, patting him on the butt. *Damn, what a fine ass.* He knew what *he* wanted for Christmas. "Going to make hot chocolate, Cowboy, you want any?"

"Nah. Go ahead."

When he came back with his hot chocolate in hand, Fred was barking at Ethan. She'd deposited the last two decorations that he'd laid out for her at Ethan's feet.

Ethan groaned. "Okay, okay! Hold on a minute, you're getting ahead of me. Slow down."

Fred barked again.

Jamie shook his head. Too cute! He sat back down and lined up more decorations, gaining Fred's undivided attention and giving Ethan time to remove the two at his feet to hang on the tree. They were having a great time when Bill came in with Margie.

Jamie waved to them from the floor. "Hey, y'all! Is it cold out there?"

Margie nodded. "Freezing." She walked over and leaned down to give him a kiss on the forehead, then walked up behind Ethan and put her hands up the back of his sweater.

Ethan jumped. "Mean old broad."

She chuckled, then wound her way to the couch. She looked up at the tree and raised her eyebrows.

Jamie knew she was thinking. He gazed at the tree, too, as he took a sip of chocolate. Yeah, it was still ugly.

Bill sat down next to Margie. "Damn! It's even uglier than last year's! Boy, decoratin' that tree is like puttin' glitter on cow shit."

Jamie laughed with the hot chocolate in his mouth and snorted it through his nose. "Shit! That burns."

Everyone chuckled as he blotted the warm liquid off himself with a sleeve, then got up to find a towel.

He went upstairs and changed shirts, then returned in time to hear his sister's voice.

"It's not the size of the tree that counts, but what you do with it."

What the hell did that mean? It was a damned big tree. And more grotesque than hell. "Jules, it's huge."

She nodded. "I know, that's what I mean."

Okaaay. Jamie sat back down on the floor, taking up his post at the box of ornaments again. He glanced over at Bill and Margie. They both shrugged, so he went back to sorting the different items.

Jules flopped down next to him, then peered up at Ethan and the tree. "It's ugly, Ethan! It's big and ugly, and decorating it isn't making it any better."

Jamie chuckled. "We tried to tell him."

Ethan took another decoration from Fred. "Y'all don't know what you're talking about."

Jamie wasn't going to argue. His cowboy liked the damned tree, and it brought Ethan pleasure. But next year, he was picking out the tree.

They finished embellishing the thing and had a great time, talking and teasing. Just being family. It felt perfect, normal, just like it had before the shooting. Better, really, because Julia and John had decided to join their Sunday suppers, too.

Jamie wasn't sure, but he thought maybe Ethan's getting shot had taught everyone a tough lesson about taking people and things for granted. It sure had for him. At any rate, John and Julia had both invited themselves to their weekly gatherings and for Christmas the following week.

Ed, Hayden, and Cam, the new hand, were coming later tonight, closer to suppertime. And somehow, Jamie had lucked out. Since this was the first Sunday get-together since Ethan had been shot, Margie and Bill had volunteered to do the cooking, saying that Jamie needed to spend time with Ethan. So, an hour after Julia's arrival, he was doing just that.

He sat on the couch with Ethan leaning against him, the two of them watching the tree lights and Fred. Now that she wasn't helping, Fred was stealing stuff off the tree, or trying to. Every time, she got too close, Ethan would growl out in warning, "Fred! Get!" It was pretty funny but seriously cutting into his necking time.

Hell, everyone was in the kitchen cooking—he *should* be making out with his cowboy.

"Mmm, this is nice. Love getting to sit with you like this."

Ethan leaned his head back against his shoulder, smiling up at him. "Me, too."

He bent a little to kiss Ethan's neck, nibbling just a bit, bringing up goose bumps and a shiver from his lover. He chuckled and fished his hands under Ethan's sweater.

"Feels good, Blue Eyes." Ethan kissed his jaw, then snuggled deeper against him. He began to rub up and down Jamie's thighs.

Ah, yeah!

"Damn it, Fred! Get!"

Jamie groaned. Apparently Ethan needed a better distraction than a few itty bitty kisses on his neck. He pinched and pulled on a nipple through Ethan's sweater, drawing it up tight.

Ethan's hands stilled on his legs, and his breath rushed out against Jamie's ear. "Ah, fuck, Jamie!"

"Yup, that sounds like a good idea. Fucking Jamie, that is. Think anyone would notice if we went upstairs?" He nipped

Ethan's throat and twisted his other nipple, then slid his other hand inside the waistband of Ethan's jeans—

"Oh, good God, Ethan! Do you *have* to pick the ugliest damned tree in the lot every year? When are you going to get over your Charlie Brown Christmas Tree syndrome?"

Ethan stilled, then flipped John off.

Jamie removed his hands and sighed. Maybe it wasn't so nice having family over.

* * *

Ethan turned off the lights, then slipped into his office.

Christmas was wonderful. Well, Christmas Eve had been. He felt good, better than he had in a while. He wasn't as stiff as he had been, and the pain was pretty much nonexistent. He was already doing his own work again, and pretty soon he'd be able to help outside more. Well, as much as either he or Jamie could with the fucking shooter still out there.

Neither of them had been taking risks more than necessary. Jamie was pretty much doing all his work in the barn or stables. It was really chapping his ass to be forced to do so, but the important thing was he was doing it. Thank God! Jamie had sent the hands out to work in the open and did all the things he could indoors.

Ethan was still worried about someone hurting Jamie, but he was dealing with it. He knew deep down that taking a stand had been the right decision, but he'd feel a whole lot better about it once the sheriff found out who had been responsible not only for shooting him, but for the vandalism, as well.

Thankfully, everything had been pretty quiet since the attack. He thought some folks might have felt the sniper was a bit of a coward since Ethan had been shot from the back. Even nowadays, that wasn't something that was looked upon kindly. Whatever the reason, people in town were either polite and respectful or they ignored him and Jamie entirely, which was fine with him. He could deal with being ignored. He'd much rather be snubbed than have slurs shouted at him or any other aggressive actions take place.

Even Jacob Killian had been unusually quiet of late. There was no way to tell whether it was from the suspicions facing the man over the ambush or John's doing, but Ethan wasn't going to discount small favors. He wasn't quite convinced that Jacob was responsible for anything other than running his mouth off, which he had done—the feed store and town council confrontations cases in point—but Ethan wasn't naïve enough to think it was over, either. Whoever—and he wasn't ruling Jacob out entirely—was responsible for the vandalism and his attempted murder, maybe even slipping Jamie that date-rape drug, was more than likely biding their time. No doubt Jacob was doing the same. Ethan was just glad that the man hadn't upset Jamie any more of late.

Jamie. He didn't know what he'd do without his Blue Eyes. Didn't even want to think about it. Jamie was not only his love and his friend, but he'd also become his partner and right hand. He had really stepped up to the plate when Ethan had gotten hurt. The man hadn't buckled under the extra hard work—and the responsibility or commitment. He'd done what was necessary and never once complained. Heck, Ethan was positive that Jamie could single-handedly run the Tin Star if he had to. And honestly, he'd probably do a better job of it than Ethan.

He grinned and grabbed the papers out of his filing cabinet. There was no time like the present to show Jamie how much he meant to him. Everyone had gone home at last, and they both could finally be alone. They had agreed to save their presents for each other for the morning, but he really had to give Jamie the big one tonight.

When he walked into their room, Jamie was just leaving the bathroom, buck naked, rubbing his hair dry with a towel. Ethan moaned and almost dropped the folder tucked under his arm.

Damn, what a beautiful sight!

And Jamie knew his reaction, too. The damn tease leered at Ethan. He tossed the towel toward the hamper, then strolled over to the bed. Lying down on his back, he began stroking his already semi-erect cock. "You see something you like, Cowboy?"

Ethan swallowed. Hell, yeah, he did. But no way was he going to let Jamie distract him this time. He was a man on a mission. He sat down on the bed beside Jamie and threw the covers over him.

"Hey!" The tone was both surprised and indignant.

"Hey, yourself." He tossed the folder onto Jamie's chest. "Merry Christmas."

Jamie raised a brow and propped himself upright, then picked up the file and started to go through it.

Ethan knew the exact moment he realized what it held. Jamie gasped and looked up at Ethan, his mouth hanging open.

Ethan grinned. "Well?"

Jamie remained wide-eyed. After a few seconds, he looked back at the papers, then asked quietly, "Are you sure? This is a lot, Ethan."

He reached out and grabbed Jamie's chin, raising his face to see him. "Absolutely positive."

"You really put the Tin Star in my name, too? This is half the ranch."

Ethan dipped his head and brushed a tender kiss across Jamie's lips. "It's more than that, Blue Eyes. This not only makes you co-owner and full partner, but if anything should happen to me—"

Jamie knocked him over and rolled on top of him, papers flying everywhere and crushed between the two of them. His mouth ground down on Ethan's, his tongue pushing for entrance.

"Not gonna let anything happen to you, Ethan. Not anymore, and not if I can help it."

Ethan pushed him back up. "I love you, Jamie. We might not be able to get married, but we can make it near enough."

Jamie blinked again, and suddenly tears were running down his face. "I love you, too." He kissed Ethan and slid off him, leaned to the side. Before Ethan could protest, Jamie had reached into the nightstand drawer and pulled out a small, red velvet jeweler's box. He wiped the back of his hand across his eyes, then smiled at Ethan.

"Now I don't feel so goofy giving you this."

Ethan took the box from Jamie.

"Well, open it already."

Ethan grinned. "Impatient!"

Jamie snorted, snatched the box, opened it, flipped it around and put it back in Ethan's hand. Inside were two gold rings, wide, masculine and attractive. Wedding bands.

His heart swelled with a wealth of feelings. He was not going to cry. Jamie was the emotional one, not him. But when he looked up at Jamie, he lost control. Something wet streaked down his cheek. *Damn!* He dropped the box into his lap and grabbed Jamie, hugging him tight, then kissed his throat.

Jamie kissed his neck, too. "Merry Christmas, Ethan."

"Merry Christmas, Blue Eyes."

Jamie pulled away first. He picked up the box again and removed one of the rings, holding it up in front of Ethan. "Look at the inscription inside."

Ethan looked closely and read, *I love you, Cowboy. Forever your Blue Eyes.* More wetness hit his cheeks, dripping one by one off his face and onto the sheets.

Jamie slid the band onto Ethan's left ring finger, then kissed his hand. Ethan smiled and wiped his eyes. He got the other ring and inspected it. No inscription. Yet. He'd take care of that later. He seized Jamie's left hand and put the gold circle where it belonged.

Jamie waited about ten seconds before he tackled him again. This time, though, the urgency was gone. There wasn't the rushed heat of coming together that they usually experienced. It was slow and easy, soft and sweet.

Making love.

Chapter Twenty

Ring.

Ethan managed to get one eye open before Jamie's arm thrust past him to attack the poor, innocent alarm clock.

Life was good. There was nothing quite like routine to make a man feel content way down in his bones. Especially when the normal had been disrupted so often of late. He was tired of waking up and finding Jamie already out of bed, too. But not today. Today, his Blue Eyes was still in bed, all snuggly. He reached for Jamie's hand and kissed the gold band before wrapping his lover's arm around his waist and grabbing the phone. "Hello?"

"Ethan." John's voice broke. Then he cleared his throat and tried again. "Ethan, Daddy had a heart attack."

Ethan sat up, the warm, snuggly feeling leaving him. Jamie blinked up at him, startled awake by Ethan's abrupt movement, but still groggy. He stroked Jamie's face absently.

"What? When? Is...is he alive?"

Jamie sat up, suddenly wide-awake. "Who? What happened? Is John all right?"

He nodded, whispered, "John's fine," and pulled Jamie in close.

"He's still alive, but on his way to have a triple bypass done. I'm at the hospital with Julia. I don't expect y'all to come, but I wanted to let you know."

"We'll be there in about two hours. Is there anything you need us to bring you?"

"Not right now. Call me on my cell when you're on the road."

"All right, John. Bye."

No sooner had he hung up than Jamie went into "Julia mode."

"What happened? Who's dead? Where is John? Where are we going? What does he want us to bring?"

Ethan took a deep breath. He knew what Jamie had said about how he felt about his dad, but Ethan still couldn't be sure how he was going to react to this news. After all, Jacob was still his father.

"Your daddy had a heart attack. He's going to have bypass surgery."

Jamie stared at him without saying a word, then lay back down.

Okay. He hadn't expected tears exactly, but…Oh, hell, he didn't know what he had expected. Fuck it. He wasn't even entirely certain what he himself felt.

"Jamie?"

"What?" He pulled the covers up and appeared to make himself more comfortable.

"You, uh, you going to get dressed so we can go to the hospital?"

"Hadn't planned on it, no." He turned onto his side, away from Ethan.

Ethan was at a loss from Jamie's reaction and didn't know what his next steps should be. Was Jamie upset? In denial? Shocked?

So he lay down beside Jamie and spooned himself around his lover and kissed his stubbly cheek. He was pretty sure that Jamie would talk to him eventually, give him some clue as to how to act. His Jamie wasn't one to keep things to himself, which was good. Ethan was never going to have to wait long to find out whenever he screwed up. Jamie would let him know.

"He never loved me, Ethan. Didn't even like me. Why? I was his kid, not Mama's, but he only tolerated me for her. If she hadn't wanted me, hadn't loved me, he'd have gotten rid of me." He stopped talking for a moment. "So why do I feel bad? Why do I even care what happens to him? I shouldn't. Hell, the man is probably responsible for nearly killing you. But I somehow can't bring myself to wish he were dead. Why is that, Ethan?"

He kissed Jamie's cheek again and squeezed him tightly. "Because he's your daddy."

"But it doesn't matter to him that I'm his son. To him, I'm just his one big mistake." Jamie rolled over, nestling closer. There were no tears in his eyes, no sorrow, no hatred, just wonder.

"You are no one's mistake. You are the best thing that ever happened to that old bastard and, quite frankly, I'm glad he's too stupid to notice. Otherwise, we probably never would have found what we have together."

Jamie kissed his nose. "I guess I should go to the hospital. If for no other reason than to show support and be there for John and Julia, who do love me."

Ethan nodded. "Yeah, they do. Almost as much as I love you."

* * *

When they walked into the waiting area they were surprised to see Grayson Hunter sitting and talking quietly to John and Julia. He smiled when he saw them.

Jamie wrinkled his brow and glanced at Ethan.

Ethan shrugged. "Let's go find out."

The sheriff stood up, held out a hand to Jamie, then Ethan. "Sorry about your dad, Jamie, but I do have good news for you both."

"Yeah?" Jamie asked.

"Oh, yeah! Come have a seat. I just got here, so you haven't missed anything. John and Julia will need to hear this, too, as it sort of involves your daddy."

Jamie started to question him, but Gray was already walking over to a bank of chairs, Ethan hot on his heels.

"I got a visit this morning from Carl Blake. He came to tell me that Tom Cooke shot Ethan."

Ethan stilled. Looked at Jamie, then the sheriff.

John stared and Julia gasped.

"What?" Jamie was almost afraid to believe that this crazy mess might finally be over.

Hunter nodded. "I arrested Tom Cooke for attempted murder before I headed over here. It seems that Carl had loaned Tom his new rifle. When he heard about Ethan getting shot, he put two and two together and got scared. He didn't want to be charged with the shooting or as a possible accessory to attempted murder, given how most people in town know he's threatened one or the both of you at least a couple of times since y'all chucked him off the Tin Star." His smile looked menacing. "The conversation Melissa Hatcher overheard a few months ago between him and Tom Cooke wouldn't help his case much, either. So he came and told me all about it. I'm not sure if y'all know this, but all new guns sold in the U.S. are now shot beforehand. The ballistics are kept on record in case a crime is committed with the gun. I got the ballistics report back this morning. They compared what we found to what was on file and confirmed that the shot was fired from Carl's gun."

"So our daddy had nothing to do with it?" John leaned forward, almost smiling.

The sheriff shook his head. "Not exactly."

"Not exactly?" Jules looked as puzzled Jamie was sure they all felt.

Hunter held up a hand. "Let me finish. Carl claims that your daddy had them cut the fence and write the graffiti on the tractor. He says your daddy also bought the drugs Jeff slipped into Jamie's drink—"

"Son of a bitch!" Ethan gritted his teeth and started to stand. Jamie wasn't sure what his cowboy might do, but he yanked him back down beside him. He nodded at Hunter to finish.

"Apparently, they were trying to scare Jamie, not do him any real harm—or so Carl says. But he swears that neither he nor Jacob, nor Jeff, for that matter, had anything to do with damaging Jamie's truck or almost killing Ethan. Said he spoke to your daddy this morning and told him that he was going to tell me. He thinks that's probably what gave Jacob a heart attack."

John took in deep breath of air and let it out slowly. "Carl did leave the office just before Daddy collapsed. Told me he'd come in to talk to Daddy about business."

Hunter nodded. "Good. Then this confirms Carl's story."

Jamie sat back. Holy shit! "Does this mean it's over? Are you sure Tom was the only one involved in the shooting?"

"Pretty sure. Carl was damned convincing, but I'm going to work on Tom. You can count on it." He looked at each of them. "Carl swears that his, Jacob, and Jeff's intent was never to hurt Jamie but to run him off. I'm pretty good at reading people, and I think he's telling the truth. Got the same vibe from Jeff. Both of them are in custody, charged with destruction of private property and assault...for now. Your daddy will be charged with the same. As for Tom Cooke, he still had Carl's rifle in his possession, and Jeff and Carl are willing to testify to the fact that he's had it since the night Jamie's truck was vandalized."

The sheriff continued, but Jamie didn't hear him. He was...happy? Relieved?

Part of him was glad that his daddy hadn't wanted him dead, after all. He looked at Ethan. "Well, *does* this mean it's all over?"

Ethan nodded. "It means *this* is over."

He knew what Ethan meant. There was still going to be hatred and prejudice, and maybe even more trouble, but this particular chapter in their lives was over. And damned if it didn't feel good!

Epilogue

The steakhouse opening was a huge success, if a little boring. The investors had eaten a nice supper at the restaurant, then moved their party over to one of the ballrooms at the Sheraton so there could be dancing. Which was where they were now.

Ethan was feeling full and mellow, watching people mingle and dance and just plain have a good time. Everyone was turned out in their best clothes and looking sharp. He thought he was dressed pretty exquisitely, too. He'd pulled out a charcoal-gray, pin-striped suit for the event. His black boots and black felt hat looked really good with the gray. And the tie... He grinned. Okay, he was being a bit ridiculous, but silly or not, it hadn't gone unnoticed by his Blue Eyes that he'd worn a red tie, the man's favorite color.

"What are you smiling at, gorgeous?" Julia slid an arm around his waist and dropped her head on his chest.

He looked down at the low-cut, long, blue dress she was wearing. It matched those Killian eyes to perfection. "Just happy, I guess. You look damned beautiful yourself, darlin'. I can already see that we are going to have to escort you home to make sure you get there unmolested."

She snorted. "You better not! I don't want to get home unmolested." She waggled her eyebrows and pointed. "You see that man over there? The one in the navy blue suit? Is he hot or what?"

His look grazed past navy blue and landed on gray. Gray suit with matching gray cowboy hat. *Fuck yeah, he's hot!*

Jules chuckled. "I know where you're looking, and that isn't the one I was talking about."

He shrugged. "Yeah, but that one is the best-looking man here."

She chuckled. "Yes, but I have it on good authority that he's gay."

He laughed. "Get out of here, pest! Go mingle and find yourself a man."

"Oh, if you insist." She tiptoed up and kissed him, then walked back into the crowd, stopping to talk to people as she went.

John came up, looking stylish in his brown suit and tan hat, and handed him a longneck. "The woman is a menace! God help the man she finally snags."

"Thanks." He took a swig of the cold beer. "Dollars to donuts, she turns him gay within a year."

"Yeah, that'd do it for me!" John chuckled and left.

Something tickled the nape of his neck. Warm lips slid across his skin, leaving the slightest hint of moisture. His hip was nudged, then Jamie grabbed the beer out of his hand and took a swig. "You ready to leave?"

Ethan raised a brow, snatched his beer back and tossed back a swallow.

"Come on. I have a surprise for you." Jamie winked and walked off.

Ethan was no fool. He set his beer down on the tray of a passing server and followed that fine ass right out the door.

Jamie gripped his hand and pulled him into an elevator to the right of the ballroom. He pushed the button for the tenth floor, caught Ethan's gaze, and winked at him. They had the elevator to themselves.

Ethan grinned. "So this is why you disappeared this morning for six freakin' hours? To get us a room for tonight?"

"Part of the reason, yeah. I even packed us a bag for tomorrow. But that wasn't the only reason. I told you, I have a surprise for you." Jamie leaned in.

Ethan bent, tilting his head so they could kiss without knocking their hats off. He stepped back when Mr. Octopus Hands started tugging at his red tie. *Damn!* His cock was rock solid. And when had Jamie undone his jacket?

"I love red. Especially on you."

He grabbed Jamie's hands, "I know you do. Cut it out; you're making me look like a circus freak."

Jamie let go of his tie and went after the buttons on his shirt, peering down at Ethan's groin as he did so. "Well, hot damn! If this is what constitutes a circus freak, you better start looking for a new foreman, 'cause I'm joining the circus."

Ethan stilled those busy fingers again. "Quit undressing me in the elevator. If anyone is waiting when those doors open, they are going to get quite a shock."

"Prude."

"Tease."

The elevator dinged and the doors glided open. Fortunately, there was no one in sight. Jamie seized his hand and towed him into the hallway. "Nope. I put out, remember?"

Ethan groaned. Oh, yeah, he remembered, all right. So well, in fact, that he had to pull his jacket closed in front, to hide the proof as Jamie hauled him along the corridor.

Jamie stopped in front of room 1010 and pulled a keycard out of his pocket. "This is us."

He followed his Blue Eyes inside, then locked the door. "So where is this surprise?"

Jamie was in his arms in an instant. "Hidden somewhere on my body."

Ethan chuckled, immediately reaching down and clasping Jamie's cock through his slacks. Oh, yeah, fucking ready for him. "Found it. I'm not complaining or anything, but how is it a surprise when it's already mine?" He squeezed and was rewarded with one of those sweet whimpers.

"Oh, fuck!"

"Thought that's part of the plan, Blue Eyes." He kissed his way down Jamie's jaw to his throat, nipping a little before caressing with his tongue.

Jamie nodded, then dropped his head back. "Yeah, great plan." He bucked his hips into Ethan's hand.

Ethan walked him backward to the bed, yanking their hats off and tossing them onto a nearby chair, then nibbling Jamie's chin. "Unwrap my surprise for me."

Jamie blinked up at him, dazed for a few seconds, then quickly started shucking boots and clothes.

Ethan chuckled and did the same. Peripherally, he became aware of those soft, sexy sounds that always accompanied sex between them, including wet, sucking noises. When he looked up, Jamie was in the middle of the bed, legs spread wide in invitation, three fingers buried in that sweet little cowboy ass.

"Oh, fuck! You're incredible!" Ethan climbed onto the bed slowly, his own cock dribbling come at the delicious sight of his lover.

Jamie's long cock was straining and dripping on that toned belly as he writhed on his own fingers. Those lean hips pumped upward slightly with every thrust of his calloused digits. Blue eyes stared up at him, glazed with pleasure; his bottom lip was caught between straight white teeth.

"So goddamned beautiful!" He crawled forward, plucking the bottle of lube from Jamie's abdomen. He slicked himself up in no time at all and reached for those long fingers, pulling them out from his lover's rear. Ethan lined his cock up with that tight little hole and pushed in.

Jamie gasped and ground down on him, impaling himself all the way on his dick. "Oh…" That dark head dropped back and those knees went higher.

Ethan looped each of Jamie's legs over his arms and thrust. He shifted his lover until Jamie's ass tightened on him. *Good!*

Jamie's head snapped back, his gaze meeting Ethan's. "Right freaking there!"

Oh, yeah, he'd found the perfect spot. He grinned, feeling rather smug. "Right there, baby?" He punctuated his question with another lunge.

"Ohmygod, ohmygod, ohmygod…harder!" Jamie came up on his elbows, panting, his eyes wide.

Ethan groaned at the tight heat gripping his cock. He let go of Jamie's legs and grasped his hips, dragged them up. *What the—?* His fingers hit plastic or something.

Before he could investigate, Jamie plunged down hard, fucking himself on Ethan's cock. Jamie stiffened. The tight heat around Ethan's dick clenched more and he thought he'd die from the ecstasy.

He thought about trying to hold back. He wanted this to last, but when Jamie started begging, whispering, "Please," over and over again, he knew he wouldn't last. It wasn't like they couldn't do it all over again later. He drove into his Blue Eyes repeatedly and, from the look on Jamie's face, pegged the gland every single time.

Jamie's breathing was choppy, his body slick with sweat. In seconds, he arched and let out a hoarse roar. His long, pretty dick jerked and sprayed semen all over his magnificent belly.

"Fuck!" Ethan's own orgasm took him by surprise. As he watched Jamie come, his balls drew up impossibly taut. He tensed, then shot deep into that sweet ass, even as Jamie's lean body stopped shuddering with aftershocks.

He stayed there, pressed deeply into Jamie, for several minutes, simply listening to the sound of Jamie's breathing. It gradually went from rough panting to smooth and even, until a soft snore finally escaped.

Ethan chuckled and shook his head. He was supposed to be the one who got all tuckered out and fell into a sated sleep immediately. "Good God, Blue Eyes, when you're my age, you'll be practically comatose after sex." So much for a repeat performance. Well, maybe after a short nap. He sat back on his heels, slipping from Jamie's body.

He suddenly remembered the plastic and cloth on Jamie's hip. *A bandage?* What the hell had he done to himself? Ethan rolled him over to investigate.

"What the—?" There was a piece of gauze taped to Jamie's left butt cheek, just below his waist. Concern gnawed at him that Jamie had somehow hurt himself. "What the hell'd you do to yourself, baby?"

Jamie chuckled sleepily, then yawned. "'S your surprise, Cowboy."

His surprise? Ethan peeled the tape and pulled the small bandage down. His breath caught and he got a little misty-eyed. He bent forward to kiss the small of Jamie's back above a newly inked tattoo.

It was the Tin Star brand like the one he had on his own arm, except under the star was added: *Property of Ethan Whitehall.*

~ * ~

J. L. Langley

J.L. writes M/M erotic romance, among other things, and is fortunate to live with four of the most gorgeous males to walk the earth...ok, so one of those males is canine, but he is quite beautiful for a German Shepherd. J.L. was born and raised in Texas. Which is a good thing considering that Texas is full of cowboys and there is nothing better than a man in a pair of tight Wranglers and a cowboy hat as far as J.L. is concerned.

To contact J.L. Langley email: langleyjl@gmail.com.

Titles NOW AVAILABLE In Print
From Loose Id®

ROMANCE AT THE EDGE: In Other Worlds
MaryJanice Davidson, Angela Knight and Camille Anthony

CHARMING THE SNAKE
MaryJanice Davidson, Camille Anthony and Melissa Schroeder

HARD CANDY
Angela Knight, Morgan Hawke and Sheri Gilmore

TAKING CHARGE
Stephanie Vaughan and Lena Austin

SHE BLINDED ME WITH SCIENCE FICTION
Kally Jo Surbeck

THE PRENDARIAN CHRONICLES
Doreen DeSalvo

Check out these other titles in print from Loose Id®

WHY ME?

Treva Harte

THE SYNDICATE: VOLUMES 1 AND 2

Jules Jones & Alex Woolgrave

STRENGTH IN NUMBERS

Rachel Bo

REBEL ANGELS 1: BORN OF THE SHADOWS

Cyndi Friberg

VIRTUAL MURDER

Jennifer Macaire

VOICES CARRY

Melissa Schroeder

FOR THE LOVE OF…

Kally Jo Surbeck